DANGEROUS DESIRE

"So whoever controls the stones of fire controls the ark?" Jessamine cupped her hands over his. A spark passed between them at the intimate contact. It brought a soft gasp to her lips. She should pull her hands away, stand, anything to break the contact between them. Instead, she gazed into his piercing blue eyes and felt a strange lightness at her core.

"Aye," he said softly. "But suddenly it's not the ark or the stones that interest me, but something else entirely." He abandoned the chest on the ground and stood, pulling her up with him until they faced each other, their bodies only a hairbreadth apart.

"Jessamine. We are entering dangerous territory." The words seemed dredged up from his very soul as he pulled her even closer, his gaze on her lips.

She knew he didn't mean the dangers of following the prophecy, but the dangerous way desire flared each time they touched.

"I like adventure," she breathed.

Other *Leisure* books by Gerri Russell:

TO TEMPT A KNIGHT
WARRIOR'S LADY
WARRIOR'S BRIDE
THE WARRIOR TRAINER

GERRI RUSSELL

Seducing the Knight

LEISURE BOOKS   NEW YORK CITY

My deepest thanks to Pamela Ahearn for your unwavering support; and to Pamela Bradburn, Teresa DesJardien, Karen Harbaugh and Nancy Northcott. You all know what it means to be warrior women. You inspire me, always.

A LEISURE BOOK®

May 2010

Published by

Dorchester Publishing Co., Inc.
200 Madison Avenue
New York, NY 10016

ISBN 10: 0-8439-6260-7
ISBN 13: 978-0-8439-6260-4
E-ISBN: 978-1-4285-0850-7

The name "Leisure Books" and the stylized "L" with design are trademarks of Dorchester Publishing Co., Inc.

Printed in the United States of America.

10 9 8 7 6 5 4 3 2 1

Visit us online at www.dorchesterpub.com.

Seducing the Knight

They shall make an ark of acacia wood; it shall be two and a half cubits long, a cubit and a half wide, and a cubit and a half high. You shall overlay it with pure gold, inside and outside you shall overlay it, and you shall make a molding of gold upon it all round. You shall cast four rings of gold for it and put them on its four feet, two rings on one side of it, and two rings on the other side. You shall make poles of acacia wood, and overlay them with gold. And you shall put the poles into the rings on the sides of the ark, by which to carry the ark. The poles shall remain in the rings of the ark; they shall not be taken from it. You shall put into the ark the covenant that I shall give you.

The Holy Bible, Exodus 25

The Ark of the Covenant is, perhaps, the most sacred object mentioned in the Bible. It is said to have contained the stone tablets upon which the Ten Commandments were inscribed by the hand of God.

Legends about the ark's location and purpose are many. This story is just one fictional interpretation. . . .

Chapter One

Jessamine Burundi ran through the streets toward her only hope. Her mother's church. A place of refuge and sanctuary. The church had to protect her from the conde.

Tears streamed down her cheeks. She hated to cry, almost as much as she hated this feeling of helplessness. She raced through the stark white buildings of Teba. She would rather die than become the Condesa of Teba.

A quick glance over her shoulder as she neared the open doorway showed her the Spanish pig's mottled red cheeks and blazing eyes. Maybe death would catch her after all.

Her heart was pounding so hard she could scarcely breathe as she slipped into the building, one of the few Catholic churches her mother's people had salvaged out of what had become a Moorish Spain. She didn't have time to pull up the veil that had shifted down to her neck and shoulders. She prayed God would understand. The heavy scent of incense assailed her. The scent of death. She stumbled, then caught herself. A funeral had no doubt taken place here earlier this morning.

Heavy footsteps sounded on the stone floor behind her. He was gaining on her. She ran toward the altar. A tall, thin man knelt there.

Jessamine's breath came in harsh sobs. Candles shimmered at the altar. Silent. Serene. Someday she wouldn't have to run. Someday she could be silent and serene.

"Father!" she gasped.

Father Gabriel twisted toward her; then his gaze shot past her to the Conde Salazar Mendoza. He stood swiftly, his black robes rustling with the movement.

"Help me." She ducked behind the priest, praying he would shield her from the conde.

The conde skidded to a halt. Beads of perspiration dotted his temples. His disheveled black hair and dark eyes made him appear demonic, and he wore a black velvet jerkin, breeches, and polished black boots. Only the redness of his cheeks gave the man any color. "Move aside," he demanded.

Wild despair tore through Jessamine. She'd been a fool to hope for rescue. If her uncle, King Alfonso XI, couldn't protect her, why had she allowed herself to hope Father Gabriel could? She touched the side of her head where the conde had struck her earlier, and winced at the pain.

"Whatever is going on here?" Father Gabriel asked. He turned halfway toward Jessamine, while keeping his gaze on the conde.

"She is to be my wife," the conde said. He lunged for her.

Father Gabriel shuffled backward, sheltering her with his arms. He reached for her hands. "Jessamine, explain." He started at the sticky moisture between their joined hands. He pulled back and stared at the blood on his fingers. "You're hurt."

Hurt? The pain she'd suffered already was nothing compared to what the conde intended. Instead of answering the priest, she spoke to the conde. "My uncle has not approved."

"This sounds like a matter of royal politics. . . ."

Jessamine stared at the priest in disbelief. He would desert her as well. "He and his men killed my guards. They broke into my quarters while my uncle and his men were engaged in battle outside of town. There is no marriage agreement, just treachery and brute force."

"Release her to me, Father, or things will go badly for you." The conde's eyes were fierce and filled with unchecked violence. "One word from me, and my men will take you down along with this church."

Father Gabriel turned pale and took another step back from her. "Jessamine, I'm sorry, but I cannot risk so much for one life."

"No," she cried, feeling suddenly exposed. The conde gripped her arm and jerked her toward him. She slammed against his chest. The hilt of his sword bit into her hip. He twisted his fingers in the flesh of her arm, then smiled.

Jessamine gasped.

His smile broadened.

Terror flooded her. He wanted her fear. He thrived on it.

"Come along, Princess. I've wasted enough time, trying to secure a place in the House of Castile. You are my last chance. You won't get away from me."

"You murdered my mother!" She jerked backward.

He held tight. "Regrettable, but necessary. Now, come with me. Once I've taken you physically, no one can argue about formal vows. You'll be ruined. By me." He propelled Jessamine forward, his grasp cruelly tight.

Jessamine realized she couldn't break free of his grip, but she could fool him. Acting as though she'd given up, she walked silently beside him.

In the middle of the cemetery, they stopped. The conde's lips tightened until they formed a thin line.

"You're suddenly quite meek. I'll hope for more spirit when I delve between your thighs."

Jessamine brought her heel down hard on the man's foot, then thrust her knee between his legs with all her might. He bellowed, released his grip, and clutched his groin. She jerked away and streaked through the cemetery. She ran around the headstones, across a freshly turned grave. When she came to the headstones of her mother and father, her steps faltered. Tears she'd been fighting filled her eyes. Blinded, but desperate to escape, she pushed herself forward, past the last earthly remains of the family she'd loved.

She was alone now, with only minimal protection from the royal court. And the conde had taken advantage of that fact.

She quickened her steps.

A dull roar sounded in the distance.

The conde shouted something.

Jessamine tore through the graveyard.

Footsteps sounded behind her, as did the clash of steel upon steel.

Blood drummed in her temples. She headed for the shrubbery that enclosed the cemetery. Branches lashed her face and clawed her arms as she pushed through the bushes. The delicate peach silk of her dress caught, ripped. She lifted her skirts and kept running.

"You'll pay for your insolence." The conde crashed through the bushes behind her.

Jessamine ran faster. She had to outdistance the demon in black. *Mother of God, I don't want to sacrifice myself to that pig.* She broke through the other side of the shrubbery and into a dense copse of trees beyond. The shadows of the trees covered her in slivered light.

Her feet flew over the ground, her pace frantic.

She couldn't hear the conde any longer. Was it because he'd given up or because the soft earth absorbed the sound of his footfalls? She couldn't look behind her to find out.

Her heart pounded painfully. She fixed her gaze on the morning light streaming through the trees at the opposite edge of the copse of trees. The edge of town. Beyond the trees was only desert. But what choice did she have? She couldn't loop back without the conde capturing her. She broke through the trees.

The shouts of men mixed with the shrieks of horses, punctuated by the clang of steel upon steel. The violent sounds of battle rushed over her as she stumbled down the hill. She tried to stop, to slow herself down, but the loose rocks beneath her feet made that impossible as she skidded into the periphery of the battle.

Dust surrounded her, choked her. She cried out as her feet nearly slipped out from under her. She could hear the crunch of the conde's feet close behind. She had no choice but to go forward onto the battlefield. The acrid scent of smoke and the coppery smell of blood overwhelmed her senses. Her stomach lurched.

Blood. War. Death.

Heavy footfalls sounded dangerously close.

A single sob escaped her throat. She would die this day. The only choice was whether her end came at the hands of the conde, or by the blade of a sword.

A sudden chill gripped her. She preferred the latter.

Bracing herself for the pain to come, Jessamine hurled forward into the fray.

Sir Alan Cathcart, known to his brothers in the Scottish Templars as the Falcon, gripped the hilt of his sword and prepared for the onslaught as ten thousand Moors swarmed toward him. He studied their numbers, calculating the odds. It would be difficult to win the day, but if the Templars stuck to the strategy he'd planned, they just might have a chance with luck and the Lord on their side.

Alan felt his horse's muscles bunch beneath his legs. Even the animal sensed the odds were against them. He stroked the beast's neck, trying to soothe its fear. The Templars were here to take back the Castle of the Stars from Moorish occupation at the request of King Alfonso XI of Spain. The Scottish Templars and the Spanish had joined forces to rid the country of the heathens under the direction of Sir James "Black" Douglas of Scotland, the Templars' commander.

Though they'd come through Spain intent on making their way to the Holy Land, Black Douglas didn't mind a little diversion along the way. The Templars he commanded would triumph as they had so many times before.

Despite Alan's attempts to calm his horse, the beast quivered at the Moorish forces lined up on the hillside opposite them. This had a different feel to it from other battles they'd fought. Was it the sheer numbers opposing them? Could it be the high desert air, which Alan and the other Templars were unused to breathing? Or was the odd feeling that tightened his chest an omen of something more?

Alan sloughed off the disquieting sensation and focused on the enemy. A shout went up, followed by the thunder of hoofbeats and the swirling of dust. The moment had arrived. Men dressed in black robes and turbans bore down on him and his brothers. They were one hundred yards away.

"Hold steady," Alan crooned to the anxious beast beneath him as again the horse quaked. "We'll get through this." Beside Alan, Sir James Douglas sat upon his warhorse, clutching the silver vessel containing the heart of Robert the Bruce. The Bruce had promised to see them through to the Holy Land. He'd promised his heart would protect them.

And along with that promise, Alan had accepted from the Bruce an additional burden. Once they reached Jerusalem, even an army of Moors wouldn't stand in the way of fulfilling it. He'd find the Ark of the Covenant and bring it back to Scotland.

Fifty yards, and closing fast. Black Douglas gave the call for the Templars to charge.

Alan set his horse in motion. As he surged forward, his thoughts wandered back to a more familiar land, that of his ancestors. Where the wind blew gently through the grass, where the heady scent of heather permeated the senses, where blue-black hills dotted the land and clouds roiled overhead, promising rain. But not here in the land of his enemies. Nay, the grass was dry and brown, the soil a rocky gray, the air heavy, and the constant heat prickled his skin beneath his white Templar tunic and heavy chain mail.

Ten yards away. Alan could see the men's dark eyes framed between their turbans and beards. He tightened his grip on his sword.

Alan could feel the air move past him as Moors on horseback came within reach. A shiver of anticipation stilled his breath as the first man attacked. He swung at Alan, bringing his sword down at an angle, intent on slashing the Templar's torso. Alan deflected his stroke, watching the sparks fly as their blades clashed. That attacker retreated and two more approached on foot. Alan kicked one in the chest, sending him tumbling backward, then struck the other man in the chest with his sword. The man dropped to the ground, dead.

When the two fell away, two more replaced them. His enemies were a tide of unending black. The Templars

broke formation. Alan tensed. Nay! "Keep to the line!"
he shouted over the roar of battle. No one listened. The
Moors swarmed in, separating the men from each other.
Alan's mind raced, looking for ways to pull them back.
Together they were strong. Apart they'd be easy prey.

Alan felt himself losing ground. The Moors forced
him back, farther from his men. He could see the Templars' white tunics in the distance, but there was no way
to reach them. A knot clenched his gut as Sir William
St. Clair of Rosslyn went down. A swarm of black surrounded the knight. Sir Simon Lockhart raced for
their fallen brother, but he was too far away. The Moors
closed in.

Desperate to help, Alan hacked at the men around
him, trying to break free. To no avail. As soon as one
man went down, three more surged forward. They
pressed him back toward the fringes of the fighting.

Sir Walter Logan and his brother Sir Robert surged
forward to try to help William. A cry of despair tore
from Alan's throat as a hooked blade pierced Walter's
body. Another blade split Robert's chest. Alan felt their
pain in his own body as he pitched himself and his
horse forward. But too late.

The sea of black kept coming. They cut off his vision. He could no longer see the Templars. Were they
all dead?

Frustration and anger drove his actions as he sliced
one Moor with his sword and broke another's nose with
his hand. He could feel the bones crunch beneath his
fist. Blood soaked his hand. Blood was everywhere.

His eyes nearly blinded by the red haze of rage and
pain, Alan kept fighting until eventually exhaustion
and the sting of his wounds dampened his rage. From
the corner of his eye, peach-colored silk fluttered at the

edge of the fighting. *Not a Templar*, his mind warned, as a streak of bright silver steel swung close to his head.

He ducked, shifted his horse to the left, then countered with a boot in the face of one man and the flat of his blade against the head of the other. The flash of peach came to him again.

His breath caught. A woman? Dark hair streamed out behind her as she ran at the edges of the fighting, avoiding swords and scimitars, men and horses.

A woman? Something inside him lurched to life as he shifted his weight forward. His horse understood the command. Together they charged through the sea of black toward that strangely incongruous femininity floating in a sea of death. As he came ever closer, he could see a thin, graceful form, a riot of shining dark hair, and wide frightened eyes.

He sliced through the fighting, the carnage, almost as if his drive to reach her was aided by Providence. Never slowing his horse, he came up beside her and scooped her slight body into his arms.

She screamed.

He kept on going, taking them farther from the fighting, through the dead and the dying.

The clash of steel and cries of men echoed all around him. Alan tried to block out the sound. She struggled in his grip.

"Cease your writhing, woman! There's a sea of blood beneath us." His voice was harsh, but at his words she stilled.

"A sea of blood?" she responded in perfect English. Her eyes, if it were possible, grew even wider as her gaze dropped to the red cross of the Templars upon his chest. "Turbans and crosses," she breathed in disbelief.

Alan slashed his way past two Moors that blocked his

way to the edge of the battlefield. The woman remained still until the danger passed.

"It's as the prophecy predicted." Her voice cut through the cries of men and horses. The tension in her face eased.

As his warhorse dodged the worst of the fighting, Alan studied the woman in his arms. Her features were finely drawn. A pair of ruby lips, full and tempting. Large almond-shaped eyes set above high, chiseled cheekbones. Lush, dark lashes, a straight nose, all set into an oval of perfect honey-colored skin.

A hesitant smile came to those full red lips, and relief entered her eyes.

"My thanks," she murmured.

Her voice was low yet melodic, with the slightest hint of a rasp. She leaned closer, and the faint scent of jasmine teased his nose. He tore his gaze from her at the sound of hoofbeats behind him. "Save your thanks until we are safe." As though in response to his words, a swarm of black-cloaked men raced toward them.

Chapter Two

Alan forced himself to relax, to keep his muscles loose yet ready, as he searched for a way to escape. One horse with two riders would be less maneuverable than his enemies' mounts.

Flashes of steel sparked in the sun. Alan drew a sharp breath. "Lean down against the horse's mane and hold tight. Close your eyes," he said next to the woman's ear. "No matter what happens, don't let go."

She did as he asked without question. He put his heels to his horse's sides. The beast shot forward. Tendrils of the woman's silken black hair caught the wind, caressing the back of his hand as he held the reins. A soft tingle snaked up his arm. He forced the odd sensation away and fixed his attention on the men whose curved swords slashed at the two of them. He charged.

Death followed each swipe of his sword. There was no consolation in dying on the battlefield, save that a man would go to God with the knowledge that he'd died for his king. Pain tightened Alan's chest at the memory of his brothers falling beneath the Moorish swords. Why had the Spanish held back? They hadn't joined the Templars in that first charge. The Templars had entered the battle alone.

Without the support of the Spanish, they'd been doomed from the start. The Scottish Templars were undone. Defeated.

All he could do now was try to survive—to finish what his brothers could not. He gripped the reins a little too tight, sending his horse's front hooves dancing in the heavy air. Alan forced himself to relax, to bring the horse under control. There was no option but to push past the fighting.

With a cry of anguish, Alan turned his horse toward the desert. The Moors would win this battle. All that remained was to save himself and the woman. Alan blocked one sword, then another and another. His breath rasped in his throat as he severed the Moors' flesh, vessels, bone.

He wove his way through the conflict. Bodies, blood, and weapons littered the ground. The screaming of the enemy, the shouting of the remaining Templars, the ranting of the bagpipes filled the desert air.

He had to survive. If these men got their hands on the girl . . . He blocked the thought.

Alan distanced himself from the sounds, from the streaks of pain that shot through his thighs, from the relentless pounding of blows on his mail. He blocked out his horse's shrieks of pain as the animal, too, took blows to his armored rear flanks, but Alan kept charging forward, into the rocky desert and toward the coast he knew lay in the distance.

Not one sound came from the girl's lips as she clung to the horse. Alan frowned at the blood spatters on her peach-colored gown. Was she hurt? Or was the blood a result of the conflict? He couldn't take the time to find out.

Behind him a banshee wail sounded. He turned to look back. A crossbow bolt struck his side. He felt it penetrate his mail, felt it pierce his flesh. That fleeting twist of his spine had saved him. Flame bloomed in his side. The bolt hit his rib and stopped. As he pulled his sword arm back, blood seeped from the wound, pain seared him, but injury could not stop him. Not after everything he'd already sacrificed. He'd done the unthinkable and abandoned his men. Death would not turn him from his last honorable deed.

With a mighty tug, he pulled the bolt free. For a moment, his vision clouded as pain exploded in his side. Alan forced his brain to clear. He had to stay sharp. The Moor who'd shot him closed in on him, but Alan was prepared. He waited for the man to raise his scimitar. Then Alan brought his own sword up, into the man's chest. The Moor fell back.

Alan spurred his horse into a reckless, zigzagging dash. He allowed himself one glance back. One last look at the slaughter of Teba. His body coiled with tension. Breath rasped in his throat and his heart pounded at the sight of his fallen brethren. Their army lay in ruin at the foot of the Andalusian hills. A sound erupted from him—a growl, a groan, an expression of sheer frustration and anger, of grief. So many men killed, yet their mission to reach the Holy Land had failed.

He'd been robbed of his brothers, of any connection he had to Scotland. All that remained was his oath to his king and his Templar's spirit. He must not forget his true purpose.

A wholly unexpected loneliness washed up from the depths of his soul, painful, intense. The loss of his brothers would haunt him for the rest of his days.

He drew a sharp breath of the dry air. *My brothers*, his heart cried in anguish. But Alan pushed his grief away. Not yet. He couldn't allow himself to feel yet. There would be time. . . . His gaze shifted to the girl still hunched against his horse's mane.

He frowned at her slender back. Why had she been anywhere near the battlefield? Only a fool would run into such mayhem.

Was she a fool, or was something else at play here? Did he truly care? Nothing could change the outcome of that battle. Nothing.

But he was in control of what happened next. He would take her to safety. Then he'd continue on his journey to the Holy Land, alone.

The task he'd been entrusted with was far too important to let anyone or anything stand in his way. Alan struck his heels against his horse's sides. The animal responded with a surging bound, lifting his hooves and springing forward, away from the battlefield, heading deeper into the desert toward the unknown.

Conde Salazar Mendoza had watched Jessamine throw herself into the chaos of the battlefield, and he'd been tempted to follow her until she was plucked from the ground by one of the Templars who had come to help the king of Spain.

As the two rode out of sight, the conde released a throaty growl as raw anger surged through him. "Damn, stupid girl." The Templars were foiling his plans to kill the king and wed his niece. Marriage to Princess Jessamine would bring him one step closer to the Spanish crown. It was a goal he and his mother had dreamed about for the past ten years.

His thoughts shifted from Jessamine to his mother, imagining her waiting for him in the ladies' parlor of their mansion on the outskirts of town. Feelings of happiness flooded him as he pictured her sitting on their finest settee in her red satin gown, with her voluminous skirts spread wide about her legs. She'd always been a regal woman, as grand as any condesa should be.

Some of his pleasure faded as he pictured her there, gazing at him expectantly.

"Did you convince the king that you should marry one of his daughters?" he heard his mother's sweet voice ask in the echoes of his mind.

The conde frowned. "No, not yet."

"You're not trying hard enough. Only naughty boys take no for an answer. And naughty boys deserve to be punished, my son." Her voice cut through his thoughts as did the memory of her rage.

When he was little more than a boy she'd punished him by locking him in a cold, dark chest without any food or water for a week, until he'd promised to alter the situation.

"I deserve to be linked to the royal family," she'd cooed to him adoringly when she'd set him free.

He'd promised her then that he'd marry into the royal family one way or another. A heartbeat later, his hands had snaked around her neck, and he'd strangled her.

Ever since that day, he'd been trying to live up to that promise. When his attempts to attach himself to the royal princesses had failed, he'd had to settle for second best. He'd set his sights on the king's sister. But even she had refused him, saying she still loved her dead husband too much. After that, the conde had had only one choice, to poison her. With the king's sister out of the way, it had been easy to home in on the newest object of his desire— Jessamine. She would ultimately bring him everything his mother had wanted.

A rush of pleasure shot through him. He could hardly wait to introduce Jessamine to his mother. Then her dull expression, he could imagine, would turn to joy. For once in his life he would have succeeded in pleasing his mother.

If only he could get his hands on the princess.

The conde stared coldly at the battle raging before him. He'd plotted and planned and incited the Moors for months, aggravating the foreign invaders in the hopes that they'd attack the king. Today his plans had borne fruit.

Today was the day the king would die. The conde clenched his fists at his sides. Or so it had seemed until the Templars intruded. With the knights bearing the brunt of the Moors' attack, the Spanish could hold back. There was no chance for the king to die if he didn't engage in battle.

The conde growled. Would nothing go as planned this day? Because it looked as though Jessamine had escaped her fate also, but only temporarily.

The conde had no intention of giving up his last hope for gaining the crown of Spain. He would see one last glimpse of pride in his mother's partially decomposed eyes. The princess would be his, one way or another.

Chapter Three

The Templar had ordered her to keep her eyes closed, banishing her to darkness. She knew only what she could hear or smell. The sorrowful cries of the dead and dying had stopped. Thankfully, the smell of death had vanished as well, replaced with the salty, musty scent of sea and earth. She squeezed her eyes shut as the knight had commanded.

Irritation mixed with understanding. She knew why he'd bidden her to block out the horrific sights of the battlefield. Yet another part of her prickled that once again she'd been told what she could and couldn't do. She'd learned long ago that as a princess, she had to do what was commanded of her, whether that order was to close her eyes or marry a conde. Her choices were rarely her own.

But today she had changed all that by running away from the conde. Her first truly independent action. She drew a startled breath at the realization. Her uncle had not chosen the conde to be her bridegroom. The king had intended to use her marriage as a way to cement the alliance between the Spanish and the Moorish people. The bloodlines of the House of Castile and the House of Burundi mixed in her veins. And she had run away from it all. Perhaps she was braver than she'd imagined herself.

Jessamine tried to open her eyes—to continue her

streak of defiance. Instead, her fists tightened in the mane of the horse beneath her. She knew what she could expect from her uncle and the conde now that she'd defied them both. But the man behind her was still a mystery. Perhaps she'd tempted fate enough for one day.

With a soft sigh, she relaxed against the horse. The sounds around her were amplified by the darkness. The animal's steady gait matched her own heartbeat. She could hear the rhythmic breathing of the man behind her, feel every shift of his body against her own. High overhead, a bird of prey circled. She heard the flap of wings, a whoosh of air, an occasional piercing call. She could smell the tangy sea air and could feel the warmth of the sun radiating off the rocky ground beneath them.

If she wanted release from the darkness, it appeared she'd have to challenge him. "May I open my eyes now?"

She heard a low muttered curse. He slowed the horse to a walk. "Of course you can open your eyes. Why the hell shouldn't you?"

She opened her eyes. "Because you commanded me to close them." Slowly she sat up, flexing the muscles of her back and giving a low, relieved sigh. She turned to look at the man behind her. He towered over her, a dark, austere presence. His eyes were the color of a summer night, deep dark blue that should have seemed warm, but they were cool and watchful as they rested on her. His hair was dark. His mouth . . . She swallowed roughly. His mouth was tender, sensuous, determined.

His mouth turned down as her gaze lingered there. "Have you no sense?" he snapped. "I didn't mean for you to keep your eyes closed endlessly."

Jessamine met his gaze. Anger flared in his eyes. Was it anger at the situation they'd just left, or anger directed at her? "You have every right to be angry—"

He laughed mirthlessly. "You have no idea." His lips tightened. "Your escapade forced me to abandon my men back there."

"I'm sorry," Jessamine said simply.

"You can't say 'I'm sorry' and make it all right." He stopped speaking, straightened, and relaxed his clenched fists. "Shouting at you won't bring them back either." He drew a sharp breath. "It's done. Where we go from here is what matters now." He pulled the horse to a stop. "What's your name?"

Jessamine tried to keep her lips from quivering. "I am sorry," she repeated.

"Your name."

She moistened her lips, hesitating. She didn't want to tell him who she was. People always treated her differently when they knew she was a princess. More than ever, she simply wanted to be someone who'd lost her way. "Jessamine." She hoped he would let the lack of a surname pass.

"Sir Alan Cathcart, a knight of the Scottish Templars." He bowed his head, then met her gaze boldly. "Now that the pleasantries have been observed, tell me what you were doing on that battlefield. Are you really so foolish?"

Twice now he'd called her a fool. She gave the Templar a level look. "Don't underestimate me, Sir Alan Cathcart. I'm no one's fool."

She slid off his horse, straightened, then stalked away. "I am no one's fool," she muttered to herself. She would keep walking; she would do anything and everything she could to escape the conde and his plans.

The knight brought his horse around in front of her, blocking her progress. "Where are you going?" He drew his sword and pressed the tip of his weapon against her chest.

She could feel the heat of the desert wash over her in waves. Perspiration beaded up on the back of her neck. She swallowed hard. *Dios*, was he as dangerous as the conde?

"You cannot walk your way out of this desert."

Jessamine clenched her fists at her sides. "I'm tired of people telling me what to do."

"Perhaps if you did what was expected, then they wouldn't have to."

She tried to walk around the horse, but his extended sword blocked her way. "What do you know about expectations?"

A sudden glint of humor appeared in his eyes. "You might be surprised."

She narrowed her gaze. The man was beginning to annoy her. But he was right about one thing. She was acting unreasonably. She needed his help, whoever he was. Insulting him or angering him further might be unwise.

"The battlefield?" he asked again, his gaze moving to the gemstone necklace at her throat and the rings upon her fingers. "You're not just some peasant out wandering the streets."

Jessamine twisted the large gemstone ring on her finger with her thumb, turning it so that it faced the palm of her hand. Did she dare tell him the truth? About who she was? About what had happened? Would he force her to go back to the conde if she did? Men were hard to read sometimes when it came to their allegiances. Would returning her to the Spanish court benefit his own goals? She didn't know enough about him to take that chance. "I had no other choice."

"You couldn't see the ten thousand Moors on the hillside, or the Spanish soldiers and Templars opposing them?"

"As I said, I had no other choice." She dropped her

gaze to the bloody ruin that was her gown. She *did* sound like a fool. No wonder he'd called her as much. "Can we just leave it at that for now?"

Jessamine heard him sheathe his sword. "As you wish," he said, suddenly sounding exhausted. He brought his horse closer to her and offered his hand. "I'll see you as far as the next town; then you and I shall go our own ways. Agreed?" A Scottish brogue was evident in his speech, the soft rhythmic cadence taking some of the edge from his words.

"Agreed." She accepted his hand. He drew her up onto his horse's back. A groan escaped him as he settled her before him.

"How badly are you hurt?" She turned to look at his wounded side. A brownish red splash of color soaked his white tunic, mixing with the matted black coat of his horse. Which was hurt worse, man or beast?

"You're bleeding."

His frown deepened. "I'll make it to the town, if that is your concern."

Jessamine grasped the veil that had fallen to her shoulders. She drew the fabric into her hands, folded it, then tucked it against his side. "You were hit."

He tensed at her touch.

"Am I hurting you?"

He shook his head.

"I can hold the compress to your side while we ride."

He brought his hand down to cover hers. Warmth flared across her fingers at the contact. "The damage is not as serious as it looks."

She met his gaze. "It will be serious if you continue to lose blood."

He withdrew his hand and shifted his gaze to the distance as though considering her words. Finally he said, "If you are so determined, very well. But let's make your ride more comfortable. Release the wound for an instant."

She lessened the pressure against his side, only to find herself picked up like a feather on the wind and repositioned facing him, with her legs off to one side. Her outer thigh pressed against that most intimate part of him. Despite the heat of the desert, a shiver snaked through her. "I'll make certain you don't die."

His lips drew up in a half smile. "I'm so relieved," he said before spurring the horse into motion.

Instead of glancing at him, at the big broad chest displayed before her eyes, Jessamine looked beyond him to the haze of dust and smoke that rose above the desert below the town of Teba. They'd managed to escape the battle, but she was sure the conde had as well.

Jessamine knew that the coastal village of Mijas lay just over the hills in the direction they rode. No doubt it would also be the first place the conde would search for her. It would take the better part of the day to reach that town on horseback. She had to keep the knight from bleeding to death until they could reach the town and find help. She also had to figure out a way to escape the conde when he pursued her. He would follow her to the village. Of that she had no doubt.

"Thank you," Jessamine said, breaking the silence.

"For what?"

"Now that we know we're safe, I'd like to thank you for saving my life."

He inclined his head to acknowledge her words but didn't speak. They rode on in silence, and as they did, Jessamine studied the flat, rocky desert that stretched before her, but eventually her gaze came back to the man who held her in his arms.

Sir Alan Cathcart's arms rested around her securely. She'd never been held so intimately by any man before, and an odd tingle of sensation passed between them where his arms rested against her.

She could tell by his torso, broad shoulders, and well-muscled arms that he was a warrior. Her gaze moved back to his face, to the blue of his eyes—eyes that spoke of some deep pain as well as kindness and intelligence. His hair was dark and cropped close to his head, setting off his high cheekbones and strong nose. His was a compelling face. It was the kind of face a woman couldn't help staring at with interest and desire.

A fist tightened around her heart. Desire was the last thing she wanted in her life. Had her parents' experiences not warned her of its dangers? They'd both been killed because of their desire: Her father, because his desire for her mother had threatened the Moors in Spain. Her mother, because even death had not dulled the desire she'd had for Jessamine's father. When she'd refused to marry the conde, he'd had her poisoned.

And now the man was after her. Jessamine shivered. Nothing could ever convince her to marry that man, or any man for that matter.

The dream that filled her heart was to see the prophecy that had been made at her birth come true. The prophecy was the last link she had to her parents. Following its path would help her stay connected to them for just a while longer.

She brought her gaze up to meet the knight's dark eyes. Somehow this man was a part of that path. "Where are you headed after we reach Mijas?" she asked, suddenly needing to know about him and his plans.

An awkward silence hung between them as his gaze became hard and assessing. "Why would you want to know that? Our association will end once we reach the first town along the coast."

Jessamine shifted uncomfortably, uneasy with his

scrutiny. She was the one who usually studied people. It was disconcerting for him to look at her and see . . . what? What did he see? Because he didn't look at her with the same cool calculation the Spanish courtiers did.

He leaned forward. Jessamine felt the soft intake of his breath against her cheek. It was warm and strangely reassuring. She looked up into his compelling blue gaze. Her throat went dry. There was something in his eyes. It was as though he could see right through her pretense at bravery into the frightened yet determined woman within.

She opened her mouth to speak but he shook his head, silencing her. She stared at him, stunned.

"You and I will part ways the moment we reach the coast. Is that understood?"

For the first time all day, Jessamine felt a glimmer of hope lighten her soul. The man was leaving Spain. She didn't know why or how she knew that, but she did. She could see the red tile rooftops of Mijas in the distance. Mijas was a port town. Her heartbeat fluttered. He intended to board a ship—a ship she would be on.

A shiver of nervous excitement pulsed through her. Not only would she leave the conde far behind, but boarding the ship figured in the first of the four parts of the prophecy. The Moorish seeress had predicted this day would come. A day that had started with turbans and crosses.

The prophecy will rise when the turban and the cross come together in blood. Then shall a night of white and the holy waters of a deep blue sea reveal the things you cannot see.

Never had the second line of the prophecy made any sense until this very moment, nor why the seeress had delivered the prophesy in English. *A night of white.* In English the words night and knight sounded the same, but held different meanings. Jessamine had always assumed the *night* sky would turn white for some unknown reason. She dropped her gaze to the blood-spattered tunic Sir Alan Cathcart wore. He was the *knight* predicted by the prophecy. He had to be.

Had the seeress meant to confuse her? Or were her own assumptions at fault here? It hardly mattered now. She'd learned the information she'd needed when the time was right. Her thoughts returned to the prophecy.

Holy waters of a deep blue sea. The words could only indicate the journey the man would soon embark upon. He'd sail toward the Mediterranean, to where the sea was a startling blue somewhere near the Holy Land. Was there a holier place upon this earth?

Her thoughts returned to her knight in white and she smiled. The prophecy involved him as much as it did her. He'd never be able to leave her behind once she revealed the truth to him.

Jessamine gazed up into his stony face. For a moment her enthusiasm faltered. Her mouth went dry. The words she longed to say lodged in her throat. Perhaps she should wait to tell him of the prophecy until they were safely on their way across that deep blue sea.

Chapter Four

Alan straightened on the horse as the red-tiled rooftops of the port town of Mijas appeared in the distance. His mission was about to begin—a mission with even worse odds than the battle he'd just survived.

Despite his claims to the contrary, he could feel the energy drain from him in equal proportion to the blood that left his side. The cloth the girl pressed against his body with her bejeweled fingers was soaked through. He needed to stop, to find a barber who could mend his wound before he set foot aboard a ship.

As the rooftops of Mijas grew closer, Alan shifted his gaze to the girl in his arms. He tried not to notice the softness of her thighs as they pressed against his legs or the gentle feminine scent that filled his head. He braced himself against the rush of warmth the thought brought to his groin. It'd been far too long since he'd had the pleasure of holding a woman this close.

And this one in particular smelled of exotic mysteries. Intriguing and dangerous. Alan shifted slightly away from her. He could have nothing to do with this woman. His vows forbade it. All his efforts must be focused on getting to the Holy Land and finding the Ark of the Covenant.

Robert the Bruce had wanted the artifact securely stowed with the rest of the Templar treasure. After living a lifetime of wars and fighting, the king had wanted to make certain no one could use the legendary holy relic as a weapon. Never once did the king talk of using the weapon for himself. He merely wanted the Scottish Templars, and Alan in particular, to make certain the countries of the world remained safe.

I shall not fail. Alan steeled his resolve. It was his duty, his obligation, to see the task through.

Robert the Bruce had been the first person ever to see something of worth inside Alan when the king had asked him to join the ranks of the brotherhood. Alan had always been different from the other boys when it came to fighting games and real combat. Other boys had charged into the conflict between the warring clans without fear and without thought. Yet Alan had always held back, wanting to reason things through before he proceeded. He wasn't afraid of conflict; he simply had a different approach. He wanted to plan before he proceeded—a trait that had made him the object of ridicule and had left him isolated from the others in his clan.

Yet it was his reasoning skills that had eventually brought him to the notice of Robert the Bruce. His strategic approach to battle had helped the Scots win many recent conflicts against the English. The Bruce had rewarded him and encouraged his efforts by selecting him as one of the ten knights who made up the Brotherhood of the Scottish Templars. It was because of that faith and trust that Alan had to succeed. He must fulfill his promise to his dying king.

Banishing a moment of doubt, Alan straightened and spurred the tired horse into a final run toward Mijas. It didn't take long before they entered the city. The streets were crowded in the late afternoon. He and Jessamine, their clothes bloodied and torn, drew more attention than Alan would have liked. People scurried up and down the narrow cobbled streets, their bodies flowing and ebbing like the tide, brushing against his legs, then away. At the close contact and the open stares, Alan found his hand drifting to the hilt of his sword.

He watched the crowd part and turned his horse into the opening and through to an inn yard off to his right. He brought the horse to a halt. "We are here," he said as he lifted the girl to the ground.

For a moment, he mourned the loss of her closeness before he slid from the horse himself. His feet hit the packed earth, and he swayed, suddenly realizing just how weak he'd become. He gripped the horse's side for support, but his hand slipped against the blood his wound had left behind, and he found himself falling.

A second later he was in Jessamine's arms. "Careful," she said, allowing him to find his feet once more.

She was stronger than she looked. "My apologies." He widened his stance and brought his gaze to hers. "This is where you and I must part ways." He kept his tone low as others strode by, their gazes lingering on his white Templar tunic.

Realizing he had better do something quickly, before someone challenged him about wearing the garment of a disbanded order, he released the hilt of his sword and unfastened his belt. He meant to pull the tunic up over his head, but in the next moment, the world swayed before his eyes. White edged his vision, narrowing to black. The black threatened to swallow him whole. A cold sickness knotted in his stomach as he hurtled into the darkness.

Jessamine knew she shouldn't be so pleased that the man had slipped into unconsciousness, but she was. She ignored the dip and sway of the boat as she tucked the blanket around the knight's shoulders.

It had taken some arranging to have him treated by a

barber, then transferred to the docks. There they'd boarded a fishing ship under the pretense that they were husband and wife. In fact, it had taken all her jewelry except the locket with miniatures of her parents to make it happen.

She had no idea where the knight was going, but the prophecy indicated holy waters that were a shade of deep blue. She smoothed the woolen blanket across the knight's chest. She'd needed his protection from the conde as much as he'd needed her assistance in treating his wound.

Her own wounds were superficial. She looked far more injured than she was, with her tattered clothing that bore the knight's bloodstains. Perhaps it was her appearance that had finally convinced the barber and the fishermen that she needed their help. They'd been hesitant at first, but eventually bent to her wishes. If she'd been willing to identify herself as Princess Jessamine, she could have commanded their aid. Yet she'd accomplished the same thing on her own.

Basking in her simple accomplishments, Jessamine stared down at the knight's silent, pale features. Asleep, he didn't look nearly as dangerous as he had before. Dangerous or not, the man would be furious at what she'd done. But his anger would come too late. They were heading east. The only way to rid himself of her would be to toss her overboard. Her fingers stilled. No honorable man would do such a thing. Would he?

Jessamine looked across the deck of the fishing vessel they had boarded. The fishermen had allowed her to build a pallet for Alan on the deck just below the forecastle. Two men were stationed on the forecastle above—one at the wheel, the other bent over a small table filled with charts. The rest of the crew were several yards away from them, scattered upon the deck, checking netting or minding the sails. No one seemed to pay their two passengers much notice, except for the occasional curious glance darted her way.

For that reason, Jessamine was grateful for the weapon she had removed from Alan's scabbard and placed between the two of them. She couldn't wield it effectively, but the sailors didn't know that.

Alan moaned.

Jessamine tensed as the knight's eyes fluttered open. "Jessamine." Her name was a whisper on his lips.

"Yes," she replied, drawing closer.

His hand snaked out, capturing her wrist. "We are at sea." His eyes opened wide. "Why?" His tone was tight, tense.

"We're on the ship *Media Noche* en route to the Holy Land."

"The Holy Land," he echoed, his grip lessening on her wrist. "How could you possibly know where I'm headed?"

"I don't." Jessamine tensed, suddenly uneasy.

"Then why?" His gaze pierced her. She tugged at her arm, feeling too close to him, too confined. He didn't release her.

He pushed himself up, attempting to sit. With a groan he fell back against his pallet of straw. "My side."

"You lost a lot of blood. I found a barber to sew you up, but he said you should rest. Your strength will return in time."

He released her. "Why'd you do it?"

"Find you a healer?" She shrugged. "You needed one."

"People don't usually go out of their way to help others. What's in this for you?"

"I need your help too." A queer twisting sensation followed the admission. She needed to tell him the truth. Jessamine straightened. She'd lived with the prophecy for so many years, allowed it to give her hope that her fate would be different from her parents'. "You are part of a prophecy," she explained. "A prophecy that has been guiding my life since birth."

His piercing blue gaze moved over her with skepticism. "Prophecies are few and far between. What makes you believe you're the subject of one?"

"The prophecy exists, whether you choose to believe me or not." The wind sharpened, sending Jessamine's hair cascading around her face. She gathered the length in her hands and twisted it across one shoulder. She didn't return her gaze to his face. She might have started this journey because of the conde's demands, but now she intended to make the most of it. The prophecy would guide what happened next. She turned to him. Preparing herself for more disbelief, she stated, "The first part of the prophecy says the turban and the cross will come together in blood."

He said nothing.

Jessamine held her breath, hoping he wouldn't turn away from the destiny that had brought them together.

"What does that mean?" he finally asked.

She smiled. He was interested. It was a start. "I didn't know until I was on that battlefield surrounded by turbaned Moors," she said in a rush. "Then you appeared out of nowhere, dressed all in white with a bloodred cross on your chest. You and I are part of this prophecy, whether we like it or not."

With a frown, his hand moved to his chest. "My Templar tunic?"

"Is safely stowed." She cast a quick glance at the fishermen. They seemed to be ignoring the conversation, but because of their proximity, she lowered her voice. "The looks of anger and scorn we received in the inn yard indicated that it might be wise to remove it. You tried to do so yourself before you lost consciousness."

A faraway look appeared in his eyes, as though he was trying to remember. "Again, what's in this for you? Why were you on that battlefield?"

"I was running from a future I didn't want."

He pushed against the straw in an effort to sit. This time he managed to lean back against the rise of the forecastle at his back. "Running from what? Imprisonment? Your family? The king?"

"Marriage."

Alan gazed at her incredulously. "You risked your life because you were too frightened to marry? Are you mad?"

Heat flooded her cheeks. "Do not judge me," she said fiercely. "You have no idea what I've suffered." She stood and moved with stiff steps toward the nearby railing, where she stared out at the open sea. She shouldn't have told him anything. Not about her plight, not about the prophecy.

Jessamine closed her eyes, allowing the seaborne breeze to rush against her cheeks, cooling her anger. Somewhere deep inside herself, she knew without a doubt that the prophecy was vital, not just for herself, but for the world. The man, the knight, was a part of it, whether he chose to believe or not.

"Tell me more about the prophecy." His voice came from behind her.

She spun around to find him disturbingly close. "What are you doing?" she demanded. "You're injured." His nearness caught her off guard. She pressed back into the wooden rail.

"A warrior must heal quickly." He leaned down, bringing his face closer to hers. "Tell me more." When she hesitated, he said, "I promise to listen."

Still she hesitated.

It took every bit of strength Alan possessed to remain standing. He leaned toward the girl and the rail that would provide him some support. Again, the soft scent of jasmine teased his senses. He drew in the soft scent, allowing it to give him strength. He needed to discover what she knew and why she had chosen to sail with him to the Holy Land. Would she stand in the way of his achieving his goal? Because he would allow no one, no matter how sweet she smelled, to stand between him and his mission.

"Tell me about the prophecy." Alan smiled faintly.

"I really don't know what any of it means. The first part only made sense because of you." Her frown vanished and a spark of eagerness glowed in her eyes. "A Moorish seeress came to my parents a day after my birth, proclaiming, 'The prophecy will rise when the turban and the cross come together in blood. Then shall a night of white and the holy water of a deep blue sea reveal the things you cannot see.'"

She straightened. "It was from the first part of the seeress's words that I determined you were headed for the Holy Land." She paused and searched his face. "Are you traveling there?"

"Jerusalem," he admitted.

She nodded. "The prophecy continues, 'Only without sight will you know what is real and bring to the world the hidden seal. Day into night and night into day, a whisper of I Am That I Am will pave the way.'"

The intensity vibrating in Jessamine's voice was reflected in her luminous expression. Alan gazed at her, transfixed. She'd come alive when speaking about the prophecy. She was either very passionate about this prophecy, or delusional. "What is it you hope to accomplish by coming with me?" he asked cautiously.

Her brow rose ever so slightly. "It was my efforts that got us on this boat. Perhaps it is you who are coming with me?"

He frowned. "It's too dangerous."

"Can you speak any other language but English?" she asked.

"Gaelic," he said pensively, not liking where this conversation was leading.

"I can speak English, Castilian, Arabic, and Hebrew. Such skill might be useful in a country filled with Jews, Muslims, and Christians. Don't you agree, Sir Alan Cathcart?"

He frowned. "I can't allow it."

"I have no intention of going home, or giving up." She straightened her shoulders and would have appeared almost regal if it weren't for her bloodstained and tattered clothes. "You're going to have to be sensible at some point. I can wait. We have a journey of several days ahead of us."

Alan found himself watching her with something close to fascination. High color rose in her cheeks. And he could just make out the rapid throb of her pulse in her delicate temple. He felt a sudden urge to reach out and touch that pulse, to trace his fingers over the silky smoothness that would be her skin.

He glanced away a heartbeat later. What was wrong with him? For a fraction of an instant he had actually felt a thickening in his groin. He, who had never strayed in thought or deed since taking his vows of obedience, chastity, and poverty to the Templar order.

At his silence she added, "I can't be dissuaded."

Lord, the lass was stubborn, Alan thought, trying to smother a spark of admiration. He steeled himself. Giving in to her would do no good. "Where I'm going is no place for a woman, especially an unchaperoned one.

It would be best to put an end to this journey before *my* quest becomes too dangerous. Your reputation has already suffered by being here with me in this boat."

She offered him a slight smile. "Not as badly as you think."

He frowned. "What does that mean?"

"I told everyone we were married."

"You what?"

She continued as though he hadn't spoken. "My reputation is safe as long as we remain together. Fulfilling the prophecy is my life's purpose. Perhaps you feel the same about your quest? They are actually the same purpose." She paused and a momentary doubt flickered in her eyes. "What are we questing for? Why did the prophecy not include such an important detail?"

A jab of exasperation shot through Alan as well as another emotion he refused to examine too closely. "I don't care what kind of tales you've concocted. My answer is still no, for your safety, my sanity, and a million other reasons. No." He pushed away from the railing and returned to his pallet, feeling suddenly exhausted and weak.

As he went he saw the color ebb from her skin, and her solemn eyes widened. He braced himself against a rush of sympathy. This was for the best. Besides, there was no softness left in him. The kind of life he'd led had allowed him to exercise little compassion, only duty.

As he sat he heard her voice carry on the breeze. "I'll change your mind." The words came softly but with a note of confidence. "I'll find a way to wear you down."

Jessamine kept her shoulders straight until the moment he lay down. Her bravado vanished the instant he turned his back on her. Her shoulders slumped, and she drew a long, quavering breath. It was just her luck that the prophecy would lead her to a man who would bluntly refuse her. In fact, the man had been more than eager to rid himself of her unwelcome presence.

She turned away and gazed back out over the Mediterranean Sea. She had two days to convince the knight to give in to her demands. Dear Heaven, how would she do it? How did one persuade a man to do something he didn't want to do?

Jessamine released a heavy sigh, suddenly weary. She would think of something. She had to. If she didn't go on this quest with the knight, she might soon find herself a victim of the conde's lecherous desires.

Chapter Five

The setting sun hung low on the horizon when Conde Salazar Mendoza appeared in the inn yard of the town of Mijas. Leaving ten armed men outside with the horses, the conde strode through the small wooden door and into the public room. He searched the hazy darkness of the chamber and the throng of men and women seated at long wooden tables for a familiar head of black hair.

It always annoyed him that Jessamine never wore the traditional Spanish headdress of her mother's people, preferring her hair loose and uncovered. As he searched the room, rage flared inside him. She wasn't there. A tall, skinny man skirted him, carrying a tray laden with piping-hot bowls of stew. The conde's arm snaked out, caught the man's arm, pulling him to a stop. The tray crashed to the floor.

"God's teeth." The man's angry cry silenced the chamber.

Every eye turned toward the doorway. The conde frowned impatiently at the gawking crowd. "I'm looking for someone." He reached for his belt and the purse of coins he kept there. With his free hand he removed a silver coin and thrust it at the server as compensation for the meals he'd ruined.

The server seized the coin with his free hand as he tried to shrink out of the conde's grasp.

The conde held tight. "There's more if anyone has

information," he said to the room at large. "The senorita I seek has long dark hair. She may have come into town on horseback with a foreigner, a man dressed in white." The conde tried to keep the venom from his voice as he continued to scan the room, searching for signs of recognition.

"Someone must know something?" The conde's fingers tightened on the server's arm.

"Let me go," the server whined as he tried once again to twist free of the conde's iron grasp.

Instead of releasing the server, the conde clenched the man's skin so hard he drew a sharp cry of pain.

The conde smiled. When he got his hands on Jessamine, he would take great pleasure in reprimanding her in a similar way. She would writhe in pain when he was through with her. A surge of satisfaction tightened his groin. He'd give her a good lesson on how to treat her husband.

"I might know something." A voice interrupted the conde's pleasant thoughts.

He scowled as a squat little man pushed back his chair and strode forward. "There was a girl who came into town today. She bartered with some fishermen to take her and the man you described on their boat."

"Who were these fishermen?" The conde thrust his fingers into his purse and withdrew three more silver coins. Two he tossed to the man. One he held up for all the room to see. "Who were they?"

A gray-haired old woman shuffled away from the crowd. "They spoke Hebrew."

They were headed for the Holy Land. "You're certain?" the conde demanded.

She nodded. "And one thing more." The old woman shuffled closer. "The girl addressed the man in white as her—"

"As her what?" His voice was tight.

"Husband."

For a moment, the conde's heart stopped. The word sank in. Jessamine had refused to marry him, then flung herself at a total stranger? Rage pulsed through his veins. He thrust the server at the old woman, knocking them both to the floor. Further venting his rage, he launched the silver coin at the woman. She yelped as the coin hit her cheek, but scrambled after it a heartbeat later. If he hadn't been so angry, he might have been amused by her desperation to keep what she felt she'd earned.

His anger so hot it was close to pain, the conde left the inn. "To the wharf," he directed his men. He would have to commandeer a ship that could overtake the fishing vessel Jessamine had hired. He had to find her and take back what was rightfully his.

The conde mounted, then led his men toward the smattering of boats just beyond the whitewashed inn. He curled his hand into a fist. When he found the bastard who was posing as Jessamine's husband . . . The man would be no good even for fish food, when the conde was done with him.

The next morning, after waking from an exhausted sleep, Jessamine stretched her neck, trying to ease the kinks left by a long, cold night. Mediterranean nights were cool and clear, and Jessamine had spent half of the last one staring up at the stars, wondering what she could do to sway the knight's opinion.

The ship was silent except for the gentle slap of the waves against the hull. By the first light of dawn, nothing had come to her. So she'd decided to simply be near him. Her presence seemed to irritate him. And she much preferred to irritate and annoy than to be dismissed.

She sat at the edge of his pallet and waited. A whistle

sounded, signaling the change of watch. The silent seamen who had seen the ship through the night moved belowdecks as others, fresh from sleep, emerged.

As each man stepped on deck, his gaze turned to her. Interest flared in their eyes. And lust. Her heart leaped. She glanced down at the knight. He was still lost in sleep, and her heart pounded jerkily with a queer sort of panic. No one had ever looked at her in such a way before. Not even the conde.

The men didn't take their posts, but stepped closer to her and Alan. Jessamine shivered with uneasiness as her hand slowly moved toward the knight's sword, which lay near her knees. Nervously, she counted them. Eight bearded men looked at her with lust, insolence, and anticipation.

Her gaze flew to the water. She could see the faint outline of land in the distance, but the ship was still too far away to hope for help from that quarter. Her fingers touched the sword's hilt, and she grasped the weapon. "Don't come any closer," Jessamine warned. When two of the sailors did, she leaped to her feet and held the lethal sword before her, hoping they didn't see how her fingers trembled.

The two men laughed. "We've decided your jewels weren't payment enough for this voyage." A young sailor with pale, beady eyes edged closer.

An older man with a hard, square jaw leered at her. "You've got other treasures we plan to enjoy."

Jessamine's stomach lurched. How could she have been so foolish to believe she'd be safe with a partially unconscious, injured man?

The shortest man in the group stepped closer. "This will be the easiest spoils we've ever earned."

Jessamine clutched the hilt, aiming the sword first at

one man, then another. She couldn't fight them all. She could hardly keep the heavy sword upright.

In a heartbeat, the knight surged upward from right beside her. He drew a dagger from his boot and jabbed one man in the shoulder while he kicked the second in the kneecap. Both men groaned from their pain and staggered backward, collapsing on the deck.

He turned back to her, extending his hand. "My sword?" he asked politely as he placed himself between her and their attackers.

Her heart hammering, she handed him the weapon, then watched him engage the men who'd rushed forward with deadly intent. The sound of steel echoed loudly in the silence of the morning. Alan caught one man with a blow to the back, another with a blow to the head. He didn't kill them, merely took them down, leaving no doubt that he could do more if the fighting continued.

The eyes of the men farthest away widened as Alan kicked one sailor in the gut, sending him crashing back into two more. He held another sailor at sword point. "Enough of this insanity. Four men are injured. How many more must follow?"

The men ceased their movements.

"The woman paid you for the voyage. Let that payment serve." His hard gaze passed over each man. "Get back to your posts."

With sullen faces, several of the men turned away as ordered. Four other sailors came forward and grasped the arms of the injured men, dragging them to the opposite end of the boat.

Alan sheathed his weapon. His hands shook and his face was decidedly pale as he turned to her. "Are you unharmed?"

Jessamine reached for his arm to steady him, but he

straightened, pushing her hand from his arm. "They must believe I'm capable of fighting them."

She nodded her understanding.

He moved to the stairs of the forecastle. He gripped the railing with a force that turned his knuckles white. "Are you unharmed?" he repeated as she followed him up.

"Yes, but I can't believe I was so foolish as to trust them."

"You did what you thought was best." Alan's response surprised her.

"What are we to do now?" she asked, looking nervously at the sailors gathered at the opposite end of the ship.

He offered her a tight smile as he took the wheel in his hands and turned the boat slightly to the north. "They won't dare bother us again until we make port. They're outmatched, and they know it."

"You know how to sail?"

He nodded. "I love the sea. I always have."

Jessamine gazed at the knight who'd taken control of the ship. "You seem remarkably well today despite your injuries."

This time his smile was genuine, and its impact left her a little breathless. "I told you. I heal quickly."

Jessamine fell silent. After a time she brought her gaze back to his. "Has the night also helped to change your mind about my coming with you?"

Any humor in his face vanished. "These men have proven that you'll be safer with me than by yourself." Alan focused his attention on the horizon before them. "You wanted a quest. Looks as though you are part of one now."

"Truly?"

He nodded.

"Thank you," she said, filled with relief and gratitude. He would not send her back to Spain . . . or to the conde.

His gaze moved to hers, his features rigid and unyielding. "Your coming along doesn't mean I believe your prophecy. It simply means I wish to protect you."

She nodded. She would convince him otherwise in time.

"I won't lie to you," he continued. "The quest before me is not an easy one, but I do promise that while you are with me you'll be safe."

She would finally have a chance to fulfill the purpose of her life. A million questions flooded her thoughts. "Where are we going?"

"We cannot discuss that now." This time his gaze moved to the sailors. "Discretion is essential."

Jessamine turned toward the land she could now see clearly in the distance. Sparkling waters of the deepest blue led to shimmering silver sand. Beyond, the golden stones of a seaside fort glinted beneath the rays of the morning sun. A bubble of happiness that she had not experienced for a very long time rose inside her. Suddenly she felt entirely at ease. Unafraid. Empowered by her destiny.

Their quest was about to begin.

Chapter Six

The girl wasn't a fool. He was, for bringing her with him. Alan frowned at the teeming throng of people who surged across the pier where he'd tied the rowboat that had brought him and Jessamine ashore. People drifted through the marketplace. Some were buying merchandise. Others sold their wares. A din of voices mixed with odd religious wails swirled around them. The sounds were nearly as oppressive as the hot desert air. Alan drew a labored breath beneath the heavy weight of his chain mail, feeling as though the heat seared his lungs. The water and wind at sea had masked the heat until now. He drew another breath, then another, until his breathing came easier.

Jessamine appeared not to be as affected as he was by the heat. She matched his steps as they moved through the crowd.

Odd scents assailed him as he wended his way through the market toward a young boy in the distance who might be able to help them. The sharp tang of unclean bodies mixed with the pungent scent of salt. The odors of dust, smoke, ripening fruit, and dung closed in around him. Alan forced himself to breathe normally as he approached the boy. "Are you for hire?" he asked.

When the boy gave him a puzzled look, Jessamine

asked the same question in what Alan could only assume was Hebrew. The boy nodded with an eager smile.

"What would you like to ask him?" Jessamine prompted Alan.

He held out a copper coin. "Ask him to take the boat back out to the ship for the others." She efficiently took care of the transaction and sent the boy on his way. All the while, Alan couldn't help frowning. Jessamine had been helpful. He had no doubt she would continue to be so.

But could he put her in the kind of danger she would experience on this quest? He couldn't abandon her in a city filled with strangers who would try to abuse her as the sailors had tried to do on the ship. It would be un-Christian of him to abandon her now, despite the fact she would slow him down.

His reasoning seemed logical if he didn't think too hard—about the way her scent made his heart race, or why the idea of other men looking at her the way the sailors had twisted his gut. He shook off his thoughts as he took her arm and led her deeper into the city of Jaffa. They needed to be away from the docks as quickly as possible, before the sailors aboard the ship could rally others and cause trouble.

Jessamine remained at his side as they walked through the streets of the fortified city. Jaffa had been at one time a glorious fortress held by the Templars. A momentary pang of regret stalled Alan's movements. His brothers had walked these same streets. He drew a sharp breath. He was here now to continue what the Templars had been unable to accomplish during their occupation. He would find where they'd hidden the Ark of the Covenant and bring it home.

Jessamine stopped beside him. An odd eagerness

warmed her features. "It's beautiful," she breathed. Her gaze traveled from the golden bricks of the city to the copper hills of the desert beyond. "Is that where we are going?"

Alan nodded. Jaffa was beautiful. He'd never been here before—he'd only heard stories from the other men. "Aye," he replied. "We'll hire a horse to take us to Jerusalem. That's where our quest begins.

"I'll not lie to you, Jessamine." Alan turned to her. "I do you no favor by allowing you to come with me. As I said before, it will be dangerous."

"I'm prepared." Determination lit her dark eyes.

"Then come," Alan said, continuing toward a stable yard. There he purchased a horse and helped Jessamine onto the animal's back before he mounted behind her. The cloth saddle was different from what he was used to, but he had to admit the design made it more comfortable to ride two astride, with only a small saddle horn between them.

Harsh, bright sunlight streamed down on them as they made their way through the streets of loose sand. The horse's plodding progress sent up a plume of reddish dust into the air. A thin layer of grit settled on their skin, and Alan knew they would have to make one more stop before leaving town.

When they came to a small wooden building with the symbol of a loom hanging from a hook near the door, Alan reined in his horse. "Stay here," he said as he dismounted. "I'll be right back." It didn't take long to buy what they needed. Even without the proper language skills, he was able to communicate what he wanted. He returned to the horse and tied the package to the back of the saddle before mounting once more.

Eager to put some distance between themselves and the town, Alan pushed the horse into a slow run. Once they'd cleared Jaffa, he let the horse fall back into a walk. In the distance he could see nothing but desert, but he knew the ancient city was out there. They headed east.

The air became still and silent. There were no more voices or soft wailing sounds. No slap of the waves against the shore or vendors hawking their wares. There was only the occasional spiraling of a bird through the open blue sky, the slithering of a snake across the cool morning ground.

The sun continued its slow, inexorable trek across the sky. Spiky and thorny scrub brush dotted the ground, with an occasional acacia tree breaking the monotony. The landscape should have been dreary when compared to the lush greenery of Scotland. But it wasn't.

Against the golden sand beneath their horse's feet, the bluish green of the scrub brush sparkled like gems set into a rich setting of gold.

"We'll be stopping here for a moment." Alan reined the horse to a stop near an acacia tree. He dismounted first, then helped Jessamine down.

She didn't step away. She stayed there in the circle of his arms and reached up. With a silken palm, she cupped his cheek. "You have risked so much for me in the last few days."

As she spoke, he couldn't seem to tear his gaze away from her full, tempting mouth. Her lips were red and inviting. No doubt they would be even softer than her hand. . . .

The screech of a bird broke into Alan's wayward thoughts, and he pulled away. He went to the saddle and untied the package he'd purchased from the weaver. Unrolling the fabric, he handed Jessamine a lightweight butter yellow gown of the softest wool, a chemise, and a cream-colored veil. "To replace your torn and soiled garments," he said. "This garb will be cooler out here in the desert and help us to look like the locals."

She nodded before she withdrew from him, heading behind the acacia tree.

The sweet scent of jasmine still clung to his body where she'd pressed up against him. His gaze followed her to the tree. She struggled to unlace her gown. With a groan, he turned his back on the sight and pulled his mail hauberk over his head, followed by his quilted ake-ton. Once he was free of the heavy armor, his breath came easier. He would have less protection without the mail, but at least he'd be able to breathe. A soft breeze seemed to caress his flesh.

He turned slightly, his gaze once again moving to the base of the tree, where a splash of peach-colored silk lay. His gaze moved up. She stood with her back to him, but that didn't hide her long legs or the rounded buttocks that danced in and out of sight beneath her long black hair as she struggled to pull the new chemise over her head.

Alan's body hardened as he took in Jessamine's dark beauty—her honeyed skin and lean body. Something about her compelled him like no other woman he'd met before. He watched her slip the chemise over her head, watched it slide down her naked flesh. She followed the same movements with her gown. He fisted his hands as her fingers smoothed the fabric in place.

He wrenched his gaze away from Jessamine and back to the black beast that would be their transportation. The animal nuzzled the ground in an attempt to find food. Alan drew comfort from the familiar sight. Horses he was used to. Women . . .

He grabbed the long muslin shirt and long brown robe he had purchased for himself and fastened the robe around his body as he'd seen the other men in the marketplace do. When Jessamine reappeared, he was mounted and waiting. He offered her his hand and drew her up onto the horse, settling her before him once more. The now familiar scent of jasmine caught him in its grasp again. His body instantly tightened and his mind flashed back to the sight of her naked backside. With a silent groan, he set the horse in motion. This would be a long, frustrating quest if he didn't shift his mind to other things.

A black buzzard glided effortlessly in a giant, spiraling arc through the cloudless sky overhead, reminding Alan that along with beauty, there was also death in the desert. He had to stay sharp, anticipate danger before it arrived.

"Now that we're alone, may I ask what it is we are searching for?" Jessamine's delicate voice broke into his thoughts. "You said we are heading toward Jerusalem. Why there?"

"Because that is the first place I must search for the Ark of the Covenant."

She faced him, her eyes wide. "The Ark of the Covenant?"

Alan nodded. "I have two letters from a Templar knight who came here during the Templar's occupation of the Holy Land in 1291. He and his men claim they found the ark. But all communication with the knights ended abruptly before they could reveal the hiding place."

If it were possible, Jessamine's eyes grew wider. "You know the location of the ark?"

"I know its probable location."

She frowned. "Then you don't know."

"I've spent the last two years studying the legends and stories. I've read the letters and memorized the clues left for us in the text of the Bible itself." He caught her gaze and held it. "It's in one of four places."

She nodded, knowing where he was headed. "Jerusalem and the Temple Mount are where we begin this search?"

"Aye. The Temple of Jerusalem is the most fought-over patch of land in the world. In ancient times the Egyptians, Babylonians, Persians, Greeks, Romans, and Jews all fought and died for control of it." He paused for a moment before continuing. "More recently, the Arabs and the crusaders shed their blood to take, hold, lose, and retake the sacred mount."

"My people and yours," she said softly.

"Exactly."

"Maybe that's why you and I are here together. To unite our purposes for the common good."

He shrugged. A part of him still wondered if Jessamine had some hidden reason for being here with him. Time would reveal the truth. In the meanwhile, he would be careful.

The remainder of the journey passed in silence. The sun started its descent as they entered the outskirts of Jerusalem and headed for the Dome of the Rock. A call to prayer hung in the air as they reached the interior of the city. Cobbled streets led through the Jewish Quarter and the Jaffa Gate. Once inside the city it was hard to look anywhere but at the dome of copper that glinted in the sun like a divine beacon.

Alan brought their horse to a stop. "We need to leave the animal here." He dismounted, then offered Jessamine a hand down. She slid from the horse into his arms. A wave of heat suffused Alan that had nothing to do with the sun beating down over them. Jessamine must have felt it too, because her cheeks flushed and she stepped back. "Is that the Dome of the Rock?" she asked, avoiding his gaze.

"Aye. Cover your head and face before we approach

the Western Wall," Alan said, pulling his own head-dress over his hair. "No one can stand in sight of the Western Wall without a head covering."

He led Jessamine through the crowd to the plaza at the foot of the Western Wall. Men stood on the left side of the wall, women on the right, rocking rhythmically and reverently before the ancient, weathered stones. Bowing repeatedly, they dutifully recited their prayers.

"Come," Alan said, leading Jessamine away from the holy sight. "We need to walk through what used to be the Royal Portico of Solomon's Temple to reach the underground tunnels."

"Is that where you think the ark can be found?" Jessamine whispered, close to his side.

He didn't answer as they approached the south side of the plaza. Two guards flanked the tunnel entrance.

"How will we get past them?" she asked.

He turned back to the Western Wall as though searching for something. "Trust me." With a hand on the small of her back, Alan guided Jessamine slightly past the tunnel entrance. Quite suddenly a warbling cry rent the air, and the two guards moved away from the passage to face the worshippers at the wall. They dropped to their knees in response to the call to prayer.

"Now." Alan turned back to the tunnels and they stepped inside unchallenged.

A series of openings lay before them, what remained of ancient rooms and passageways that would have been at street level at one time. Alan's thoughts drifted back to the research he'd done. He knew the way to go even though he'd never been here before. The route was clear in his mind.

He guided Jessamine to the tunnel on the left. Torches lit the passageway through a series of vaulted chambers and into another tunnel. The temperature dropped sharply and the musty smell of mold and ancient, crumbling brickwork hung in the air.

They hurried through one vaulted chamber after another until finally they entered a much larger and differently designed chamber. The other spaces they'd passed through were plain and clearly functional, whereas the roof of this one was supported by ornamental columns and the walls were adorned with stonework. "This chamber is known as the Hall of the Hasmoneans. It dates back to the time of Herod the Great."

Jessamine moved about the chamber, careful to avoid the large, round rocks stacked in the corners. "What are these?" she asked.

"They are what remain of the missiles that were flung from catapults by the Romans when they stormed Jerusalem after the Jewish Revolt. It was during that time that the Romans looted the temple as they pillaged and sacked the city. Some scholars believe that the Ark of the Covenant was among the spoils taken."

Jessamine stopped her exploration and turned to him. "You don't think the ark was taken then?"

He shook his head. "I believe that the ark was removed by the priesthood shortly before the Romans descended on the city."

She turned startled eyes to him. "Then why are we here?"

"To make certain my suspicions are correct. Shall we find out?"

When she nodded, Alan grabbed a torch from the wall sconce and headed deeper into the labyrinth. The passageway seemed to twist and turn randomly.

"How do you know where we are going?" Jessamine asked.

"I studied ancient records." He said nothing more,

caught up in the excitement of the search. With each step, the temperature dropped as they made their way through the part of the maze that would have been underground even in Herod's day.

They'd arrived at yet another chamber, one deep within the tunnel complex. A bricked-up archway took up the far wall of the room. Alan handed Jessamine the torch, then drew his dagger from his boot. He moved to the archway and, with powerful strokes, hacked at the mortar at the edge of the archway. "Behind this wall is where the Ark of the Covenant was kept in the Holy of Holies."

In the torchlight, Jessamine's face turned ashen. She gazed nervously up the passageway. "What would happen to us if they caught us digging here?"

Alan shrugged and kept digging away at the ancient barrier. "They would most likely put us to death."

Jessamine gasped.

Alan continued to dig. Small chunks of stone pinged against the dirt floor as he created a hand-sized gap in the mortar.

"But you really don't know if the ark is there or not, do you? We could be risking our lives for nothing."

"Perhaps, but is it not your own prophecy that tells you we're not searching in vain?"

"You believe in the prophecy?"

"I said no such thing." He paused suddenly, listening to the shuffle of feet in the passageway beyond. Chance passersby would not be this deep in the temple complex. Had they been discovered? Alan palmed the dagger, ready to strike.

Jessamine's gaze went wide and shifted between the doorway and him. "Do you honestly believe the ark isn't behind that archway?"

"I do."

She turned toward the door. "Then let us be away from here. I have no wish to die in this dark chamber."

Alan sheathed his dagger in his boot. If they didn't leave now, they'd be trapped, and he already knew they would find nothing inside. Halfway up the passageway they came upon an old man with shockingly white hair, garbed in a long white robe.

For a moment, he blocked the doorway, studying both Alan and Jessamine with an intensity that sent Alan's pulse thudding. Despite the man's age, Alan sensed strength in him. Alan clenched his fist, fighting the urge to draw his sword. He wouldn't fight in this holiest of places unless provoked to defend himself and Jessamine.

Finally, the man uttered something in Arabic as he moved aside to let them pass. Yet even as they stepped around the old man, Alan could feel his watchful gaze upon them. Alan was grateful to note that the old man didn't follow.

Together he and Jessamine moved back through the endless maze of passageways. It seemed like forever before they reached the end of the long narrow tunnel and emerged into the waning evening light, to be met by an overly large man wielding a sword. The man was dressed all in black. Yet the look on his face was darker than his garments. Ten heavily armed men closed in around Alan and Jessamine.

"The conde," Jessamine breathed at Alan's side.

Chapter Seven

Jessamine looked past Alan at the man she'd hoped never to see again. Bile rose in her throat at the murderous look in the conde's black eyes.

"My bride," the conde growled. "You've put me to a lot of trouble."

Jessamine wrapped her arms across her chest to ward off a sudden chill despite the evening heat. "I'm not your bride."

"Do you know this man, Jessamine?" Alan's lips tightened grimly. The men flanking the conde moved in, yet Alan's hand didn't go to his sword. Instead, he widened his stance, preparing for a different method of attack.

"Unfortunately, yes. But it's not as he says. We're not married."

The conde lurched forward. "The hell you say!"

Alan's arm came up to block the conde's movements, his palm flat against the conde's chest.

The conde flinched back. "How dare you?" He drew his sword.

"Come no closer to Jessamine." Alan's voice was like steel.

Neither man moved.

Jessamine's gaze moved from Alan, whose expression was intense but not frightening, to the conde, whose eyes glittered with rage. Tension made the air seem suddenly heavy and still. She'd known the conde would follow her, but she couldn't go back to Spain with that man, to the life of abuse and servitude he intended for her. She had a prophecy to fulfill. And more than that, she wanted her freedom. Her throat grew thick with unshed tears.

The conde broke the stillness, signaling his men to advance. "You cannot defeat me alone."

The men rushed forward, their hooked swords drawn.

"Cease!" Alan's voice boomed. "This is a place of peace. Sheathe your weapons at once."

The Spaniards froze, startled. And Alan took advantage of that momentary pause. He grasped Jessamine's hand and hauled her toward the Western Wall, where they vanished into the crowd.

Jessamine looked back over her shoulder. The conde and his men had tried to follow, but the two guards stationed at the tunnel entrance had returned and blocked their way. She saw no more as she and Alan ran back through the Jaffa Gate to the horse that waited there.

Alan swung her up on the back of their horse. She barely had time to settle before he joined her and spurred their mount through the city streets. They flew across town while people scurried out of their way. By the time they'd reached the edge of Jerusalem, Alan had slowed the horse to a walk. "Stay alert," he warned as he pulled her farther into his arms, protecting her. "We cannot risk staying in town. We must head for the wilderness."

The conde had followed her. Her chest tightened. His presence threatened everything—Alan's quest for the ark and their fulfillment of the prophecy. If Alan hadn't been there to protect her . . . She shuddered.

But he had been. He was part of the prophecy as well. She frowned. Had the seeress known that? Was Jessamine's relationship with Alan directed by fate? Her heart sped up. Was the conde part of the puzzle as well, or was his interference something the seeress had not counted on?

No matter, the conde presented an urgent problem. Somehow, they had to get rid of him before the man ruined everything.

When they reached the outskirts of town, Alan slowed the horse. "Who was that man, Jessamine? And this time, I want nothing but the truth."

Jessamine gazed at Alan. "He's the Conde Salazar Mendoza, and the reason I ran onto the battlefield. He wants to force me to marry him."

A tic started in his jaw. "He followed you to Jerusalem. Why would he do that?"

She was tempted to turn around, to shield herself from his searching gaze, but she met his eyes. "I want to follow the prophecy, not bind myself to a man who has no right to me."

His gaze narrowed. A flash of anger darkened his eyes. "You will tell me all you aren't saying when we bed down for the night, so prepare yourself."

Jessamine nodded stiffly. They fell silent as Jessamine grappled with what she would say to him when the time came. Her fear slowly receded as she listened to the sound of Alan's breathing against her ear. She found the sound comforting despite the fact he was angry with her. She couldn't blame him. He'd come here on a quest and he'd ended up with trouble.

Despite it all, a sense of exhilaration moved through Jessamine because she was finally doing something with her life, not just meekly accepting her fate. She was taking a stand, reaching out for what she wanted—to follow where the prophecy led her, for better or worse. For a short while, she would have her freedom.

Idly, she traced the threads of her new gown. She liked the simple garment. She especially liked the way it made her look. Ordinary. Until three days ago, she would never have dared to try leading an ordinary life. Having left the court, the palace, and all the responsibilities of being a princess behind her, she was filled not with fear, but joy.

She realized that for the past nineteen years she'd been a prisoner. Her uncle loved her, but since she wasn't his child, and her parents no longer lived, she was often ignored, and isolated.

Out here, in the desert, she was free from the demands of court, the king, and all his expectations. Out here, she was simply Jessamine. She could blend into a crowd. She could do whatever she wanted for the first time in her life. A shiver coursed through her as both exhilaration and fear tightened her chest.

Alan wanted answers. She'd tell the knight at least some of the truth. But nothing would make her admit to being a princess.

She glanced up at the darkening sky. The sun was setting quickly.

As if in response to her thoughts, Alan said, "The darkness will offer us protection, fear not."

"With you, I'm not afraid," she admitted, gazing back into his face.

His eyebrows drew together. "You shouldn't say such things to me."

"Perhaps not, but it's the truth, and that's what you asked me to give you."

"So I did." Regret tinged his voice.

Jessamine drew a long, shaky breath. "I'll tell you what you want to know now." She felt his muscles tense against her back. "The truth is," she said softly, "when you found me on the battlefield—"

"You could have died," he interrupted.

"For a moment I wanted to. That outcome seemed preferable to sacrificing myself on the altar of marriage."

"He is your bridegroom?" Alan inquired in a harsh voice.

Jessamine shook her head. "No. Never. He wants to marry me only for the—" She stopped abruptly. She'd almost betrayed herself. Any mention of political advantage would only raise more questions. "He's a brutal man," she admitted. Alan had witnessed some of that brutality today. She prayed that one glimpse would garner his support.

"He's hit you?"

"Yes," she replied, pulling back her hair to reveal the bruise on her cheek. "He would have done worse had I not run onto that battlefield. He killed my mother."

"God's teeth! No woman deserves such brutality." His eyes grew stormy.

Jessamine closed her eyes, fighting back tears once more. She would not be so weak as to cry in front of this knight. She wasn't the kind of woman who manipulated men through female weakness. She straightened her shoulders and opened her eyes.

"Not all men are brutal, Jessamine," he said softly against her ear. "You deserve someone to love you, not cause you pain."

The husky sincerity in his voice stole her breath. She met his eyes. His gaze was personal, intimate. Again her breath faltered. This wasn't the foolish repartee she was used to from the men at court.

This man might be a Christian warrior monk, but he was dangerous. With him, she felt as breathless as she did protected. A dangerous combination.

Disturbed by her thoughts, she turned to face the open expanse of desert. The only sound was the whisper of their breath in the cooling, motionless air.

When he finally stopped the horse, the stars hung high in the velvet black sky. "The horse needs a rest, as do we. We'll stop here for the night."

Jessamine searched the moonlit darkness. They'd stopped near a rock outcropping that towered high overhead. Alan dismounted first, then helped her down. As she slid down beside him, she could feel his hard length. Instantly, the tension that had built between them before surged back to life. His hands encircled her waist, gentle, yet firm. She should have felt threatened, overpowered, engulfed. Instead, she felt the stirrings of passion. Her gaze rose to his face. A somber and tender expression lingered there.

"We'll sleep in the open then?" she asked. Her voice sounded strange to her own ears.

His gaze lost its softness. "We'll be safe enough. I can see and hear anyone who approaches."

"Won't you sleep?"

"Not likely."

"But you'll need your rest if the conde—"

"You'd be surprised how little sleep one needs to battle an enemy."

She could imagine he'd known many sleepless nights. She had too, in the past few days since they'd met. It wasn't Alan that caused her sleeplessness. It was the conde. She would do anything she could to escape the man who'd killed her mother.

"He's my enemy," she said quietly, hearing the catch in her own voice.

"For now, it makes him mine as well," Alan said softly.

As she gazed into those mesmerizing blue eyes of his,

with his hands on her waist, Jessamine's breath stilled in her chest. At that moment the conde and the threat he offered were the furthest things from her mind. Nothing seemed to matter except the sound of Alan's deep, compelling voice.

Heat came into his eyes. His body remained rigid, yet he pulled her slightly forward and his lips nearly brushed her hair before he set her away.

A dull ache of disappointment tightened her chest as they looked at each other in silence. "Where do we sleep?" she asked, trying to break the tension.

"On the ground would be most appropriate."

"Do we sleep now . . . ?" Jessamine's voice trailed off as she looked at this tall, handsome man who was completely off-limits to her. Not only was he beneath her socially, he was also a self-proclaimed monk. Swallowing, she tried again, "Are you tired?"

"My thoughts have little to do with sleep," he said in a husky whisper. Suddenly his eyes were smoldering. He shifted toward her, then went utterly still, as if waiting expectantly for her to take the final step that would bring them close once more.

She took that step. His arms encircled her and a warm, searching mouth descended on hers. Parted lips, both tender and insistent, stroked hers, molding them, shaping them to his. Just when she felt she would melt in his arms, the kiss deepened. His hands tightened on her back, her shoulders, caressing and possessive.

A needy sigh escaped her as she reached up, her hands grasping his broad shoulders, clinging to them for support in a world where nothing mattered anymore except experiencing more of this dangerous passion.

When he finally dragged his mouth from hers, he kept her close in the circle of his arms. She laid her cheek against the rough texture of his robe, feeling his lips brush the hair atop her head. His heart thudded in his chest, matching the cadence of her own frantic heartbeat.

What had just happened? Never had she felt so swept away by a force outside herself. She drew a shuddering breath. Was this the kind of passion her mother and father had shared? The kind of overwhelming desire that stole logic and reason—the kind of madness that had made her father give up his crown in order to spend his days in exile with her mother?

"That was a mistake," he whispered into the darkness. "God help us both."

"You're right," she admitted, placing distance between them. "That was a mistake."

When Jessamine felt more in control, she brought her gaze to his. "We . . ." She spoke the word with emphasis, praying she would find the strength to put into words what must be said. "We must never give ourselves over to such abandon again. From this point on, we need to behave with proper decorum."

The glint of his smile shone in the dark. "Is that how it's done in Spain?"

"We need to behave twice as properly now to make up for our lack earlier."

"If you insist," he said, bowing, then extending his arm out to her. "Milady, it would be my pleasure to escort you to your bed for the night."

His words were probably not the most proper, but she understood his meaning. She placed her fingers on his arm and allowed him to walk her to the outcropping. In the moonlight, she could make out a smooth patch below it. She released his arm and settled on the ground. Jessamine curled her legs beneath the skirt of her gown. She leaned her head back against the rock outcropping. "The moon and the stars are so beautiful tonight."

He settled on the ground beside her, careful to maintain a proper distance. "That is one thing we all have in common."

"What is that?"

"The night sky. The moon and the stars follow us wherever we go."

"That's a comforting thought." She tipped her head back and concentrated on the stars. She searched for familiar star patterns. Instead, her attention was caught by a strange blue star that hovered slightly lower than all the rest. It hung in the night sky just off to her left. Now it shifted its position to directly above them.

A chill moved along her flesh. "That star . . ." She pointed to the small blue orb, which moved yet again to her right. Jessamine tensed. "Are stars supposed to move?"

Alan must have seen it too, because he got to his feet. "I've seen flashes of light in the night sky that were falling stars."

Jessamine stood beside him. "This one isn't falling."

"Nay, it's slowly spiraling downward," he agreed with a note of wonder. "Perhaps it's lightning. I've heard tales of lightning that forms in balls instead of streaks across the sky."

Jessamine stepped closer to Alan's side as the orb descended toward them. She reached for his arm, needing the feel of something solid as she realized that the star was actually a blue light no larger than her fist. "Alan—"

"I see. It is no star."

Chapter Eight

The fist-sized orb of blue light came closer, until it hovered at Alan's eye level. The odd light hung there, as though waiting. Alan stepped away from Jessamine, drew his sword, then positioned himself in front of her.

Jessamine felt her mouth part in wonder. Despite the nervousness that rooted her to the ground, she could honestly say she wasn't afraid. A strange kind of calm descended over her in the light's presence. The blue orb moved from Alan to her.

He shifted, and raised his sword. Jessamine stilled his movements with a hand on his sword arm. "I don't think it wants to hurt us," she whispered.

"That's good, because I doubt my sword will have any effect on it." A heartbeat later, the blue orb swirled around both their heads, then spiraled into the night sky and disappeared.

Jessamine stood silent, staring into the dark space the light had just occupied. The soft whoosh of leather against steel sounded as Alan sheathed his sword.

"It's a sign," she whispered.

"Of what?" he asked.

"That we are blessed."

Alan shook his head. "Sometimes, there is no meaning behind things that happen."

"I refuse to believe that. The blue light meant something special." She straightened and turned to face him.

"I'm taking it as a sign that we're on the right track with our quest. It's one more affirmation that destiny is showing us the way."

"Believe what you like." He motioned with his hand toward the rock outcropping behind them. "Come, let's try to get some rest, even if neither of us can sleep. We'll need to start off early tomorrow morning to make certain we stay ahead of your bridegroom."

"He's not my bridegroom."

He released a soft chuckle. "It was a joke."

"Not a funny one," she replied as they repositioned themselves on the ground. "Where do we go next?"

He leaned his head back against the rock and with his hand beckoned her to lean against his shoulder. She stiffened. How she wanted to lay her head down on his shoulder, but she knew she must not. Touching him now, when she was tired and still baffled by the mysterious light, might prove a dangerous combination. She had to resist what he offered.

"Tomorrow morning we enter the Judean wilderness on the western side of the Dead Sea."

"Why? Is that where you believe the Ark of the Covenant is?"

"It's where the clues lead."

Silence hovered between them for a time as the stars glittered and the heat of the day slipped away to leave a bitter chill. "Alan?" Jessamine sat up. "Why do you think the prophecy brought us together?"

In the half-light provided by the stars, his features shuttered. "It was the war, not the prophecy that brought us together."

"I don't believe that any more than I believe the blue light was nothing but a coincidence," she said softly. She leaned back slightly and studied the man beside her. His eyes were his most arresting feature—as light as the sky one moment, and as dark as midnight the next. His eyes commanded attention, and at times seemed to probe too deeply. His gaze moved over her now, assessing her. Did he find her wanting?

"I'm your partner in this quest, just as the prophecy revealed," he said.

"But you don't believe in the prophecy," she reminded him.

"I believe in God, not in fate or destiny. I believe in things I can see and touch."

She laughed. "And you've seen God, have you?"

A dark look crossed his features. He grasped a handful of sand and allowed it to run through his fingers to the ground. "Nay, but I can see the proof of God in this sand and the rock at my back. I can see his goodness in your eyes, and feel his divine presence in the whisper of the night air."

"I believe in all that, and more." She leaned her head back against the rock. "Sometimes there are other forces that guide our lives. It's been my experience that people are led to the things they need. They must then open their eyes and accept the gifts they've been given. It's not some divine being who's acting on their behalf, it's free will. People are given choices that determine what happens next in their lives." She let her words trail off at the irritated scowl he turned on her.

She crossed her arms over her chest and looked away. "Fine. We are at an impasse. Let's just leave it at that."

"Aye, we'll drop it for now," he replied with a thicker brogue than usual.

Silence hung heavy between them until finally he sighed. "If you want me to believe in the prophecy, then tell me what else it foretells, more slowly this time."

Was he laughing at her again, or was he truly interested? Jessamine frowned. "The second stanza of the prophecy talks of a mount or, I've always assumed it to mean, a mountain."

"Tell me."

"'Thunder and lightning, a cloud upon the mount, and the voice of the trumpet shall call out loud. Only without sight will you know what is real and bring to the world the hidden seal.'" The words rolled off her tongue as they had so many times before, except now they had meaning and context. Alan had said they were heading into the wilderness—mountainous wilderness, from what she'd seen before the sun had set. "Does that make sense to you?"

He nodded. "In my research, I came across a reference to the trumpet of God found in the ancient city of Petra."

"Petra?" she asked.

"The city of stone."

Jessamine had no idea what or where Petra was, but the very word sounded exotic. She stared out into the vast expanse of darkness and felt her tension and nervousness evaporate. The conde would never find her in the wilderness. She was safe to follow the prophecy and her own dreams.

Jessamine shifted away from Alan and settled against the rock at her back, careful not to touch any part of him. She needed the distance to center her thoughts—something she found increasingly harder to do when Alan touched her.

She tipped her head to look at the wondrous display of stars overhead. The sky was so immense, the stars were so sharp, so clear. She felt as though she were falling into those stars instead of looking up at them. A sense of awe moved through her, and for the first time she felt a touch of gratitude toward the conde. If he hadn't come after her, she would never have found the courage to leave her uncle or her home, to follow the prophecy.

She drew a deep breath and quietly reveled in the breeze that brushed against her cheeks in soft, cool waves. The night stilled and she heard the ripple of the leaves in the distant acacia trees, the slip of the sand as it drifted across the desert floor. And beside her, she heard the soft cadence of Alan's breathing. The sounds were hypnotic, lulling her into a quiet peacefulness where sleep awaited.

Alan came awake with a start. Nothingness curled around him. The stars had faded from the night sky. The world around him seemed suddenly thick and suffocating. The air held a tension that had not been there before. He felt swallowed by the nothingness, surrounded, watched. His hand moved to the hilt of his sword as his heart sped up. The sound of his heartbeat pounded in his ears. He'd felt such nothingness many times just before an enemy struck. It was as if the physical world could sense the coming conflict, the pain, the death, and responded with silence.

Nay! He chided himself, trying to banish his fears. Someone was out there, but this was no war. He was in control of the situation because he'd been warned. He gripped his sword and silently withdrew it from its sheath. His eyes adjusted to the darkness and he could now make out the dark shape of the rock behind him, the trees in the distance. The world was not black but a deep, hazy gray. Alan focused his thoughts and listened to the only other recognizable sound—the regular intake and release of Jessamine's breathing.

He slid his fingers to the left until he felt the warmth of her body. To his surprise, her fingers tightened around his own. She hadn't been asleep. She must have felt it too, the odd tension in the air.

At the snap of a branch, Alan tightened his fingers around hers, then released them. Their eyes met in the darkness. He could see fear in her expression. He prayed she could see the silent warning in his. "Whatever happens, stay behind me," he whispered in an almost imperceptible tone.

She nodded. Together they stood. With a tip of his head, he signaled toward the horse. The hairs on the back of his neck rose as the awareness of others pressed in upon him once more. Robbers? An ambush? The Moors' attack still lingered fresh in his mind as grief clawed at his senses. He'd abandoned his Templar brothers.

The breath caught in his chest as pain swamped him, weighed him down. He staggered to one side. He'd failed to keep them safe. Images of their torn and bleeding bodies battered at the closed door of his mind, slipping through the cracks, drawing strength from his remorse. The pain of grief flashed through him with blinding force. His sword was too heavy.

Then the warmth of Jessamine's hand curled around his elbow, her grip strong and supportive. He clung to the sensation, allowed it to ease the pain in his soul. His breathing slowed, his strength returned. The darkness of the night seemed to ease as pale moonlight spilled across the desert sand at their feet.

That hell lay behind him. Jessamine was here with him now. No harm would come to her. Not while he could do something to prevent it. Alan concentrated on the sounds of the night, the soft shuffle of feet coming from the west. One man, two, three. They approached slowly, like snakes ready to strike.

Alan tightened his grip on his sword. He was ready.

A flicker of movement came on the left. Farther back on the right a streak of black appeared.

A flash of light illuminated the area as one of the men lit a torch. Three men dressed in dark clothing approached. Each held a hooked sword in his hand. Alan's heart thudded. He forced his breathing to slow, centered his thoughts, allowed the men to come closer, step by step.

Jessamine remained silent, but her body tensed, waiting.

For a brief moment he considered fighting them, then banished the thought. Three men to one. He couldn't endanger Jessamine that way, not when they could reach the horse and escape. Alan waited until the invaders massed together as the rocks narrowed. The closer they were to each other, the harder it would be for them to maneuver. Two more steps and Alan darted backward, taking Jessamine with him.

He reached the horse and tossed her onto the animal's back. As he joined her, the horse surged forward, understanding Alan's unspoken command. The two lurched into the darkness, away from the men who closed in on them.

Angry shouts filled the night air. The men raced forward, but they were too late. Alan guided the horse around a rock outcropping. A man's shape separated itself from the dark mass. He leaped from the rock, toward them. Alan managed to maneuver the horse away before the man could pull either him or Jessamine to the ground.

"Hold tight to the horse's mane," Alan warned Jessamine as he kicked the horse into a gallop. They flew across the sand, illuminated only by a pale silver light. Shadows cast by rocks or brush or possible brigands appeared at every turn. Alan tensed as they passed each one, fearing more attackers. Another rock outcropping appeared ahead. He gave it a wide berth as they sailed by.

Another man leaped out at them. He stepped toward the horse but didn't attack. Instead, the man raised a tube-shaped object to his lips.

Jessamine gasped. Her hand moved to her neck a moment before she collapsed against the horse.

"Jessamine." Alan searched the darkness ahead and headed the horse farther into the desert, away from the attackers. He clung to Jessamine's body as she sagged against the animal. Had they used poison? If that was the case, she needed immediate help. But he couldn't stop now. "I'm here with you," he said, more for his own comfort than hers. He had to put some distance between them and their attackers.

She lay so still, her weight tugging against his arm. Even in the hazy darkness he could see a protrusion at the side of her neck and feel the trickle of blood that slid down her skin and onto his. They'd hit her with some sort of blow dart.

Alan maneuvered the horse back toward the rocks. He had to find a cave. The Judean wilderness was riddled with them. "Hold on, Jessamine."

It didn't take long to find a cave that looked deep enough to hide the two of them along with the horse. He circled the area several times, laying down several sets of tracks. It would do no good to enter the cave to treat Jessamine's wounds if it became a trap for them both. When he was certain no one would be able to follow his trail, he headed back for the cave.

Once they were shielded by the darkness, Alan dismounted with Jessamine cradled in his arms. As he set her down, her head lolled back. Silver light from the moon illuminated the cave, and he could see her skin was a pale, deathly white.

He quickly grasped the edge of the dart that protruded from her neck and yanked it out. She flinched. In the next heartbeat he flicked the dart against the tip of his tongue. Snake venom mixed with something else he couldn't identify—some other poison that had robbed her of consciousness.

He knew what he must do. He drew his sword and set it on the ground beside him, then withdrew his dagger from his boot. With a steady hand, he traced the tiny puncture wound in her neck with the edge of the blade, drawing a rivulet of blood. Setting his dagger on the ground beside her head, he brought his lips to the new incision and sucked the poison from the wound. As his mouth filled, he spat the blood onto the ground and repeated the process. Over and over he drew the venomous blood from her system until the bleeding slowed.

Carefully he set her head down on the sand, then stood. He moved to the horse and removed a bladder of water from the saddlebag along with a smaller bag containing crystallized honey before he returned to her side. He cleansed the wound with water, then wiped it dry before applying a poultice of honey. He'd learned on the battlefield that honey helped to draw putrefaction from the body. Perhaps it would have the same effect on poison.

When he was through, he wrapped a clean strip of linen loosely about her neck, then sat upon the ground and positioned Jessamine's head in the crook of his legs, cradling her gently. He'd done all he could for her. Now time would be either his friend or enemy.

At that thought a cold chill invaded his chest. He didn't know the woman he held in his arms, not really. Yet the thought of losing her brought a wave of deep regret. He tried to shrug it away, but the feeling of hopelessness he'd tried so hard to control over the past few days simmered below the surface, waiting to erupt. He had to stay in control. Jessamine needed him.

He wiped his forehead, feeling the grit of sand roll beneath his hand. Lord, he was tired. So very tired. And so damned hot.

Alan shook off his exhaustion and returned his attention to the woman in his lap. He carefully tied a length of fresh linen around her neck, protecting her wound. It was his fault she had been injured. If he'd left her back at the port where they'd disembarked, she wouldn't be in this position now.

Or she could have been in an even worse situation, abused by the sailors, or the conde. He took slight comfort in that thought as he studied her in the half-light. A dark swath of her hair had fallen across her cheek. He gently brushed it back to tuck it behind her ear, and jerked his fingers away.

Alan clenched his jaw, suppressing the urge to gather her tightly against him and keep her safe. He balled his fists, resisting the urge. Lord, what was wrong with him? He'd never had this kind of reaction to a woman before.

He stared off into the darkness. His emotions had been veering from one wild extreme to another since leaving Teba behind. But losing control now wouldn't help. He took a deep breath and unfurled his fingers. He had to think about the present, not the past.

"Jessamine?"

No response. He swallowed, tucking his pain further inside himself and concentrating on the night. He heard the soft, whispered rush of wind blowing against the mouth of the cave. He longed to turn his face into that wind to find some relief from the heat, but he couldn't risk it. The enemy could be anywhere. He pulled the hilt of his sword closer to his side.

"Alan?" Her voice was barely a whisper, but the very

fact that she had survived the poison brought a warm glow to the center of his chest.

He touched her cheek. "Jessamine, can you hear me?"

Her eyes fluttered open. She turned toward his voice.

"How do you feel?" he asked.

"I don't know." Her dark, compelling eyes searched his face. "What happened?"

"You took a blow dart in the neck that was laced with poison."

Jessamine's eyes widened as her fingers crept up to her neck to find the bandage he'd wrapped around her delicate flesh. "Those men?"

He nodded. "Assassins."

"Why were they after us?"

"They could have been bandits. But my guess is it's more than that. We must be getting close to some truth about the ark."

Jessamine struggled to sit up. "We should keep going."

He helped her into a sitting position beside him. She leaned against the rock at her back. She'd never relax enough to find sleep that way. With one hand, Alan reached up and gently drew her toward his shoulder. Gradually he felt her body soften against his. Her warmth enveloped him, as did the soft smell of jasmine. He drew a slow, deep breath of the intoxicating scent, drawing it into himself.

"Alan?" Her soft voice broke through his thoughts.

"Yes."

"I've been wondering about something."

"About what?" he asked when she paused.

He felt her shift beside him, but in the darkness he could see only the hazy outline of her body. "Why do you want to find the ark?"

At the question, his breath hitched. Duty, honor, a promise to his king demanded he do so. And yet, there was another reason too. "I need to make the deaths of my Templar brothers count for something. I don't want them to have died in vain. Bringing the ark back to Scotland will memorialize them as well as keep it safe through the ages."

Silence hovered between them for a long moment before she replied, "How will the ark be safer in Scotland?"

"The Holy Land always has been an area of great conflict. The ark is a powerful weapon. In the wrong hands, it could bring the world to its knees. The Templars will make certain that no one uses the ark for evil purposes. With the ark in our protection, the world can be at peace."

"A noble cause."

"It's my duty, Jessamine."

"Your duty means that much to you?" she asked.

The question lodged in his brain like a shard of metal. Why was he here, avoiding everything else, including his own grief? A chill crept across his flesh. Seven years ago he had become a Templar because he'd had nowhere else to go, no one else who'd cared about him. Now here he was again, just as he'd begun: alone. "My duty is all I have."

Duty is all I will ever have. Could it be true? Was that all the Almighty thought he deserved? He'd been given a family of brothers for a short while, only to lose them. His gaze moved to the silhouette of the woman beside him. Because of her, he'd lost them all.

Did he blame Jessamine? If she hadn't come onto the battlefield, would the outcome have been different that day?

The darkness of the cave melted into gray and he saw

himself back upon that battlefield, surrounded by his brothers. The battle cry went out. They charged into the fray as ten thousand Moors advanced. A veil of death descended. There was no hope any of them would survive. Pain clogged his throat. He'd been the lucky one to escape. Because of Jessamine, he'd lived to fight another day.

He'd lived to try to fulfill his duty to his king, and to protect others, like Jessamine, from the evils of the world.

Alan straightened and drew a deep, calming breath. Duty was all he had, but it filled the void his brothers' deaths had left inside him.

She must have noticed a change in his posture or felt the lessening of the tension in the darkened cave, because she leaned back against the wall once more and rested her head on his shoulder. "Will we find the ark?"

"For certain."

"How can you be so sure?"

"I know that the ark is waiting for us to find it."

"It's your heart that tells you so."

He frowned. What did she know of his heart?

She snuggled closer and drew a long breath. "My heart tells me to have faith in you." A moment later her breathing changed to the soft, slow cadence of sleep.

Her words lingered in the silence. She had faith in him. She had faith in her prophecy. She had faith in so many things. Lord, what would it be like to have that kind of confidence, confidence that allowed a person to dream about the future?

She had dreams.

He didn't have a single one.

Chapter Nine

Where were they? The conde frowned at the teeming streets of Jerusalem. He'd sent his men out in every direction, looking for some clue as to where Jessamine and the man had run.

The girl was his. His princess. He deserved to have her after everything he had suffered. He would be overlooked no longer. When he had the princess, people would have no choice but to take him seriously. Respect him. Give him the power he deserved. Especially his mother.

A growl of rage startled the peasants who strolled by. They scattered to the opposite side of the street. The conde scowled. Let them flee his anger. Jessamine would not. When he caught up with her, he would demonstrate the full force of his displeasure.

Aye, once they were married, he would set his plans in motion to take control of the throne of Spain. Poison would ensure that each and every surviving heir to the throne died, leaving only a distraught Jessamine. Despite her half-blood connection to the royal family, the court would have no choice but to recognize her. And through the benefit of marriage and manipulation of his wife, the conde would become the ruler of Spain.

The conde could feel a flush heat his cheeks. But nothing would ever come of his plans if he didn't find the girl. Perhaps it was time for a different tactic. He kept his gaze on the crowd, watching, waiting, until the perfect specimen of womanhood strolled by unescorted. His hand snaked out and clasped her arm. She yelped, struggled, but the conde held firm.

Others in the street stopped momentarily, taking in the girl's ragged clothing. Assuming she was a slave, and he her master, they continued past the two of them.

He pulled the girl tight against his body. "I want information," he said, his voice velvet smooth.

She rattled something off in incomprehensible Hebrew. Her eyes were wide, her face pale. Her chest rose and fell, emphasizing the firm breasts hidden beneath her dark clothing.

A frisson of lust pulsed through his veins. So innocent. So tempting. The conde moistened his lips. If he didn't need her so desperately for information, he might have indulged himself.

He pulled her closer against the hardened length of his manhood. "You'd best understand me, or take me to someone who can." With one finger, he reached out and stroked a loose strand of soot black hair that had escaped her headdress.

A shiver racked her body. She nodded.

He loosened his grip ever so slightly, allowing her to lead him toward a row of small stone buildings at the edge of the market. As they moved through the streets, he watched the sway of her young hips beneath her gown and his body hardened again.

He clenched his jaw against the jab of desire. He needed a tracker to lead him into the desert far more than he needed to slake his need with this girl.

Once he found someone who could follow Jessamine's trail, she would pay for all the inconveniences he'd suffered since entering this godforsaken land.

* * *

There were no signs of the men who'd attacked Jessamine and Alan the night before when they left the cave on horseback the next morning. Although the sun had barely risen in the sky, the day was already hot. A warm breeze curled across the desert floor, doing little to relieve the heat.

Jessamine batted impatiently at the ends of hair that fluttered about her face. What she wouldn't give for something to tie the loose ends back. No sooner had the thought formed than a silken gold cord dangled before her.

"Take it," Alan said, his arm brushing against her shoulder, sending a shiver of sensation through her.

She accepted the cord, then gathered the heavy length of her hair in her hands, quickly securing it at her nape. The breeze flowed against her skin and dried the moisture from her hair. Her neck still bore the bandage he'd placed there last night. She tugged at the cloth with her fingers.

He pulled the horse to a stop. "Here, let me help you. Your wound should be healed enough to remove the bandage." With gentle and adept fingers, he removed the fabric. A moment later, he pulled his water bladder from his saddlebag to moisten the cloth, then drew it back over her wound, cleaning away the sticky substance that covered her skin. "Better?"

"Blissful." She smiled up at him. He studied her, his blue eyes clear and free of the shadows she usually saw there. She felt as though she could see straight into his soul. Something subtle had shifted between them last night. She felt it in the way he held his body against hers and heard it in the tone of his voice. The tension that had tightened his muscles was replaced by a warm, supple strength. "I never did thank you for saving my life last night."

His eyes shuttered. "Then neither of us is in each other's debt any longer."

She nodded and turned back around, feeling suddenly bereft. He set the horse in motion. He'd put a wall up between them again, one that was just as real as the natural rock walls of the desert. Huge, red mounds of sandstone were now visible in the distance. And red, pointy spires thrust up from the ground toward the sky like the scarlet bones of an ancient skeleton.

Was it the kiss they'd shared last night? Did he think about that one brief moment of connection as much as she did? Her lips tingled at the thought of their passionate exchange. She'd claimed she wanted to keep her distance, to be proper in their interactions with each other. Yet another part of her wanted to kiss him again, just to see if the passion that had flared between them had been real or something she'd imagined.

What kind of man was the knight behind her? His commanding presence and power were undeniable. But the shadows in his eyes also spoke of deep pain and vulnerability. This was a man who'd had a hard, harsh life. Much harder than the pampered existence she'd known in the palace. "Alan?" she asked quietly.

"What, Jessamine?" There was a note of tension in his voice.

"Where is your home?"

"Home," he said, his tone wistful. "It seems like a lifetime since I've stepped on the shores of Scotland."

"Scotland is your home?

" 'Tis the land of my birth." A soft brogue lingered in his words.

"Tell me about it."

He sighed. "It's so green, with wide open spaces, craggy black hills . . ."

At the wistfulness in his voice, she turned to look at him. "It sounds lovely."

She saw a slight lifting at the corners of his lips and his gaze moved to her face, sweeping her features as softly as a caress. Her breath caught as he shifted to look at her lips. "You have no idea how lovely it is." His voice sounded raw. He leaned slightly forward. A long silent moment stretched between them.

Then the screech of a hawk sounded, vibrating in the air, breaking the moment. He pulled back.

He'd wanted to kiss her as much as she'd wanted it. She took a deep breath and turned back around to stare once again at the desert. Heat rose off the sandy earth in radiant waves that distorted vision.

Over the course of the morning she'd been staring at the red, craggy peaks in the distance, and yet they appeared no closer now than when they'd started their journey. The hills almost seemed to retreat at the same pace as she and Alan advanced.

But by the time the sun had reached its zenith, they'd finally arrived at a deep, narrow opening in the mountainside. Alan stopped the horse at the entrance.

A shiver of fear rippled across her neck as she gazed into the dark unknown. The prophecy would take them inside that deep recess. Why was she suddenly afraid to follow the driving force of her life?

"I won't let anything happen to you, Jessamine," Alan said as though reading her thoughts.

The words brought a small measure of comfort. "Where are we exactly?" she asked, staring toward the dark, narrow space.

"The Valley of Edom," he replied with reassuring calm. "We must enter what the locals refer to as the Siq here if we are to reach Petra."

Jessamine closed her eyes and nodded. When she felt a gentle caress against her cheek, she opened her eyes to find Alan smiling down at her.

"Those men will never get another chance at you. I'm forewarned. We'll be safe within these walls. Trust me."

"I do."

His smile widened. He encircled her waist with his arm and pulled her firmly back against his chest, then kicked the horse into motion. They surged forward into the cleft to follow a long, winding gorge that was no more than fifteen feet wide. The farther they progressed, the narrower the path became until sunlight no longer shone down between the sheer walls to either side. Chill air prickled Jessamine's flesh, but she refused to let her fear break free. It was just the dark, confined space that had her on edge. Nothing more. Her knight of white was with her.

They rode for what felt like forever, and just when the long, dark corridor seemed about to close in on them completely, it turned abruptly and opened wide. Jessamine gasped at the scene before her. Rising high above them on the opposite cliff was a gigantic edifice with two tiers of columns, colossal pediments, statue niches, and carved urns, all cut into the sheer rock face. "It looks like the entrance to a royal palace."

"In its day, it was the entrance of a tomb," Alan breathed beside her, sounding as awestruck as she felt. "The locals call it the Treasury of Petra. Behind this facade are a number of vast chambers cut deep inside the mountain."

"Who used the tomb?"

Alan shook his head. "It was built by the Nabataeans in the fourth century before Christ." Alan swung down from the horse, then assisted her down. He moved back to his saddlebag and withdrew a small leather book that he concealed inside the folds of his robe. Next, he took out a small lantern and a tallow candle, along with a flint stone.

He set the lantern on the ground and positioned the candle on the sand at his feet. He drew his sword. With a quick clean stroke of the flint against his sword, Alan created a spark that he guided toward the candle's wick. Moments later, the candle glowed brightly in the lantern. He sheathed his sword, replaced the flint, then held out his free hand to her. "Come, let's have a look inside."

Jessamine curled her fingers around his. She'd never held hands with anyone before. The courtiers weren't allowed to touch her. For one breathless moment his smoldering gaze studied her feature by feature, then he gave her hand a squeeze and led them through the entrance that rose some twenty feet high overhead.

With a sense of awe, Jessamine followed Alan into the ornate structure. Inside, the air was still and cold, a stark contrast to the suffocating heat outside. Golden light from the lantern splashed the nutmeg-colored walls, illuminating a colossal doorway that dominated the outer court and led to an inner chamber. Alan led her up the seven stairs and into what she could only guess was some sort of sanctuary, if the ablution basin was a clue.

"Where do we go now?" she asked. There were two passageways off to the left and right sides of the room.

"Let's start here." He led her to the passageway on the right. When they hit a wall of stone, they retraced their steps and instead took the passageway off to the left.

They entered a large, empty space that looked almost identical to the one they'd just explored. But as Jessamine searched the empty space, a strong sense of premonition made her skin tingle. There was something different here. She stared at the only other doorway carved into the stone. The answers they sought were in there. She knew it.

Alan appeared by her side. "Ready to explore?" he asked, stepping inside.

Jessamine followed. They headed down another passageway that seemed to go on forever, until finally it opened into another empty chamber. This room was different from the others they'd passed through. It was carved out of the stone like the others, yet these walls were uneven and, from the looks of it, carved in haste.

Then she saw it—a small pinprick of light emanating from a tall, narrow crack in the wall at the back of the chamber.

"Alan?" Jessamine breathed.

"I see it," he said, moving past her to explore the human-sized opening. He held the lantern into the space. "It's unfinished," he said, bringing his free hand up to caress the poorly sculpted rock at his eye level.

"Perhaps they grew tired of chipping away the stone," Jessamine offered.

"Or perhaps they wanted it to appear unfinished for a reason. We need to go inside." Alan offered her his hand.

She took his fingers in hers and allowed him to guide her into the dark void. Her heart raced and her palms grew damp. The space was narrow and confining, forcing them to turn to the side to slip through the rock.

Jessamine's breath quickened as she and Alan moved deeper and deeper into the ever-narrowing space. The wall at her back was cold. The wall at her front nearly brushed against her chest. She clung to Alan's hand and kept moving. "If we find the ark in this place, how will we ever get it out? The walls are too narrow."

"Somehow it was brought in, so there must be a way to get it out," he replied with confidence.

Together, they felt their way along the cool, gritty sandstone wall. The lantern cast eerie shadows that twisted and danced with each step they took. The shuffling of their footsteps mingled with the quickened rush of their breathing. The darkness seemed to seep around them, outside the circle of light cast by the lantern. Alan's hand became her lifeline.

Cold dampness seeped into her clothes. Jessamine shivered. Her breath caught. She shuffled forward. "How much farther?" she whispered into the confined and darkened space.

No sooner had the words left her lips than the passageway opened up, spilling into a small chamber. The light from the lantern splashed across the walls, painting everything in hues of coppery gold. The room was empty, just as the others had been, except tucked high into the back wall was a shelf cut into the stone. It held a small golden chest that was much too small to be the ark.

Alan released her. He pressed the lantern into her hands and moved slowly across the chamber until he stood before the chest. He reached up and carefully removed it from the rock ledge.

"What is it?" Jessamine asked.

Alan turned toward her and bent, setting the small chest on the floor. "I'm not certain." He blew the dust and sand away from the lid. No ornamentation decorated the chest. "Bring the light closer."

She stepped beside him as he carefully lifted the lid from the chest. Inside were twelve formed and polished colored stones.

"What do they mean?" She set the lantern on the floor beside them.

With a grin, he sat back on his heels and pulled the

leather book from the folds of his robe. She moved to peer over his shoulder as he flipped the loose pages. When he came to a drawing of what appeared to be a ceremonial garment, he stopped.

"What is that?" she asked. "How does it relate to what we found?"

"These stones might not be the Ark of the Covenant, but they are a worthy find in and of themselves." He lifted his gaze to hers. Excitement brightened his eyes. "These twelve stones are what were referred to in the Old Testament as the stones of fire. They represent the twelve tribes of Israel and were at one time set into the breastplate of the high priest. That high priest would have worn the breastplate to control the divine fire that was said to emanate from the ark."

"So whoever controls the stones of fire controls the ark?" Jessamine cupped her hands over his. A spark passed between them at the intimate contact. It brought a soft gasp to her lips. She should pull her hands away, stand, anything to break the contact between them. Instead, she gazed into his piercing blue eyes and felt a strange lightness at her core.

"Aye," he said softly. "But suddenly it's not the ark or the stones that interest me, but something else entirely." He abandoned the chest on the ground and stood, pulling her up with him until they faced each other, their bodies only a hairbreadth apart.

"Jessamine. We are entering dangerous territory." The words seemed dredged up from his very soul as he pulled her even closer, his gaze on her lips.

She knew he didn't mean the dangers of following the prophecy, but the dangerous way desire flared each time they touched.

"I like adventure," she breathed.

No sooner had the words shivered past her lips than

his mouth descended. Shock trembled through her body. All her senses were centered on the feather-light pressure of his mouth, on the teasing, taunting dalliance of his tongue as it lingered against her lips, tasted, prepared her for what was to come.

He drew her closer, molding her to the hard contours of his body. His arms tightened and his lips slanted more forcefully over hers. Jessamine felt her knees weaken as her body became heavy and fluid as molten lead. The sensation slithered further into her with each silky, probing caress of his tongue.

Of their own accord, her fingers spread across the rough texture of his robe and inched higher, until she clung to the powerful breadth of his shoulders. She'd never experienced the surge of liquid heat that robbed her of anything but the desire to melt against him. She wanted more of this delicious madness. Her body grew tauter, tighter, with each stroke of his tongue.

With a groan, he broke free.

She inhaled sharply at the abruptness of his release. He didn't pull away, just stood there with his face poised above hers. She couldn't see much in the shadows of the room, but she sensed a shared feeling of surprise. She wondered if the thud of his heart meant he, too, had experienced a rush of warmth and pleasure.

She stared in fascination as he brought his fingers to her mouth, his index finger tracing the curve of her lower lip. "I apologize. I couldn't resist."

A shiver of desire tumbled through her at his confession. She pressed into his touch, seeking the warmth of his flesh on hers. "Kiss me again."

He dropped his fingers from her lips and took a step back as if he no longer trusted himself to remain near her. "That wouldn't be wise," he said.

She nodded and took two steps back, wishing the

distance would quell her desire. Her heart hammered in her chest as she fisted her hands. "Because you're a monk?"

"That is the last thing on my mind at the moment."

Jessamine was stunned into silence by the harsh need in his voice. She gazed up into his face, saw the tension around his eyes, in his jaw, and knew what it cost him to hold himself back.

She found herself at a loss, uncertain what to do or how to proceed. It would be so easy to forget about the world outside this chamber, to step back into Alan's arms and let whatever was supposed to happen next happen. Was that part of what the prophecy demanded of her? Was that what her newfound freedom allowed? Or was she giving in to her own wants and desires? Jessamine dropped her gaze to the stone floor as her swirling senses began to return to reality.

"What do we do next?" she asked. When she felt more in control of her emotions, she brought her gaze back to his. The shadows had returned to his eyes and his rigid stance made her heart ache. He appeared lonely somehow.

"Let's return to the horse," Alan said. "I didn't plan anything beyond the treasury. I was certain we'd find the ark here."

She nodded sympathetically. "Where else could we look? Petra appears to have many places where the ark could be hidden."

He straightened, and any hint of vulnerability vanished. "I want to consult the Templar letters. There might be a clue there." He bent down beside the wooden chest and carefully picked up each stone, placing them into a small leather pouch attached to his belt. When he'd gathered all the stones, he replaced the lid on the chest. Standing, he returned the chest to its former resting place.

"It would be best if we left the chest behind. The stones will be safe here with me." His hand moved to cover the pouch at his belt.

"Agreed," Jessamine replied as he once again extended his hand to her. She braced herself for the flare of warmth, and there it was as she curled her fingers in his.

"Ready?" The tension in his body vanished, and his expression became heated once more.

She inhaled sharply at the realization that she wanted to kiss him again, just as strongly as before. She moistened her lips and nodded, not trusting her voice. Perhaps the cold, dark passageway would help her get her senses under control. But was it even possible to keep her head clear in the presence of this man? As she followed him back into the long dark void, she was starting to wonder.

After what seemed like forever, they emerged from the back of the chamber, then retraced their steps through the maze they'd traveled until they'd reached the tomb's entrance.

They stepped outside. The hot afternoon air stole her breath as the sun's rays beat down mercilessly. Alan released her hand, and she stood there for a long moment, torn between her desire to step back into the cool tomb and their need to continue the journey.

Alan seemed unaffected by the shift in temperature as he made his way to the horse and stroked the animal's neck. Jessamine steeled her resolve and started forward, but a sudden fierce wind whipped up the dust of the valley floor, making the horse whinny and forcing Jessamine to cover her face with the crook of her arm. Hot, dry sand stung her eyes anyway. In the haze of dust, an eerie, unearthly sound rose to a high keening pitch. In the bizarre cacophony of noise, Jessamine stumbled forward.

"Hold on!" Alan shouted from somewhere nearby. A heartbeat later, she found herself pulled against the solid wall of his chest. His arms sheltered her. His cheek rested against the top of her head. He pulled his robe up around their faces to protect them.

He held her there until the wind subsided, and the noise ceased as suddenly as it had begun. The world stilled as the sand settled. Alan lifted his head and looked down at her. "Are you all right?"

She nodded and glanced up at the towering edifice of the treasury with its staring statues. A carved eagle with a fiery orb over its head seemed poised for flight, its outstretched wings lifelike in the shimmering air. "What was that?"

"I have no idea."

They stared at each other.

"The trumpet of God," a voice called from behind them.

Alan released her suddenly. He twisted toward the voice and drew his sword, stepping protectively in front of her. She peeked around Alan to see an old man standing at the entrance of the tomb. He was dressed in a long white robe with a hood that came up over his head. A white beard framed his face, making him appear more like an aged scholar than any kind of threat.

"Who are you?" Alan asked, his sword still held at the ready.

"Where did you come from?" Jessamine stepped beside Alan. She frowned. Hadn't she seen this man back at the Temple of Jerusalem?

"Jessamine, get back," Alan warned as he kept his eyes trained on the man.

Leaning heavily on a gnarled cane, the old man stepped through the tomb's entrance and onto the sand that a moment before had swirled about them. "I'm just an old man who knows his way around the desert. You have nothing to fear from me."

Alan widened his stance. "That's for me to determine."

Chapter Ten

The old man before Alan appeared harmless enough. But the knight wasn't sure he trusted that impression. Nothing had gone as he'd expected since they'd arrived in this hot, arid land. Alan's hand tightened on the hilt of his sword. He glanced at the old man, then at Jessamine, who still stood beside him, despite his warning to stay back. Both Jessamine and the old man watched him with curiosity.

Suddenly his weapon felt heavy in his hand. God's teeth! Did Jessamine have to be so damn accepting of everyone and everything? Was she truly that innocent? The old man posed no current threat, but one could never be too careful. Especially when so much was at stake.

With a lingering glance at Jessamine, Alan gripped his sword. "What do you want, old man?"

"It's not what I want, but what you need that brings me here." His voice held a hint of challenge.

Alan frowned. The man's dark gray eyes studied him. "And what is it you think we need?"

"A meal. A safe place to sleep."

"A meal?" Jessamine repeated with longing in her voice.

The old man shot Alan a triumphant look.

Alan took Jessamine by the arm and led her to a private spot a few feet away from the old man. His shadow fell across Jessamine's face. "We cannot risk this, Jessamine."

She stepped to the side, out of his shadow, and gazed up into his face. "What are you afraid of?"

Resentment surged to the forefront of his mind. He hadn't revealed his fear, and yet somehow she'd seen it—she'd recognized his fear that he wouldn't be able to keep her safe.

Her fingers slid to his cheek. He felt the warmth of her touch like a brand against his skin. Against his will, he leaned into her touch, allowed it to soothe his irrational fear. "He's an old man," Jessamine said in a soft, gentle voice. "And he's right. We need to sleep, and I don't know about you, but I'm quite hungry."

Turning, he stared at the old man, and then, slowly, he brought his gaze back to her face. "All right. We'll go with him." He sheathed his sword.

She smiled and he felt the warmth of her joy in his chest.

"Thank you, Alan." Jessamine dragged him back toward the stranger.

He was being a fool, he knew it, to trust the old man. But unlike the malice that radiated from the conde, and from the assassins, the old man had a sense of peace about him. Could Alan trust that feeling?

Alan's hand moved to his sword as it had so many times in the past. He'd stay alert. Watch the old man. One sign of danger and he and Jessamine would be on their way. Alone.

Alan and Jessamine followed the old man beyond the treasury and through the ancient and deserted streets of Petra, until another series of elaborately carved edifices came into view. "These are the Royal Tombs," the old man explained as he hobbled across the sand, moving past three separate rock facades and coming to a stop before the fourth. "The Urn Tomb." He moved to a long, narrow staircase that led past three stories of arches.

Alan guided their horse to an alcove in the rock that offered the animal some shade. He removed the saddle and set it on the ground beside the beast. From the saddlebag, he removed a portion of oats and offered it to the horse, then went in search of water. When he returned with water, he stroked the horse's neck before hitching the saddlebag over his shoulder.

"Ready?" he asked Jessamine, and signaled for her to climb the stairs ahead of him. He wanted to be able to catch her should she slip on the uneven rock. They climbed slowly, following the pace set by the old man as he struggled up the steps with his cane.

The rock face was more of a golden brown here than it had been at the treasury. Vivid striations of color rippled through the sandstone walls—streaks of yellow, gray, pink, and brown, giving the hard stone a silken texture in the sunlight's warm glow.

Finally they reached the top of the steps and stood before another arched opening in the huge wall of rock. The murmur of voices sounded from within, as well as the soft lilting of a flute.

"Welcome to the Urn Tomb," the old man said as he slipped inside.

Alan stayed beside Jessamine as they followed him. At the center of the stone chamber stood a group of dark-robed men with white headdresses tied with black cords.

"Bedouins. I've studied these people with my tutor." Jessamine's eyes went wide.

"Your tutor?"

She paled. "I meant to say, I've studied these people

along with my students. I've schooled privileged girls in history and language." She studied her hands with sudden interest.

Alan frowned. There was something not quite right about her explanation. Instructors of such disciplines were usually men. Yet it did explain her demonstrated abilities with language and why she seemed so refined. "What did you learn about these people?"

Jessamine looked up. Her gaze shifted between him and the Bedouins. "The men wear their head ropes as an outward sign that they will uphold the obligations and responsibilities of manhood. The women are required to cover their hair, and their headgear signals their status. Those two women over there, with black cloth wrapped around their foreheads, are married. The younger women wear more colorful kaffiyeh cloth."

"You do understand the Bedouins," the old man commented as he waved them closer to the fire pit.

"They have such freedom," Jessamine replied with a touch of longing.

Alan narrowed his gaze on Jessamine. Questions still lingered about her education, but her comment supported her claim. An instructor of nobles' daughters would have very little freedom.

The old man smiled. "The Bedouins know the secrets of the desert, and how to stay alive in it. This is a temporary home, for tomorrow they will journey elsewhere. Tonight, though, is a celebration. Come."

The smell of roasted meat filled the air, making Alan's stomach grumble. As they approached the group, conversation halted. The men ceased their activities and watched Alan with wary eyes. Alan curled his fingers at his sides, fighting the urge to grasp his sword. These men did not appear to be armed, but their stances didn't indicate acceptance or even welcome. Still, despite their lack of friendliness, they did nothing to discourage the newcomers from joining the group near the fire.

The old man settled himself in a seat near several heavily veiled women. No one seemed to pay him any heed as he reached out and served himself from one of the bowls the women had filled with slices of lamb. "Help yourselves," he said between bites.

Alan approached the women. One of them handed him a bowl. He nodded his thanks, not knowing what language these desert dwellers spoke. He turned and offered the bowl to Jessamine, but she shook her head. At her refusal, a brightly veiled woman offered her two plump figs instead. Jessamine accepted them with a smile and bit into the fruit with a soft sigh.

Conversation started up around them again as the men and women continued their meal. It had been a full day since either he or Jessamine had eaten, as his stomach reminded him with a loud growl. Alan followed the example set by the other men, grasping a slice of the savory meat with his right hand, then taking a bite. He closed his eyes and nearly groaned as he tasted the flavorful meat. It had been months since he'd had such good food.

The youngest of the women, in a light blue veil, brought them a platter of odd-looking fruits and nuts. She set the fruit down in front of Alan and fluttered her eyes flirtatiously.

Uneasy with the woman's behavior, Alan scooted closer to Jessamine. The woman was undeterred by his action and reached for a piece of red fruit, then offered it to him. Not wanting to be rude, he accepted the object but simply held it, not knowing what to do with the leathery fruit.

At his hesitation, the young woman giggled, took the fruit from his hand, and with a small knife that she drew from the folds of her gown, she cut the skin in half. She handed it back to him, saying something he didn't understand. He looked at Jessamine.

"Pomegranate," she said softly. "She wants you to take it."

Alan accepted the fruit and brought the bright red multiseeded flesh to his lips. He took a small bite and tart sweetness erupted in his mouth. He smiled his thanks to the girl. She giggled and thrust the other half at him before being pulled away by the other women.

Annoyance coiled in his chest as he handed Jessamine the other half of the pomegranate. The women chattered among themselves, the tone of their voices excited as they cast curious glances between him and Jessamine.

Alan leaned toward Jessamine, his thigh brushing against her leg. A soft shimmer of sensation tingled there. He pressed closer, finding comfort in her presence. "Do you understand what they're saying?"

"Yes. Are you sure you want to know?"

He nodded.

She leaned toward him. Amusement sparkled in her eyes. "They are bartering among themselves to see who gets to bed down with you for the night."

Alan started at the shocking translation. He started to respond, when an older woman in a darker blue veil thrust two wooden cups into his hands. He held them, uncertain how to proceed, and fearful of what the cups might mean.

Jessamine took one of the cups from his hand. "She wants you to drink. You're safe, for now. This is not a bridal cup."

The Bedouin woman waited expectantly for him to take a sip of the dark, thick liquid inside. Alan brought the cup to his lips and drank. The liquid tasted bitter at

first, then mellowed as the rich taste of cardamom filled
his senses. "This must be coffee," he said, recognizing
the beverage some of the older Templars had talked
about tasting during earlier crusades. "It's unusual, but
delicious." He took another long drink.

Jessamine sipped delicately from her cup before she
returned a soft smile. The firelight reflected on her face,
turning her skin a warm apricot. Her eyes sparkled.
"The coffee is the first of many temptations they will
offer you."

"Why?"

She smiled. "To make you more eager to choose one
of them for the night."

Alan choked on the coffee. "I don't want—"

She set her cup down and grasped his hand. "Then
show them." She placed his hand possessively on her
knee. "You'll have to make them believe that I'm yours,
or you'll have no peace."

He stared back at her. Her eyes were on him, urging
him on, waiting. He ran a hand through his hair and
stole a glance at the Bedouin women. They watched his
every move.

"Alan." Her voice was so quiet he could barely hear it,
yet her body called to him like a siren's song. Heat
moved from the center of his being to his groin. He
turnèd to Jessamine, uncertain what to do or say. He'd
chosen a life of celibacy, and yet his body was on fire at
the simple touch of his hand upon her knee. He felt his
resolve falter. *Just once more . . .* A voice deep inside responded. *Kiss her one last time. Prove to these women that
you are already taken, if not by Jessamine, then by the Church.*

The fire crackled, the light wandering over Jessamine's face, highlighting her cheekbones, her eyes, her
lips—her full and entirely kissable lips. His fingers
curled around her knee, barely stroking the inside of

her leg. The touch, however innocent, sent a jolt of white-hot desire through him. He leaned toward her, intending to kiss her lightly.

Yet the moment their lips touched, he lost himself. Raw pleasure flared, stealing all rational thought. Her tongue darted between his lips, then sank deeper. Needing to experience more of what she offered, he let his hand drift to her neck, pulling her closer. She gasped against his mouth and arched deeper into his touch. It took all his willpower to pull back, to leave the taste of paradise she'd offered so freely.

"Jessamine," he rasped, bringing his forehead to rest on hers. "You are a forbidden treat that I dare not taste again. The more I taste you, the more I want you."

"You say that as though it's a bad thing," she whispered against his ear.

Alan pulled back to stare into her face. Her features were luminous as innocent desire shone in her eyes. By the saints, he wanted to kiss her again. "When I'm near you, nothing but you seems to matter." His tone was low and savage.

She reached for his hand. Her fingers laced with his, the touch excruciatingly intimate. The heat tingling between them thickened in intensity. The wool of his robe felt abrasive against his skin.

"Jessamine—"

A tap on his shoulder stole his attention. He suddenly noticed that two of the younger women stood on either side of him. He'd been so intent on Jessamine that he'd seen nothing else. Alan frowned. He was behaving irrationally, losing his focus, leaving both of them open to attack. He straightened abruptly. He would have to be more alert in the future.

The women spoke to him and pulled at his arms. From their hand signals, he realized they wanted him to rise. He glanced at Jessamine, who remained seated beside him.

"They wish to dance with you." Her voice was cooler now.

"But you said—"

"They still seem to think you are available."

When had the music started up? The soft lilting of a flute mixed with the high-pitched melodic strains of a single violin. The women grasped his arms amid flirtatious laughter and hauled him to his feet. They linked their hands with his, then pulled him toward the other men and women who danced in a circle. The rhythmic music swirled around them, but he could not lose himself in it. A glance back at Jessamine sitting alone brought tightness to his chest.

Jessamine watched Alan dance with the women. They linked their arms with his and pulled him through the steps of the dance. Alan laughed, the sound rising for a moment above the music, and Jessamine smiled. It was good to see his features lighten and the shadows that haunted his eyes disappear.

She brought a hand to her neck and toyed with the long gold chain that held the miniatures of her parents. She lifted the small locket into her hands and snapped it open. Her mother and father's smiling faces stared back at her. The portraits had been painted before she was born, while their love was still fresh and unspoiled.

Tears formed in her eyes, blurring the images. She missed them both. The memory of her parents tugged at her heart, tapping into some deep, fundamental emotion. And for the first time she had an inkling of what her parents' love had been. They were not doomed.

They'd been the lucky ones, even for a short while, to share a love so precious.

She snapped the locket closed and drew in a breath.

"Memories?" a soft voice queried in Hebrew.

Jessamine turned to see that an older Bedouin woman had seated herself where Alan had sat. "Good memories." Her voice dropped. "But that is in the past."

"May I?" the woman asked, her gaze on the locket Jessamine still clasped in her hands. The dark-veiled woman opened the locket and smiled down at Jessamine's parents. "So in love. I can see it in their eyes." She brought her gaze back to Jessamine's.

"Yes, they were definitely in love to give up all that they did."

"Sometimes, one must give up one thing to receive something greater in return." Jessamine looked up suddenly. Her gaze captured the old woman's, held it. They stared at each other for a long, breathless moment. The fire hissed, sending a spray of red-gold sparks into the night air, and Jessamine felt a quiver of understanding leap between the two of them. The woman wanted to share something with her. But what?

Jessamine's heart raced. "I am open to your wisdom, if you choose to share it with me."

The woman offered her a soft smile. "I am the tribe's visionary. I cannot tell you of a future that hasn't happened yet, but I do have a gift for you." She removed her hand from Jessamine's arm and slipped it into the folds of her gown. From them, she withdrew a small packet that she opened with one hand. She brought the open packet to Jessamine's locket and poured a small portion of fine, white powder onto the miniatures of her parents.

Jessamine gasped and nearly jerked away, but the

woman's gaze met hers. *Trust me.* A peculiar sort of sadness showed in the old woman's eyes.

"These herbs can be mixed with any liquid," she explained. "You will find them useful should there be a time in the future when you need to render someone . . ."

"Unconscious?" Jessamine asked.

"Unresponsive," the old woman corrected. She snapped the locket closed, then settled it once again against Jessamine's gown. "You'll know what I mean when the time is right." The old woman stood. "I wish you well, my child. You will need all your strength for what lies ahead of you."

Before Jessamine could ask her what she meant, the woman disappeared into the crowd of dancers. Jessamine frowned as she gripped her locket in her hands once more.

Special herbs. When the time is right. What ever could the old woman mean?

Alan glanced back at Jessamine to find her staring off into the distance with a sorrowful look in her eyes. With an effort, he disengaged his hands from the two young women's. He offered them a bow and made his way to Jessamine. At his approach, her gaze met his, and she slid something metal into the depths of her bodice. He held her gaze and extended his hand. "Dance with me."

Jessamine stood and, with a slight tremble in her fingers, took his hand. Wild music filled the chamber, reverberating off the stone until it sounded as though the melody came from every direction.

Slowly that look of loneliness vanished from her gaze, to be replaced with exhilaration as they twisted, turned, and stamped their feet, mimicking the Bedouins' movements.

Alan found himself relaxing, and for the first time

since leaving Teba, he allowed himself to feel a moment of pleasure that wasn't tempered with guilt. He was alive. He had survived that devastating battle. Gratitude resonated deep within him.

A kind of giddiness bubbled up inside his chest. Jessamine's fingers brushed against his shoulders, lingered there a moment as color flooded her cheeks. Her lashes came down to hide her eyes, then her gaze sought him out again as though she was as captivated by him as he was by her.

"What is it?" Jessamine asked with a carefree laugh.

"Fate."

"You said you don't believe in fate."

"Tonight, I do." He laughed again and twirled her until they were both breathless and dizzy.

Again, the tempo of the music changed. The beat grew softer, slower, more soothing than celebratory. Alan drew Jessamine against his chest. The circles they inscribed became smaller and smaller, their footsteps slower and slower until they were barely moving at all, hardly swaying to the strains of the music. He could feel the flutter of her heartbeat, could smell the subtle scent of jasmine in her hair.

She gave an audible sigh and leaned her head against his chest.

He tightened his arms around her. As he turned his head to rest his cheek against the top of her hair, he noticed a woman standing less than five paces from them. She was older than the woman who had tried to attract his attention before. And she wore a darker veil, indicating her married status. She motioned with her hands for them to follow her.

"Jessamine," Alan said softly. He pulled out of their embrace.

A flow of words issued from the woman. Jessamine

had been right about his needing her translation skills.

Jessamine turned her head toward the woman and smiled. "She wants to offer us a bed for the night."

"We'd be safer here with the Bedouins than out in the desert," Alan mused. "The assassins we met earlier would think twice before attacking such a large group of men."

"If we are safer, then you might actually sleep?" she prompted.

His mouth titled in a quickly suppressed smile. "Aye." She had noticed his sleeplessness. Which meant she hadn't slept well either. It would do them both good to relax, even for a short time. Alan nodded to the woman.

She turned and led them to a colorful blanket on the far side of the room. At the cloth's edge, Jessamine's smile faded. He was certain she had expected more than a place upon the stone floor. He didn't know why, but he imagined she was used to great luxury in whatever life she'd fled.

"It'll be better than it seems," Alan encouraged.

"This is perfect." She spoke to the older woman, who bowed, then left. "I thanked her for her kindness." The words trailed off as she stared, ramrod stiff, at the small blanket.

"Are you certain you'll be all right here, Princess?"

"What!" She spun toward him. The color drained from her cheeks.

Silence thudded between them until finally he eased the tension with a smile. "I was teasing you, Jessamine." He drew his sword and set it at the edge of the blanket, then motioned for her to lie down first.

She straightened and looked at him squarely. "Don't call me that. I don't like it." With that, she marched onto the blanket and sat down before curling against the wall with her back toward him.

Alan frowned at her back. What had he said that had upset her so?

Chapter Eleven

Jessamine stared at the wall. She lay stiff and unmoving with her arm tucked beneath her head as Alan lowered himself beside her. She'd been terrified when he'd called her Princess. She'd been certain for a moment that he'd discovered her secret.

What would he do if he did find out who she was? Would he send her back to Spain? Would he treat her differently? She frowned into the darkness. Only one time before had she managed to slip past the palace guards. She'd experienced an afternoon of freedom among the commoners. She smiled at the memory of walking through the streets unescorted, of eating a sugared fig without the benefit of a royal taster. While walking near the river, she'd loosened her mantilla and allowed a breeze to blow through her hair. It had been the best day of her life, until today.

Her thoughts returned to the present as the music faded. The sound of footsteps echoed through the chamber as others settled down for the night. Her body tingled from her efforts to remain still. She tried to block out the feel of the rock as it pressed against her hip. The pressure increased until she felt as though her body would shatter.

With a sigh, she rolled onto her back. She could feel the warmth of Alan's body alongside hers. His musky, masculine scent filled the air between them, heightening her awareness of him.

She stared at the ceiling of the chamber. The flames from the fire sent shimmering light across the gold-hued rock. Dark shapes moved in and out of the light as the Bedouins settled to sleep. It didn't take long for a hush to fall over the room.

Relax, she told herself for what had to be the hundredth time, but she couldn't do it. Alan and she had spent the past four days together. Granted, he'd been wounded and close to unconsciousness for the first two. Last night they'd spent the night alone. But she'd been not quite herself then, thanks to the assassin's poison.

Tonight was the first night they were both themselves, influenced by nothing but the night air and the warmth of each other's bodies. Gradually she relaxed as the light from the fire died and darkness blanketed the chamber. She heard the soft, even cadence of Alan's breathing. She smiled into the darkness, pleased they'd found a measure of security among the Bedouins.

Jessamine stared into the darkness and felt the tension in her shoulders ease. They'd found the stones of fire today. It was proof they were on the right path. The prophecy was guiding them toward the ark.

Alan sighed in his sleep, nestling closer to the warm body spooned tightly against his own. Something tickled his nostrils. He wiggled his nose and pushed the offending strands of hair out of the way.

He tightened his arms around her body. He felt the slow, steady beat of his heart. A weird mix of elation and wonder filled him when he realized he'd let his guard down and slept deeply for the first time in almost a year.

A soft sigh came from Jessamine as she rolled over to

face him. Her warm, firm breasts pressed against his chest. The contact jolted him fully awake. He blinked twice at the sight that greeted him.

Jessamine curled against him with the same smile of contentment he'd felt moments before. Her face was turned up to his, and their lips were no more than a handbreadth apart. Her even, peaceful breath caressed his face and teased his lips.

He had the sudden, overwhelming urge to shift forward, to bring their lips into contact. It would be so easy to give himself over to the desire that had his pulse racing. But he held himself back, using all his willpower to remain still.

He studied her honey-colored face. Beautiful. Elegant. Innocent. She was the kind of woman who inspired men to be more than they thought they could be. He frowned as he remembered the man who'd followed her across a sea. She was also the sort of woman who drove men to great violence.

The conde was proof of that.

And she was running from the blackguard. At times, he saw shadows in her eyes when she thought he wasn't looking.

He reached out and pushed a silken strand of her dark hair away from her cheek. She sighed. Her eyelids fluttered, then opened.

He and Jessamine stared at each other for a long moment as the sounds of others moving about filtered into his awareness. Then she moved her head back, but not her body. "Good morrow."

"Good morrow," he replied, pleased she didn't want this moment to end any more than he did. He reached up and stroked his thumb across her cheek.

She leaned in to his touch. "Your thumb is calloused."

His movements ceased.

"It was just an observation." She reached up and rubbed the tip of her own thumb against the ridge of hard skin.

"I'm a warrior. My hands are covered with calluses and scars." He tried to tug his hand away, but she held tight.

"You're a survivor." Her words were little more than a whisper, and he felt the brush of silky skin against his knuckles. A kiss. Nay, more a salute. Something that had lain undisturbed inside him for years contracted, or expanded, he couldn't have said which. Only that her touch moved him beyond words.

No one but his brothers had cared about him, for as long as he could remember. His story was no different from that of so many of the Templars. They'd given up everything to join the order. He'd said good-bye to what little family he had and embraced an unknown future fighting for his king, his country, his God. Fighting. Alan closed his eyes. Always fighting.

And until Teba, they had won every battle. Pain and remorse twisted inside him like a physical thing. He drew a sharp breath at the intensity.

"Alan." Her voice was soft, yet it shattered the memories, rescued him from the pain that always followed. "Tell me something good, some happy memory from your past."

A good memory? There weren't many. He'd spent so much of his youth and young adulthood alone. "There was the time I broke my nose."

Her gaze immediately went to the slight crook in his nose. "That's not a good memory."

"It was. I think that was probably my father's proudest day. My father tended to be rather brutish. I didn't want to be like him. But that day I was mad. I won the sparring matches—every one of them—and had a bloody face to prove it. He marched me through the village with such pride."

Alan released a sigh. "I never felt much need for fisticuffs, but the older lads learned I could speak well enough with my fists when they'd earned my ire," he said, remembering the moment.

"I was feeling no pain, believe me." Even years later, a wave of satisfaction rode through him. "My father and I spent the entire day together."

"He was proud of you," Jessamine said, the words catching in her throat.

"That day. There was never another."

"Why not?"

"He and my mother both drowned a week later. They were visiting my mother's family on one of the outer isles. Their boat took on water. And although my father was a fierce warrior on land, he couldn't swim, and the sea took their lives."

She reached for his hand and lifted it with both of hers. "And because you could do nothing to save them you've been punishing yourself for their deaths ever since, haven't you?"

"Aye."

The answer emerged without any thought, an acknowledgment of a truth he had never admitted before.

She was right. That was the moment his life had changed. Afterward, he'd isolated himself even more from the others in his clan.

"Aye," he repeated. "I turned away from everyone and everything from that moment on. I became the warrior my father wanted me to become, but I did it my way, using logic and strategy, and that was what brought me to where I am today. My king, Robert the Bruce, respected my skills and rewarded me for them."

He slanted his head farther back upon the blanket

and stared at the ceiling. The course of his life had led him here, to this moment, to this quest, along with this woman.

Coincidence or fate?

He sat up and grabbed the nearby saddlebag with a sudden thrill that he could believe in *something* again. He truly believed he and Jessamine would find the ark. The Templar letters he'd been given might tell them where to look next. Perhaps Jessamine would understand the clues he'd been unable to decipher upon his last reading.

The majority of the Bedouins were still barely stirring. Jessamine and he could read the letters in relative isolation. Alan sat down beside Jessamine, who was leaning back against the wall.

"There are clues hidden in these letters about the ark's location." He could feel her gaze on him as he unfolded the first letter. "But I've been unable to figure anything out so far." He handed the letter to her, then settled back against the wall and picked up the other letter.

"The first letter was written as the knights were fleeing. The second letter came from somewhere in the Judean wilderness after they'd hidden the ark in what I'd mistakenly assumed was the city of stone."

Alan tried to concentrate on the words written by Sir William of Tyre to Bishop Baldwin Lambert, but found it impossible. He was too acutely conscious of Jessamine sitting next to him, her eyes wide as she read the story of the fall of Acre. He'd read that particular letter at least ten times already. The words tumbled through his mind, creating vivid pictures of those last moments before the Pilgrims' Castle had fallen into enemy hands.

Your Holiness,
A terrible tragedy befalls us this morn as the Sultan of Egypt and his Mamluk warriors storm the fortress of

*Atlit. Agonized screams pierce the air. Templars fall as
the enemy lays siege to the temple compound.*

*My fingers tighten on the quill. The attack is fierce
and we are vulnerable as we never have been before.
The knowledge I possess, the location of the secret, is too
sensitive to trust to pen and paper. I cannot be taken, I
cannot risk the enemy acquiring the secrets I have har-
bored in my soul for many long years.*

*To flee, with my knowledge intact, is my only option.
And yet I hesitate. My heart goes out to the men who fall
beneath the blade of our enemy. Yet they would rather
die than become slaves to those who slaughter them.*

*From the small arrow slit in the tower I can see
dark-clothed warriors pouring through the gates. They
slay the Templars with their fierce curved swords and
put their torches to anything that burns.*

*The castle is surrounded. I am afraid. Yet I must
take precious moments to send you these clues, should I
fail in my goal. The secret lies in the Judean wilderness, in a city of nothing but stone.*

*The stone will speak if only you will listen. The an-
swer lies in the stone.*
Your servant, William of Tyre

Jessamine looked up at Alan in surprise. "The city of
stone. You thought Sir William meant Petra," she said
softly.

"Aye. It was the logical location for the ark."

She frowned down at the paper in her hands. "Stone
does not speak. What does William refer to? The
sound we heard yesterday just outside the treasury?"

He shook his head. "I don't know. Such a noise could
hardly be considered speaking."

She folded the letter and handed it back to him.
"Does the other letter make anything clearer?"

"Hardly. If anything, it makes the whole puzzle even more confusing." He handed her the second of the two letters.

She absently rubbed her thumb over the red wax seal. "William must have reached safety if he wrote a second letter and was able to seal it with wax." She frowned down at the yellowed papyrus. He knew the words she read by heart.

> *Your Holiness,*
> *Flames claw at the night sky as I stand safely away in the distance, looking back on all that remains of the last Templar stronghold. My chest constricts as I grieve for the lives lost and the destruction of our home. I am out of danger and my knowledge of the secret is safe, for now.*
>
> *I hope to lose myself in the western region of Jordan, in the Wadi Rum, among the mountains of Moses, where I shall take up my calling as the secret's guardian.*
>
> *Never shall I look back on the burning walls of Atlit as I embrace my future. The hidden seal is the only further clue I offer as to the location of the secret. The seal reveals everything.*
> *Your servant, William of Tyre*

Jessamine set the letter in her lap and stared thoughtfully at the growing light of dawn creeping through the large doorway of the Urn Tomb. "Whatever happened to William of Tyre?"

"No one ever heard from him again. It was assumed he died out here in the wilderness."

Carefully, she refolded the papyrus and cradled it in her hands. "The letters came to the Templars from the bishop?"

Alan nodded. "For forty years the bishop has hoped to discover what it was William of Tyre knew about the ark. The bishop entrusted the letters to Robert the Bruce when the king talked of organizing another crusade to the Holy Land. That crusade never came about. What you saw at Teba was the end of the king's crusader dream."

"Perhaps the dream of a crusade died along with your brothers, but the king's dream lives on through you. Are you not here in the Holy Land, searching for the artifact that the bishop and the king hoped to find?"

"Robert the Bruce asked me to go on to the Holy Land should something happen to my brothers." Alan shook his head. "It was almost as if he knew of our failure before it had even come about. The king made me promise that I would go on and finish what we'd all started."

Jessamine smiled. "Prophecy affects our lives in many ways. Perhaps your king did know what would happen. Perhaps he knew your mission was of the greatest importance."

Alan chuckled. "You don't give up easily, do you?"

"No, not when I really believe in something." She absently stroked the red wax seal. "The one thing that keeps going through my mind is the reference in the second letter to the hidden seal." Her gaze met his. "My prophecy talks of a hidden seal as well: 'Only without sight will you know what is real and bring to the world the hidden seal.'"

Her words sparked something inside him. Excitement flared. Coincidence again that the second letter and the second stanza had similar language? Petra. The stone speaking. The hidden seal? What could it all mean?

Jessamine went still. Her gaze became fixed on the letter in her hands.

"What is it?"

She didn't answer for a moment. "The wax seal . . ." Her words trailed off.

He positioned himself beside her, gazing at the seal, seeing nothing but a stamped red mass.

"Do you not see it?" Her voice was a tense whisper. "This symbol in the wax. I remember seeing the same exact symbol on the facade of the treasury yesterday."

He studied the red mass more closely. Still seeing nothing, he gently lifted it from her hands and raised the seal into the light. The symbol of an eagle stood out— an eagle with a fiery orb hovering over its head.

"You saw this symbol? Where?"

"When that horrible sound came out of nowhere, I looked toward the sky, but my gaze was pulled instead to the image of an eagle at the top right-hand corner of the treasury's carved roof." Determination shone in her dark eyes. "There's an eagle there with a fiery orb over its head."

He felt his breath catch. "Are you certain?"

She got to her feet and stepped off the blanket. "Only one way to find out."

Could this be the clue they were searching for? The key that would lead them to the ark? Eagerness and excitement soared through him as he gained his feet and held his hand out to Jessamine. "Let's go find out."

Chapter Twelve

Jessamine and Alan hurried toward the stone edifice of the treasury. Morning light broke across the land at that moment, painting the city of stone in hues of pink and red. At the rock facade of the treasury they came to a stop.

"Are you as excited as I am?" Alan asked as he set the saddlebag onto the ground at his feet.

She nodded breathlessly as she dabbed at the perspiration dotting her brow. Morning had just come over the land, and already the temperature soared.

Alan tipped his head back, staring up at the mammoth two-level, carved structure standing over one hundred twenty feet high. Jessamine did the same and smiled. Even the height couldn't hide the image of an eagle perched at the right side of the roofline. Carved into the rock behind the eagle was a fiery orb that matched the symbol on the wax seal.

"I need to get up there and see if there is any kind of clue as to where we should look next," Alan said.

"Truly?" Jessamine gasped. "The roofline is twenty times your height at least."

"We've come this far." He faced her and removed his belt, sword, and the pouch containing the stones of fire, placing them gently into her hands. "Trust me."

"I do trust you." She returned her gaze to the eagle. "What if you get up there and you can't read the clue?

It could be written in Arabic, Aramaic, Hebrew, Latin. . . ."

"I can read Latin, but you have a point."

He rifled through his saddlebag until he pulled out the book he'd shown the night before. He pulled out two blank pages, then replaced the book in his bag and stood. He stepped away to search the ground, then picked up a reddish rock. "There," he said with a note of satisfaction. "If I can't read the clue, I'll make a rubbing. Then we will put your linguistic talents to the test."

Before she could comment, he turned away and strode toward the farthest column to the right of the treasury's entrance. Despite the heat, a chill prickled her flesh. If anything happened to him . . .

No. He would be fine. If the clue truly was behind the statue of the eagle, then someone had placed it there, proving the wall could be climbed.

She grasped the thought like a lifeline as Alan shinnied halfway up the column, then swung himself to the rock face beside the temple. He reached with his hands and his legs for something . . . and she saw what she hadn't noticed before. Vertical footholds had been cut into the rock, most likely to help the sculptors who'd carved the edifice. She breathed a sigh of relief.

Alan shifted himself fully over to the footholds, climbing slowly higher and higher. Jessamine bit down on her lip as she watched each stretch and extension of his powerful arms and legs. His body was finely honed, no doubt from his life as a warrior. In no time at all, he reached the slanted rooftop and stepped onto it. He moved behind the statue of the eagle. He remained partially concealed behind the statue for what seemed like ages before he emerged and started the painstaking journey down again.

Jessamine moved close to the last pillar, staring up at

him as he descended. Dust rained down upon her, but she ignored it. She wanted to be close in case . . . She couldn't finish the thought.

With each step downward, her tension mounted as he struggled for the next foothold. She clenched her fists, as though doing so would help him find purchase on the wall.

Alan's foot slipped. Loose mortar gave way beneath his leather boots, dislodging a stone that tumbled to the ground. Jessamine held her breath as he clung to the wall, regained his foothold, and kept moving downward.

A wave of relief washed over her when he finally regained the ground with a grunt, covered in golden dust. She reached out and pulled him to her, wrapped her arms around him, and held him close.

"You're trembling," he said, breathing hard. He rested his cheek against her hair and comforted her, despite the fact that it was he who had risked his life climbing the facade.

"I can't seem to stop." Jessamine drew a ragged breath. "What did you discover?"

He pulled the two loose pages from within his left boot. "I was hoping you could interpret the symbols etched into the stone below the fiery orb. There were two of them." He unfolded one paper, then bent to the ground and set the pages side by side at her feet. "What does it say?"

Jessamine kneeled beside him. "The symbols are Hebrew." She concentrated on the darker areas of red that had been made when Alan rubbed the red rock over the wall with the paper in between. "The first word is *mountain*. The second word is *God*."

"Mountain God," he put the two words together.

Jessamine nodded. "The next clue is located at the

Mountain of God." She met his gaze. "Have you heard of such a place?"

He traced a finger over the rubbings he had made. "The Old Testament refers to the Mountain of God by two different names: Mount Sinai and Mount Horeb."

"Why two?"

"That's something of a mystery. But it may have been because, like God himself, the mountain was too sacred to call by name. However," he continued, "the Bible also leaves no doubt that these two names were for the same mountain."

Alan stood and moved back to his saddlebag, removing his book again. He flipped page after page, until a smile came over his lips at one of the pages. "Here it is." He turned back to her and thumped his finger on the page. "I wrote down all the passages in the Bible that had anything to do with the ark. It was a labor that took nearly a year, but I knew it would help when the search began."

He returned his gaze to the page. "Here in the book of Kings it says quite specifically that Horeb is the Mountain of God."

"Does the Bible say specifically where Horeb is located?"

He laughed. "Nay, it wouldn't be so easy as that. But there are two incidents that occurred on the Mountain of God that might tell us where to look." He flipped several more pages.

She came to stand beside him and looked down at the bold handwriting in which he'd painstakingly recorded the words *logic* and *strategy*. She hid the smile that crept to her lips. Alan knew his strengths, and he played to them well.

"In the book of Exodus there is this passage that concerns Moses and the burning bush: After Moses was forced into exile from Egypt, he settled in the land of Midian, where he married the daughter of a local priest called Jethro. Some years later, Moses was tending his father-in-law's flock when he was confronted by a bush that burned without being consumed. It was from within this miraculous fire that Moses first heard the voice of God. This event took place at the 'backside of the desert.' In biblical times this area would have been called Edom."

He flipped several more pages. "The second clue to the location of the Mountain of God can be found after Moses went back to Egypt and led the Children of Israel to freedom. He returned with them to Horeb to commune with God on the sacred mountain. By the time they arrived, the Children of Israel had run out of water and were dying of thirst. Moses saved them with a miracle when he smote the rock and water came out of it."

Excitement radiated from him, and Jessamine couldn't help being caught up in it.

"The pieces fit." Alan's gaze met hers. "Edom was a small kingdom in the northwest of the Sinai. We are but a day's journey from the mountain of which the Bible speaks."

"Then let's be on our way," Jessamine said.

Reluctance entered his gaze as he continued to study her. "I must warn you, the area we travel to next is one of the least hospitable in the Sinai wilderness. The Shara Mountains are an arid wasteland, and the Valley of Edom is but a small, fertile vale nestled within those barren peaks. As we travel, it will be scorching during the day and freezing at night. Are you accustomed to such travel? If not, I will ask whether the Bedouins would keep you with them until—"

"We are in this together, until the end," she interrupted. "I'm not afraid of the rugged, barren terrain, or the temperatures."

Pride entered his eyes for a moment before he turned his gaze to his book. He closed the pages slowly, then replaced the small volume in his saddlebag. "One of the mountains that encircle the Valley of Edom is the mysterious Mountain of God." Alan retrieved his belt, sword, and leather pouch and reattached them at his waist. "The Valley of Edom awaits." He held his hand out to her.

"The Valley of Moses?" A familiar voice spoke from behind them.

Jessamine started and turned to see the white-haired old man they'd met yesterday. Where had he come from? She'd heard no footsteps. No movement of his cane in the sand.

"The Bedouins call the valley by that name," the old man continued.

"Why?" Alan asked.

The old man shuffled forward. "There is a fresh-water spring there that never runs dry. Ain Musa, or the Spring of Moses, as the Bedouins refer to it."

"Do they call any of the mountains Mount Sinai? Or Horeb? Are there any traditions associated with either of those names?" Alan leaned toward the old man.

He pursed his lips in thought a moment, then shook his head.

"Do you know where this miraculous spring is located?" Alan asked tentatively.

The old man's features cleared. His eyes brightened. "You'll find the Spring of Moses at the summit of Jebel Madhbah as the Bedouins call it, or Mountain of the Altar."

Alan's gaze filled with suspicion as it shot to hers, then back to the old man. "You know a lot about this area."

"I've lived here most of my life. Longer than you can imagine," he added softly.

Jessamine studied the old man. He seemed as harmless today as he had yesterday. Yet a flicker of unease passed through her. He inclined his head at her, almost imperceptibly, as though he could read her thoughts and was trying to reassure her.

"What is your name?" she asked, realizing that they'd not been introduced last night.

"You may call me Will," he answered before turning to Alan. "Would you like me to guide you to Jebel Madhbah? I'm familiar with the desert. I'd see you safely to that mountain."

Alan's brow creased as he, too, studied the man. "We appreciate the offer—"

"Did I not assist you last night?" the old man asked.

"Aye." Alan replied, frowning. "As much as we would appreciate a guide, the journey is dangerous. We cannot—"

"Don't judge me by my appearance, son." Will's face remained calm, but an edge crept into his voice. "With the aid of a horse, I can go anywhere in this desert."

"We have but one horse," Jessamine replied.

"Allow me." The old man whistled, the sound shrill in the still morning air. As the sound died away, hoofbeats echoed through the ancient streets of Petra. A moment later, two dark horses galloped toward them, saddled and ready for riding. "The Bedouins are my friends. They provide me with what I need, when I need it."

The horses came to a stop before Jessamine and tossed their heads, as though eager to be underway.

Alan turned to her. "Can you ride by yourself?"

"I'm quite capable."

"Then it's settled," Alan said. A short while later, he

fastened his saddlebag to the saddle and remounted his horse.

Jessamine could feel excitement tighten her chest as she kicked her horse into a gallop, following Alan and their guide. They'd figured out another key piece of the puzzle. They were one step closer to finding the ark.

The thought stayed with Jessamine as she, Alan, and Will headed into the desert.

By late afternoon, the sun beat mercilessly on the dusty white rocks and searing, lifeless sand of the desert. With the back of his hand, Alan wiped away the sweat that continually formed on his brow. In the distance he could see the humped red ridges of the mountains. The only sound filling the desert was the clip-clopping echo of the horses' steps as they moved over the dry land.

Alan swallowed, trying to dredge up some hidden bit of saliva to slide down his parched throat. His swallow died, unborn. He'd forced Jessamine and the old man to drink the last of their water some time ago, hoping and praying they'd find the summit and a new source of water before they died of thirst.

The mountains still looked so far away.

"Just ahead," he thought he heard Will say from behind him.

The words drifted past him, without meaning. Then, a distant part of his brain registered what Will had said. Alan straightened in his saddle. *Just ahead.*

A small patch of green appeared in the distance. Before Alan could nudge his exhausted horse, the animal's nostrils flared, as all three horses shot forward.

All his thoughts focused on the speck of green in the distance. The Valley of Edom appeared like an emerald cut into the arid landscape. They'd made it. He leaned forward, encouraging his mount to greater speed.

Jessamine and Will were right beside him as the greenery beckoned, and glistening water sparkled like a thousand diamonds at the summit of the mountain ahead. His tongue slid along the bumpy, chapped surface of his lips.

Water. Had there ever been a more welcome sight?

He pulled the horse to a stop at the pool's edge. The Spring of Moses. He led the horse to the water's edge. The beast needed no encouragement, thrusting its nose into the pool for a long drink. Alan helped Jessamine and Will down from their exhausted mounts. Together, he and Jessamine headed for the edge of the pool. Jessamine scooped up a handful of water and drank. Alan did the same.

The old man stood on the opposite side of Jessamine, looking thoroughly refreshed. Alan frowned. Had Will already drunk from the pool? Had Alan been so caught up in satisfying himself that he hadn't noticed?

Alan shook off the thought as he stood and removed his empty water bladder from the horse's saddle. He knelt beside Jessamine again and refilled the container with cool, clear water. The pool was unbelievably beautiful. There were lush blades of grass shooting up from between the rocks at the water's edge and tiny blue flowers that perfumed the air with their sweetness.

When the bladder was full, he clamped it off, then splashed cool water over his face, allowing rivulets to run down his neck, providing a welcome relief to the sun's harsh rays.

Jessamine followed his example. She scooped water into her hands and splashed it over her skin. He watched the water run freely down her neck and across the rise of her breasts, and farther down. Alan swallowed roughly, this time not from thirst but from another deep-seated need.

He forced himself to his feet, putting some distance between them. "Better?" he asked.

Jessamine stood. "I didn't think water could ever taste that good."

"Do you need more water or rest?" Will asked. "Or would you like to move on?"

"Where do we go from here?" Alan asked, grateful for the interruption.

Will pointed to a cliff face with a flight of steps that zigzagged up the side of the mountain.

"Let's secure the horses," Alan replied. "It looks as though we'll need to proceed from here on foot." He tied the horses to the nearby shrubs. The horses paid them no heed as they munched on the blades of grass within their reach.

Dusk approached, and for a moment Alan hesitated.

"What is it?" Jessamine asked.

"I'm not certain we have enough time before nightfall to make it up the mountain and back."

She frowned. "We've come all this way. . . ."

"Perhaps, if necessary, we could remain on the mountain overnight. I've food and water in my saddlebag," Alan said, hitching the bag over his shoulder.

At Jessamine's radiant smile, all reservation faded. "Let's go," he said, and the three of them scrambled up the mountainside until they'd climbed to a plateau a thousand feet above the valley floor. Despite his cane, Will seemed to have no difficulty keeping up.

"Before you lies the Obelisk Terrace," he said, pointing to an area of flat rock that stretched two hundred feet long by a hundred feet wide. Rising from the terrace were two towering pillars of solid rock. Shiny blue slabs of slate created a paving-stone walkway around the two obelisks.

"These obelisks would have been the processional

entrance to the shrine that was up there on the summit," said Will, indicating the mountaintop, which was joined to the terrace by a narrow ridge about six hundred feet long. "The Bedouins consider this plateau to be sacred ground. They call these monuments Al-Serif, meaning 'the feet.' They have a tradition that God once stood astride the monuments."

Alan's emotions veered from elation to reservation. How did Will know so much about the area they needed to explore? The old man had referred to the Bedouins often, yet he wasn't one.

Alan frowned. Will had done nothing but help them in their quest so far, yet Alan couldn't shake the feeling that there was something the old man wasn't telling them about himself and where he'd come from.

And yet, staring at the summit before them, Alan wondered if the man's origins truly mattered. His pulse raced. Had they found the right place? Will's story confirmed the link between Jebel Madhbah and the biblical appearance of God. But even more important, the appearance of this mountain matched the description of the Mountain of God in the Old Testament. "The terrace could be where the Children of Israel stood while Moses proceeded up to the summit to receive the Ten Commandments."

"Let's keep going," Jessamine said as she started up the ridge.

"What will we find up there?" Alan asked Will as they followed her up the narrow path, but the old man did not answer.

Will moved slowly along the incline. Alan fell into step behind the older man. He wanted to be nearby if Will lost his balance. None of them could afford to tumble down the mountainside, least of all Will.

The climb was harder now, and it seemed to take all

Will's efforts to propel himself up the steep incline. After a few more steps he stopped entirely. "I'm not going to make it," he said between harsh breaths. "You two go on without me. I'll make my way back down . . . to the Obelisk Terrace and wait there." He leaned heavily on his cane. "There's an open-air temple up there known in ancient times as the High Place."

Jessamine came back to them. "Is everything all right?"

"Will's too tired to go on." Alan studied the old man. His face had lost all color. His cheeks were gaunt. He did look tired.

"You must continue," Will said, leaning more heavily on his cane.

Silence stretched between them until Alan reluctantly nodded. "All right. You head back down to the horses, and we'll join you as soon as we're able."

"Take the time you need," Will said. "I'll look for shelter while you two continue to explore the temple."

"Agreed."

Alan watched Will shuffle away, then turned back to Jessamine. "Ready to keep going?"

At her nod, they strode up the steep incline together. As they climbed, the daylight faded. Twilight turned the sky into a brilliant array of pink and yellow interspersed with big, dark clouds. "We'd better hurry before we lose the light," Alan warned.

"Why is it so dark?" Jessamine asked.

"I'm not certain," he admitted. Suddenly his thoughts moved back to Jessamine's prophecy. Wasn't there something about thunder on the mount?

"Jessamine? What does the third stanza of the prophecy say?"

Chapter Thirteen

Jessamine stilled as she felt the earth tremble for a heartbeat beneath her feet. A flash of lightning streaked through the silver-gray sky. Fear tightened her throat. Then Alan was there beside her. He slipped his arm around her waist, drawing her close.

"What is it?" he asked. "Does the lightning scare you?"

She shook her head. "Do you not feel the ground tremble?"

"It's just the storm."

"It's more than that."

"Then what?" A frown creased his brow as he searched the area around them.

"I don't know. I just felt something." She drew a sharp breath as the earth trembled again. This time his eyes widened as the earth shook.

"Jessamine, the third stanza of the prophecy. Tell me."

She recited the familiar words. "'On the Mountain of God all shall be revealed when the mists of the cloud and the devouring fire meet. Day into night and night into day, a whisper of I Am That I Am will pave the way.'"

His gaze shot to the sky. "Day into night and night into day. We have to keep going." He took her hand and guided her up the incline as another blue streak illuminated the sky.

"Isn't it dangerous? What about the light?"

"The prophecy seems to indicate that we need to be on this mountain when the storm breaks."

"That's not very logical."

"I know." He laughed. "Perhaps you are starting to have an influence on me." They picked their way gingerly across a patch of rough rocks.

Couldn't he have felt her influence somewhere safe? Jessamine ducked her head as the wind picked up and tossed her long hair about her face and tugged at her clothing like tiny invisible fingers trying to hold her back.

Was it a warning?

"What if we don't find the ark?" she asked.

"We'll find it. We have to." He sounded far more confident than she felt at the moment.

"We'll find it," Jessamine whispered, trying to convince herself of that truth. She'd trusted the prophecy to get them this far. She had to have faith. Her lungs burned and her legs trembled with exhaustion when they finally reached the summit. As they crested a ridge, another streak of light flared in the night sky and a thunderous boom sounded all around them.

Jessamine flinched and nearly lost her footing until Alan's arm steadied her. In that brief flash of light, she saw the open-air temple before them. Tall walls arranged in a rectangle were cut from the solid stone. Rows of benches, also cut from the rock, faced a central altar with steps leading up to it.

The sky went dark. Jessamine frowned, wanting to see more of the temple complex. "Why is it so dark?"

"There are forces other than simple nature at work here, I fear." He flashed her a confident smile. "This is the temple we've been searching for. Here we are in the presence of God, if all my research is correct."

To be in the presence of the Almighty was more than a little daunting. "How will we find the ark without any light?"

"The prophecy seems to want us here during this storm. We need to trust that whatever forces brought us here will keep us safe until all is revealed."

The wind picked up again and another flash of light ripped the darkness right beside her. A startled cry escaped her, to be silenced a heartbeat later by a thunderous crash. The hair on Jessamine's arms stood up as an odd sensation filled the air around them.

"Come with me." Alan took her arm. He pulled her toward one of the temple's high stone walls that stood near the altar.

"What about Will?"

"He's farther down the mountain. He'll be safe there, and he'll keep the horses calm while the storm blows itself out."

At his words, the wind swirled around them, drawing with it the heat of the day. Alan removed his saddlebag and set it at the edge of the altar, then sat down and leaned against the wall. He motioned beside him. "If the prophecy wants us here in the temple during the storm, let's cooperate."

She sat and leaned into him. Her heart accelerated as he pulled her closer with an arm around her waist. His gaze fixed intently on her face.

With the flashes of light, she could see him clearly one moment, but he disappeared into shadow the next. She trembled as another flash of light brightened the sky.

"We've been on this quest for five days," he shouted over the wind and thunder. "I know next to nothing about you."

Her heart stumbled. "What are you asking?"

"Anything you want to tell me. Your favorite scent. The most beautiful thing you've ever seen. About your family." He grinned. "Anything at all."

She flattened her hands against the rough fabric of her dress. Was it time to tell him the truth? They were too far into the journey for him to take her back to her royal family. But was that the real reason she'd kept her identity secret?

If she was honest with herself, her reluctance to tell the truth stemmed more from fear of the way he'd treat her if he knew who she was. She stared down at the large, capable hand at her waist. Would he talk to her so openly, or treat her as his equal, or touch her in the same way once he knew?

She would never know unless she took the chance and trusted him with her secrets. Yet the words would not form. Experience had taught her that people did treat her differently. Once they knew who she was, people kept her at a distance.

She didn't want that, not here with him. She wanted to be just another female who was free to decide the course of her own life. Someone who could listen to her heart and follow its call. Tears formed in her eyes and she turned her face away.

What had he asked, her favorite scent? She swiped at her eyes, then leaned back and drew a slow, deep breath of musk and sandalwood. Her eyes drifted closed. He was her favorite scent, but she couldn't tell him that. She opened her eyes. "I love the smell of cinnamon." Her voice sounded raw. Perhaps he wouldn't notice. "I don't think I've yet encountered the most beautiful sight in the world. And my family . . ." She paused. "They meddle too much."

He drew her more tightly against him, and despite

the storm's song she heard his soft laughter. "Meddling isn't bad. It sounds as if you are loved. Be grateful for that."

"I am," she replied, but she wanted something her birth denied her. Maybe it was a mistake to want it . . . and maybe it was unfair to want it from him, a man dedicated to logic and war and the divine.

She looked at the sky. Again, the lightning flashed. Was it her desire for freedom that brought them here to this moment on the mountaintop? Or was it fate that had led them to Mount Sinai?

She preferred to think that fate was in charge—or at least some force outside herself. She cast a sideways glance at Alan. Warmth stirred within her. She became acutely conscious of his hand at her waist. Of the cool sandstone beneath her. The tang of metal lingering in the air after each burst of light. The moon that hung low in the night sky and threaded Alan's hair with streaks of silver.

His gaze met hers.

The wind kicked up again, caressing her face and throat with cooling fingers, pressing her gown against her breasts. Her nipples grew taut. She sucked in a startled breath at the sensation.

"Jessamine?" His voice sounded thick.

He could sense her desire. She scrambled to her feet. Sitting beside him was every bit as dangerous as the lightning overhead.

Alan followed her up and reached for her hand. Her heart pounded in her chest. She was certain he could hear it above the booming thunder.

He touched her throat with a light caress. A primal shudder went through her. Her nipples responded again, straining against her gown.

She could feel him against her. She could smell him

in the darkness. Musk and sandalwood and moonlight. She closed her eyes, allowing the scents to lure her in.

She should resist him.

He should resist her.

For one breathless moment the world fell silent. Then his lips claimed hers. She didn't resist. She couldn't. His hands slid up her body to settle at the sides of her breasts, and Jessamine felt all her will, all her resistance, crumble. She kissed him back with her whole being. She didn't care about anything but his touch in the darkness. The dark would hide them—hide their secrets and all the reasons they shouldn't be together.

Thunder sounded all around them as she brushed her lips over his, teasing, taunting. He groaned and cupped her face with his hand, pulled her tight against the hard length of him. He held her without kissing her, as though waiting for something.

He was so near, scarcely a breath away. A flash of lightning showed his eyes filled with desire. Then a low, guttural sound escaped him as he nuzzled her neck and pressed a heated kiss to her cheek, her chin, her jaw, and finally her neck. When he kissed his way to the small incision he'd made in her neck, he paused and nipped her ever so gently.

"Alan." His name was a plea for something she couldn't name.

Alan curled his fingers in her hair. He brought a thick lock up to trace the rise of her breasts that peeked above her gown. It was not her shiver that startled him as much as the tingling in his own hand. It was as if his fingers had been frozen and were now coming painfully back to life. The strands of her hair flowed against his skin like warmed treacle.

The tingling spread from his fingers to his wrists and arms. His loins were aching, the muscles of his belly knotting. For a man who was always in control of his responses, he had to admit he had no control now. He found himself trembling. Alive.

A flash of white light streaked through the night sky, followed immediately by a thunderous boom. Alan's fear was not of the storm, but of rejection. "No second thoughts?" he asked, his voice guttural.

"None."

The word had barely formed before he grasped the edge of her gown and pulled it up over her head, leaving her dressed in only the sheer fabric of her chemise. He couldn't hold himself back. He needed to see her—all of her.

Lightning flashed as she stood before him. Through the thin, pale fabric, he could see the faint outline of her body, her dusky nipples, and a darker thatch at the apex of her thighs. Forcing himself to go slow, he slipped the chemise up over her thighs, her breasts, her head.

Freed from her clothes, she was a true and utter goddess. Perfect. Small and delicate. Her taut breasts were round and firm and crowned with darker peaks that flowed down to a flat stomach and a small waist, then widened to rounded hips. His gaze moved down to her exquisite thighs and the black curls that shadowed her womanhood. His blood pounded through his veins.

Had he ever wanted anything more?

Your vows, a voice deep inside cautioned. He curled his fists at his sides. His chest rose and fell with the force of his breathing. He had tossed his vows aside the moment he touched Jessamine on the battlefield. He'd turned away from his brothers and everything to do with his old life.

He was not the same man he'd been five days ago. He'd been an empty shell before. The man who stood here now wanted to fill that shell. He wanted to feel alive. He wanted to start anew.

With her.

He unlatched his belt and set his sword at his feet. His boots came off next. He shed the rest of his clothes in the space of a heartbeat, then scooped her into his arms. He carried her to the stone depression behind the altar. In earlier times it would have been used for the sacrifice of animals. He forced the thought away. They would sacrifice themselves to each other tonight— their old lives would be forever behind them and they would emerge renewed.

Again the lightning flared and thunder shook the ground. Jessamine gasped, not from the storm, but from the sensation of Alan's flesh against her own. She could feel the dark curly hair of his chest pressed against the side of her breast, his warm muscular arm curled around her naked back. Heat. Desire. Hunger. She pressed against him, needing to be nearer.

When he set her down on a smooth slab of sandstone, she nearly cried out because the stone took his warmth from her. Then, banishing the cold, he joined her, his lips exploring her shoulder, her torso, her breasts. His tongue flicked her sensitive nipples slowly, relishing the taste and texture of her skin.

Jessamine gasped. Her fingers tangled in his hair. She wanted him closer, beside her, inside her. She'd heard the courtiers talk about sex before, and she'd always wondered what the fuss was all about. Now she understood. It was as if a fever had taken hold of her body, heating her, devouring her, stealing all but the desire to merge with him, become one.

She arched up to him, and his mouth closed over her breast. He suckled first one breast, then the other. Flame shot through her. She cried out, arching against his mouth. "What is it, Alan? Why do I feel so strange? It's as if something is missing. I want more," she gasped.

"I've not been celibate all my life. There's plenty more, I promise." His tone was as velvet soft as his calloused hands glided over her stomach to nestle in the curls at the center of her womanhood, tangling, caressing, probing as he flicked her nipples with his tongue.

Her heart pounded painfully. She couldn't breathe. Couldn't think. Could only react. She reached for his shoulders, delighting as his muscles bunched and relaxed beneath her touch. Emboldened by her desire, she slid her hands across his chest to his abdomen, and curled her fingertips in the V of dark hair that gathered at the apex of his sex, moved farther down until her hand wrapped around his pulsing hardness.

He released a low, throaty sound, and his fingers moved deeper into her curls and parted her flesh, searching.

The muscles of her stomach clenched and convulsed. He stroked her. Just when she grew used to his rhythm, he changed it, keeping her at the brink of something, waiting, waiting . . . for what?

Again the lightning and thunder sounded all around them as Alan spread her thighs, his palm running feverishly up and down her flesh until he delved two fingers inside and sank deep. She arched up against his hand helplessly as his rhythm escalated. Her hands moved back to his shoulders, clenched, held on as her head thrashed from side to side. "It's too much," she cried. "Too intense."

"Nay." His fingers vanished and he settled himself between her thighs, his rigid manhood pressing against her. "There is hunger. There is fever. And there is more."

The stone was cool against her naked hips and back, and yet she was surrounded by heat as Alan cupped her buttocks and the molten need inside her flared. She could hear the harsh sound of their breathing as it mingled with the darkness and the storm.

He bent to capture her lips. His tongue slid over the seam of her mouth, seeking entrance. Their tongues met, toyed, tangled. He groaned low in his throat. The sound was lost as she gasped. He plunged forward, met resistance, and kept going, piercing the last barrier that separated them.

Pain seared her. Her cry was muffled against his lips. Then completion, fullness. They were one.

He left her lips to look down at her. As the hunger that had driven her earlier replaced the pain, she moved against him.

He smiled his pleasure, and moved slowly at first, allowing her to adjust to the sensation, then faster, deeper, with growing desperation. The tension inside her built, tightened. Incredible pleasure streaked through her with each forceful thrust. He cupped her buttocks in his palms and lifted her to him over and over again.

She gasped for breath, held tight to his hips, urging him forward. Lightning flared over them, around them, within them. She opened herself to him, spiraling, devoid of air, engulfed in flame.

"Jessamine!" The word was savage as he buried himself in her.

She didn't know what he asked for . . . and then she did as every nerve inside her flared to exquisite life and sensation rolled over her with a dizzying intensity that robbed her of everything but the need to be swept away. Her name was on his lips as he cried out his pleasure. His movements stopped and he gathered her close.

She lay absolutely still, stunned and splintered. The lightning had abated and darkness once again settled around them.

"Are you cold?" he asked.

"No." Despite her nakedness, she wasn't cold. She was blissfully content and heavy with sleep.

He brushed her temple with a kiss, then turned her to nestle with her back to his chest. "Rest for a moment. We'll plan our strategy after that." His hands closed possessively over her breasts.

Her eyelids shut, and she felt awareness edging away from her.

She woke in what felt like only moments, but the darkness had given way to the pink light of dawn. Alan still held her as intimately as when she'd closed her eyes. His hands cupped her breasts as though he was not willing to end the intimacy they'd shared. The long, muscular length of his body was curled against her back. She smiled her contentment, but that smile slipped a moment later as she considered what had happened between them. They'd come together as one, joined their bodies, and her life would never be the same.

She was a fallen princess. She bit down on her lip. Strange, she didn't feel any different. She could detect no dark burden of sin weighing her down. There was only a slight ache between her thighs and a warmth in the center of her chest to prove her untoward behavior had had any lasting effect.

She looked at the sky and searched the small swath of pink that suggested dawn was on its way. A hawk circled high overhead, its wings outstretched and seemingly motionless as it rode the currents of air, searching the mountainside for prey. Jessamine stretched and rolled onto her back.

"Good morrow," Alan murmured, his tone as soft as the early morning light. He rose up on his elbow to stare down at her. "How are you?"

"Perfect." Emboldened by their nakedness, she

reached out and trailed her fingers over the hard plane of his chest. He inhaled sharply. The dark centers of his eyes flared and she knew he wanted her again. A smile formed on her lips, then faltered a moment later when his hands came out to stop further exploration.

"Jessamine," he said, his voice tight. "We must talk."

"About where the prophecy will lead us next?" She brought a toe up to stroke the length of his leg.

"Nay." He pulled back with regret in his eyes. "Please. We must speak about what happened between us last night."

She pushed up on her elbows, for the first time gazing at his naked body in the steady light of dawn. He was unlike anything she'd seen before. Not that she'd seen any naked men, but there had been a statue once in Spain. . . . But he was not pale marble. His flesh was warm bronze. His powerful shoulders and muscular chest flowed down to a tight stomach and corded thighs. Dark hair surrounded his maleness, which was boldly erect.

"Jessamine, you must stop looking at me like that or we'll not be discussing anything for a good long time."

She smiled. "That would serve me well." She reached for him.

With a groan, he scooted back. He sat up and placed some distance between them. "You don't know how tempted I am. But we really must talk."

She sat up as well. The dark shadows were back in his eyes. "If not about the prophecy, then what?" she asked hesitantly.

"Marriage."

At the word, her heart stumbled. "Why?"

"You deserve the safety of marriage." His voice was harsh. "What if we created a child last night?" He met her eyes gravely. "I couldn't live with the possibility of bringing a bastard into this world."

A sharp pain filled her chest. She hadn't considered a child. Grief robbed her of breath. Had she learned nothing from her parents' lives? Had she not witnessed the pain and suffering their love had brought them? Her parents had defied their traditions, their religion, and their royal status for the passion they'd found in each other's arms. She understood that passion now, understood what power it had, but she wasn't ready to throw herself down at passion's feet. Such emotion had ultimately destroyed her parents.

Jessamine drew a sharp breath and forced the old doubts and questions back into the deepest recesses of her mind. "Is that your only reason for wanting to sacrifice your freedom? A child?"

"It's as good a reason as any."

"Not for me." She stood and took several steps back. "Child or no child, my purpose is to fulfill the prophecy, not to marry you or any other man."

Chapter Fourteen

Alan watched Jessamine step back. She looked so fragile standing at the edge of the altar, naked. The long loose ends of her dark hair coiled over her shoulders, across her breasts, and teased the curves of her waist and hips. A glorious goddess. And he'd just insulted her with his emotionless proposal. He could tell by the flash of pain in her eyes that she'd wanted him to say something more.

Her lashes, spiky with the tears she refused to let fall, cast shadows on her half-veiled eyes. His heart twisted. "You have a right to be angry. I handled that poorly. But my clumsiness doesn't change what happened between us in the darkness of last night. We must face it and deal with it in the light of day."

"I cannot marry you. If last night's pleasure burdens you so much, then let's forget it ever happened."

"I cannot do that." Stubbornness mixed with guilt and another emotion he didn't want to define. "You would want to bring a bastard child into the world?"

She flinched. "Never. It's the children who suffer—"

"Then accept me. Marry me. Let's protect whatever child we might have created last night." He touched her cheek gently. "I'll be a good husband to you."

"You are a Templar. A man of God. How can you be both a monk and a husband?"

"After last night, my future is changed. I'll carry my sins as a man."

She pulled away from his touch. "I'm as much to blame for what happened last night as you. The situation forced us together, but I offered no resistance. I wanted you."

"I want you still," he said through the tightness in his throat.

Her gaze shifted to the lower region of his body, then jerked back to his face. Her cheeks flamed anew, but he could see desire flare in her eyes. "That," she said crisply, "is not why we came to this mountain." She straightened as though finding her equilibrium once more. "Daylight is almost upon us. Let's continue our quest for the ark."

"And what about marriage?" he persisted.

She met his gaze. "I'll think on it."

"Then I have no choice but to wait." Why did the words fill him with such wrenching pain? "Get dressed," he said more harshly than he'd intended. "We must find the ark."

Her shoulders eased as though relieved of a mighty burden. "You truly believe we are close?" she asked as she dressed.

He grasped his braies and breeches, throwing them on with as much haste as he'd used taking them off last night. "Aye. We are close."

The renewed flicker of interest in Jessamine's eyes almost made him miss the prickly sense of awareness creeping up his nape. He scanned the temple complex. Were they being watched? Alan frowned into the increasing light of dawn. Who would be out there? The man who'd followed Jessamine from Spain? The assassins? Alan saw nothing, yet the feeling would not go away.

He sensed someone or something out there waiting, waiting for him to fall asleep when he should stay awake, to relax when he should remain alert, to grow careless when he should be diligent.

He finished dressing and returned to Jessamine's side. "Come, we must go now."

"Alan?" Her voice sounded odd.

She stood still, gazing beyond the temple complex. He followed her gaze and froze. A ball of fiery red light, around six feet in diameter, hovered a few feet in the air above the temple ruins. Slowly, it moved back and forth, shimmering, then growing dull, then shimmering once more.

"What is it?" Her voice was a strangled whisper. She reached for his arm, holding tight.

"I'd call it devouring fire."

"The prophecy," she gasped. "What do we do?"

He gently removed her grip from his arm. "Stay here." He started toward the fiery ball.

"Alan!"

He turned to her, startled by the fear in her voice. Her eyes were wide.

"What if it's really devouring fire?"

"We need to know what it means if we are to continue our quest."

After a slight pause, she nodded.

Alan moved closer to the orb of red light, listening for sounds that might indicate what the object might be. Nothing. The earth had fallen silent. Even the hawk that had circled above only moments before had vanished. The absolute silence seemed eerie, prickling his skin with gooseflesh. It felt as if the earth itself were holding its breath. Was this what he'd sensed before? He took another step closer.

A rumble sounded, softly at first, then growing stronger.

"Alan." He twisted back toward Jessamine to see her

stagger toward him. He tried to go back to her, but fell to his knees as he was overcome with dizziness. He clutched the ground, looking for support as the mountain seemed to be rippling beneath his knees.

Rocks began to tumble from the walls enclosing the temple complex. Alan felt them hit his shoulder, his legs, as he crawled toward Jessamine. "Get down," he warned her.

She dropped to the ground, and the rock beneath her rose and fell like a wave on the sea. She gave a little scream and jerked backward as a rock tumbled in front of her.

For a suspended moment, he and Jessamine stared across the distance that divided them, the red orb forgotten, while dust and debris rained down on their heads and shoulders. The earth shook harder.

Alan forced himself forward. If he could just reach Jessamine. Soon the trembling would stop, and they'd be safe.

The trembling didn't stop. Instead the shaking grew steadily worse until the ground beneath him felt as though it were surging in great undulating waves.

For a frozen moment in time, Alan clung to the rocky ground as the temple around them seemed to ripple like a storm-tossed sea. They were part of the maelstrom whether they liked it or not. He could see Jessamine's mouth moving, but he could not hear her cries over the crack and roar as the earth split and tore around them. The ground beneath them gave way, sucking them into a dark abyss below.

Jessamine had no idea how long she lay there on the cold stone. She was just grateful the earth had stopped shaking. It was pitch-dark. There were no stars or moon. No pink light of dawn. A chill racked her flesh as she realized why there was no sky, no light, no sound. She'd fallen into some sort of cavity beneath the ground. Buried. Entombed. Yet she must not be alone.

"Alan!" She lifted her head and found she could sit up. Rubble rattled off her. Pebbles and dirt clinked against the rock beneath her and a fine, cloying dust floated in the air. She coughed and waved her arms before her, hoping to calm her breathing. She flexed her hand before her. She couldn't see anything, not even her fingers as she brought them close to her face. She wiggled her fingers anyway, noting they were undamaged. Her appendages were stiff and sore as she tried to move them. A tender spot ached at the back of her head, but she appeared to be all right.

But what of Alan?

Jessamine struggled to her feet, gathering her wits and her strength. They'd been caught in an earthshake. She'd heard about them, but had never experienced one herself. She staggered as she tried to walk a few steps. She tripped on the uneven floor and landed on her knees. She stayed down, crawling through the darkness. She had to find Alan. He might be hurt, or worse.

Then she would be utterly alone in the darkness. Panic sucked her breath from her. She quickly forced the thought away. He was here. He was alive. She simply had to find him.

She called his name again. There was no reply, only the settling of sliding stone and sand and the rapid beating of her pulse in her ears. Jessamine forced herself to calm down, taking several deep breaths. She had air to breathe. That was something to be thankful for. Now, if only she had a candle or a torch . . . or even that strange red orb to guide her to Alan.

Jessamine looked up where the sky should have been, hoping to see the red light hovering. She saw only darkness. She'd never been in absolute darkness before. There had always been some sconce in the hallways of the castle to guide her way, or a servant nearby to bring a candle, a fire in the grate. Even in a dark room, she had seldom experienced this complete absence of light.

She put her arms out before her, but couldn't see them as she took small steps forward. "Alan? Where are you?" Her voice echoed and reverberated back to her.

The sound brought with it a sense of hope. In order for there to be an echo, she must be in a large open space. Perhaps she'd fallen into an underground temple?

She inched forward and let out a tiny shriek when her hand touched something. For a moment her heart lurched until she realized the cold, hard object was a wall. She continued on. Every now and again, her fingers moved across etchings in the walls. She was certain now that she'd fallen into some sort of temple structure. Was it the one she and Alan had been searching for? Could they have literally stumbled into the resting place of the Ark of the Covenant?

Only Alan would know for certain. "Alan," she called again, staring into darkness that didn't seem quite so dense now. Perhaps her eyes were growing used to the lack of light. She'd taken one step, then another, when the earth started shaking again. Dust showered down on her, stinging her eyes, filling her mouth. She covered her face with the sleeve of her gown and flattened herself against the wall.

She waited for the earth to settle. When it calmed, she released a great shuddering sigh.

"Jessamine?"

She froze. "Alan!" Had the sound been her imagination? Or had she heard Alan's voice?

"Over here."

His voice came from the blackness, disembodied but comforting. Tears of thankfulness came to her eyes as she stumbled toward the sound. "Keep talking. I'm trying to find you."

His response was a groan. The sound came from her left.

"Are you hurt?"

A shifting sound was followed by the pinging of rocks. "Did you sit up?" She stared into the darkness, hoping to see something that might indicate where he was. "Can you move?"

"I can move, though it feels like someone is drumming on my skull."

She could hear his breathing as she edged closer. She stretched her fingers out before her, probing, searching. She connected with something soft. "Alan?"

"I hope that's you," he said with a touch of relief.

"Is anything broken?" Her fingers moved to his shoulder, his neck, his cheek.

His hand came up to cup hers against his face. "I'm feeling better now that you're safe. The last thing I remember is hitting my head, hard. Then the sound of your voice."

Her fingers shifted from his cheek to his nape and farther up over the back of his head. An egg-sized lump stood out against the back of his skull. "You must have hit pretty hard. Are you dizzy?"

He reached for her hand, bringing it to his lips. "How are you?"

"I'm unharmed." She breathed deeply, drawing in his familiar sandalwood scent. "I'm more than a little curious about the timing of this earthshake. Did that red light cause it? Was it our presence in the temple? Is this part of the prophecy that the seeress forgot to mention?"

She could feel him shift beside her.

"I'm sure all our questions will be answered in time," he said.

"So what do we do now?"

"Find a light. My saddlebag was near me when the earth started quaking. It must have fallen in here with us, somewhere. Then we'll find a way out."

She could hear him searching the ground beside them. She extended her free hand in front of her, sweeping the area. She was about to release a frustrated sigh when her fingers contacted something soft and supple. "Alan!" she gasped. "I think I found it." She grasped the heavy soft leather pouch and pulled it into her lap. The sound of sloshing water came to her ears. Her heart leaped. "Not only the bag, but the water."

He shuffled through the darkness toward her. His fingers found the bag and he took it from her. A moment later she heard the hissing rip of fabric being torn, followed by a scratching sound. The scratching came again, and again, until a brief spark of light appeared. "I'm going to need a stick of some sort. As the light increases, be ready to search for something."

Jessamine got to her feet, poised to dart in any direction as the spark became a dancing flicker. It took a moment for her eyes to adjust to the light, but when they did she hurried over to a pile of rubble to grasp what they needed—a stout tree branch. She returned to Alan's side.

He accepted the branch and wrapped the loose cloth he'd ripped from his Templar tunic around the wood. He set the fabric to the small flame, making a torch.

"It appears we've fallen into a chamber that existed below the temple complex where we spent the night."

"Could this be the place where the ark was taken for safekeeping all those years ago?"

The torch sent golden fingers of light through the

cut-rock chamber, banishing the darkness to the far corners of the long, narrow room. Two piles of debris in the center of the chamber must once have been pillars.

"It makes perfect sense," Alan admitted, "that the guardians of the ark would have returned it to the house of God, here on Mount Sinai."

"And they built an underground chamber complex to keep it safe." Jessamine's gaze shifted from the destruction to the walls surrounding them. Just as she'd imagined in the darkness, decorative scenes had been carved into the walls. She moved toward them and ran her finger over the cool, gritty surface, feeling the sharp edges of the chiseled lines. "These markings are so crisp. They look as though they were cut yesterday."

"No doubt they've been protected from the elements for many years. . . ." His voice trailed off as he joined her.

She moved slowly around the chamber. One scene depicted a large orb hovering over a mountaintop. The next revealed a man standing beneath that orb, his hands outstretched. Jessamine progressed down the wall to find the next scene depicted the orb hovering over a rectangular box. "Is this the orb we saw today?" she asked, fearing she already knew the answer.

Alan stopped beside her. His hand went out to trace the rectangular box. "The ark."

They stood side by side, their eyes glued to the scene. Jessamine went weak with hope and excitement. Maybe, just maybe, they had fallen into this chamber for a reason.

Together, they shifted down to the next scene. The rectangular box appeared alone in this scene. On the carved image of the lid sat two winged cherubs facing each other, their wings outstretched as though protecting the contents of the rectangular box.

In the next scene, Jessamine gasped at the image of a man and a woman standing on either side of the box. The man had a red Templar cross on his chest and the woman had long flowing hair. "Is that supposed to be you and me?" A chill moved through her.

"It appears so," Alan said with a touch of reverence in his voice.

She stepped away from the wall. She couldn't look at the next scene. All she could do was stare blindly at the red-gold rock that surrounded them. "I'm afraid to see what comes next."

He reached out and took her hand in his. "You are the great believer in fate. Why do you suddenly fear what it might have in store for us?"

A strong sense of premonition made her skin tingle. "I don't know for certain, but I do."

He squeezed her fingers. "All will be well, Jessamine. There are no more scenes ahead. Only a blank wall."

Her breath whooshed from her. Before she could wonder why she felt such an overwhelming sense of relief, Alan tugged her farther down the wall. "Where are we going?" she asked.

"Watch the flame."

She stared at the torch and felt a moment's thrill when the flame bent beneath a flickering breeze that came from the direction Alan led. As they progressed, Jessamine could see a crack of light in the distance.

"Is that light?"

"Amazingly, it appears to be." Alan quickened his pace. "If we want to fulfill this quest, it looks like we need to head this way."

Jessamine sucked in a deep breath to prepare herself for whatever lay ahead.

Chapter Fifteen

The torch in Alan's hand splashed light and twisting, dancing shadows across the carved walls as he pulled Jessamine through the passageway. His head pounded with every step, but he hardly noticed as excitement flared in his blood. "We're so close, Jessamine! This must be where the ark is hidden."

She gripped his hand more tightly. "All the clues fit. The devouring fire led us to where the earth could open and reveal hidden places." She slowed her steps.

"What is it?"

"Each clue we discover puts us in greater danger. The lightning, the earthquake . . . What will be next?"

"We are at the journey's end, Jessamine. What could be left for us to pass through?" He moved forward again, then turned a corner and stopped.

Jessamine thumped into his back. "What is it?"

"Oh my heavens," was all he could force past his suddenly dry throat. It was not a chamber, as he had expected, but a lush, green paradise.

Jessamine gazed spellbound into the cavern ahead, scarcely breathing. "This is what I always imagined Eden would look like."

Golden light bathed everything around them. "Where is the light coming from, this far below the Earth's surface?" Alan set the torch down on the stone floor and drew Jessamine with him into the open space.

The sandstone rock had been cut away to form an enormous chamber, a cavern, an oasis, deep beneath the arid mountain. Rocky walls soared two hundred feet over their heads. Vigorous green vines trailed down the sides of the golden rock. Palm trees and spiky green shrubs thrust out of the rocky soil. "This is impossible," Alan mused as he cautiously stepped along the gold-lined path cutting through the foliage. "This place must be touched by God. What other explanation could there be?"

As the greenery thinned, the golden path widened. They came to a double row of statues that formed a walkway leading across a wide gold-covered expanse and up ten steps to an elevated altar that held the Ark of the Covenant.

"The prophecy led us up the mountain so that we could discover the secret chamber of the ark," Jessamine said with awe.

She stepped up to one of the statues, an angel with its wings outstretched, so elegantly carved that it appeared ready to take flight at any moment. She reached out and touched the silky smoothness of the wing. "Gold." She turned to Alan, her eyes wide. "This kind of wealth is incomprehensible. I've never seen so much gold."

He nodded as he strode up the ten golden steps leading to the altar and the treasure waiting there. He could feel Jessamine behind him. Everything around them was silent and still. The only sound in the cavern seemed to be the shuffle of their boots on the golden stairs.

They approached the ark together. Alan felt the breath leave his lungs and he froze. "Dear God." He thought he had been prepared for this moment, but he knew now he hadn't been.

He heard a soft intake of breath beside him. "The Ark of the Covenant," Jessamine whispered as she took a step closer. "I never imagined . . ." She brought her hand to her chest. "It's so beautiful, and yet I feel uncertain."

The ark didn't make him uneasy. Nay, after the first stunning impact, he felt something vibrate in the air. Not a sound or a wave, but a rightness. A soothing of doubts. A rush of certainty, and calmness, and a strangely peaceful joy. Everything in his life had led up to this moment. He moved slowly forward until he stood next to the golden chest.

Four pillars made up the corners of the ark. A long pole ran the length of each side. Ornate carvings covered its exterior. Yet it was not the gold or the artistry of the carvings that drew his attention. It was the two angels that sat atop the chest's lid, wings outstretched as though protecting the ark's contents. He reached for the tip of one wing where it almost touched the other. His hand hovered over a delicate golden feather, almost afraid to touch it. When he did, it felt warm and smooth beneath his fingertip.

"Alan?" It was Jessamine's voice.

He turned to find her looking, not at the ark, but at him.

"Alan? You're scaring me."

He started. "What do you mean?"

"You've been staring at the ark for such a long time. I was beginning to wonder if you were caught in a spell."

His hand fell away from the wing. It had seemed like only a moment. He forced himself to take a step back, then another, until he stood by her side. He took her in his arms and lifted her up, twirling her around. "We did it!"

Their laughter merged, floated up to the heights of the chamber. Excitement brightened her face. Something inside his chest tightened. He slid her down the length of him. Joy shifted to desire. He drew a sharp breath when he saw his desire reflected back in the dark depths of her eyes.

They stared at each other for a long moment before Jessamine spoke. "Are you curious about what's inside the ark?" Her gaze drifted to the golden artifact. "Are the broken tablets of the Ten Commandments really inside?"

Alan's gaze shifted from her to the ark. "Nay. We should only touch the poles. My research revealed that when those whose hearts were not pure touched the ark, they were struck to the ground . . . dead." He looked at her once more.

"I agree. It's not worth the risk." Her gaze moved from him to wander around the huge chamber. "Do you wonder what else might be in this cavern?"

He nodded. "The thought had crossed my mind. Would you like to explore?"

"What about the ark?" she asked.

He smiled. "The ark isn't going anywhere. We have time to explore. Where would you like to go?"

"I want to see what else might be here. I want to spend more time alone with you."

He had barely drawn breath when her lips touched his with a pressure so soft he could almost have imagined it. And then breathing seemed irrelevant as the slow, penetrating warmth of her lips seeped into his veins, spread through his body like liquid heat.

It was a kiss of unbearable sweetness that gave and gave, growing in intensity as the tips of her fingers slid down his neck, seeking out the pulse point beneath his jaw. And her touch, when she found that pulsing point, sent a current of pure energy through him, as if she were somehow concentrating all of her being into that one spot.

It was as if, for years, his entire body had been lying dormant, waiting for this, waiting for her to kiss him into life and wake him with her touch.

Then her fingers trailed down to his chest. For a moment she laid her hand over his heart, and it too leaped to her touch. It was as though her touch were breathing warmth and life back into his cold, angry core. It was unbearably sweet, and utter agony, as every part of him, including his heart, pulsed back to life beneath her touch.

"Jessamine." He gasped her name out, but whether he wanted her to revive him or leave him in that cold dark place he'd inhabited for years, he could not have said. But something had changed inside him since he'd met her. Something that would never be the same even if she left.

"Alan?" He was suddenly aware that she kissed him no longer. "Are you well?" she asked with a note of concern in her voice.

Was he? He was feeling rather strange in the aftermath of her kiss.

"Alan!" she said more urgently.

"I'm well," he replied, then looked down at her to see concern reflected in her eyes. "I'm better than I've ever been," he said with a smile, then took her hand and led her down the stairs back to the golden walkway, through the rows of angels and to the trees beyond. They were utterly alone in this magical place. They walked for a bit among the unusual foliage until they caught sight of the shimmer of water through the trees.

"Water?" Jessamine asked at the same moment he recognized the sight.

With all the greenery, he should have expected some source of water. They broke through the foliage. Amongst the velvety, dun-colored rocks, Alan saw an oval pool. A hazy mist floated up from the water.

"What is it?" Jessamine asked.

He glanced down at the shimmering water. The mist was not mist at all, but steam that curled into the air. "A hot spring."

The pool was unbelievably beautiful, just as everything else had been in this underground cavern. There were ferns growing where the water splashed on the rocks, and tiny blue flowers bloomed in the misty air. Huge ivory lilies filled the air with their scent.

Jessamine bent down at the water's edge. She scooped a handful of water and let it run through her fingers. "It's warm." She stood and reached for the hem of her gown.

"Jessamine? What are you doing?"

"I'm going in," she said, slipping her gown over her head. She tossed her shoes at the water's edge, then pulled her chemise off, tossing it down beside her shoes.

Alan could not take his eyes off her as she stripped away her clothing without a hint of self-consciousness and stood before him as Eve. She stepped into the water and allowed the warm liquid to ripple over her, turning her skin into satin against the jet of her hair.

She turned, and their eyes met. There was something in the depths of her dark eyes that made his gut clench. A promise of passion. "There's plenty of room in here for two."

Every reason for resisting vanished in the curling steam that rose around them. Desire flared in his blood and settled in his groin. His tunic pressed against his flesh, suddenly feeling heavy and cumbersome.

Alan's clothes seemed to melt from him as he hurried after her. Water curled around his legs, brushed against his naked thighs. The steam formed a silvery curtain through which he could see Jessamine. The muscles of his belly knotted and his manhood became rigid. The scent of jasmine mingled with lilies. He drew in the heady mixture. If he touched her, there would be no turning back for either of them.

He took a step toward the woman who made him feel as though he was someone special, someone extraordinary. The woman he wanted more at this moment than he wanted to draw his next breath.

Heat surrounded her, invading her senses as Jessamine stared at Alan. He moved toward her, looking every bit the knight, the warrior, the man who'd filled her dreams. He approached her in the waist-deep water. Naked.

The golden light of the chamber limned his lean, sinewy body in gold. He ducked beneath the water, came up, and dragged his fingers through his hair. Silver-bright droplets of water fell from his dark hair onto the hard muscular ripples of his chest. She noticed a purple bruise darkening his left shoulder.

She reached out and touched him. "I'm sorry—"

"Nay. You didn't cause these."

"We've both been wounded on our quest."

"Aye." He trailed his hand in the water, sending ripples across the surface before raising his fingers to her own wound. "Perhaps now is the time for healing?"

Anticipation fluttered deep in Jessamine's core at the look of raw, unveiled passion in Alan's eyes. There was an animal-like intensity she'd never seen there before that stole her breath. It was as though he wanted more than to heal her.

As if he wanted her soul.

And she would give it to him without thinking about the consequences.

His eyes caressed her body, her shoulders, her bare breasts, her waist, until his gaze lingered at the water's surface—searching for the mysteries that lay beneath.

Warmth flared deep inside her at his look of possession. Gooseflesh rippled along her arms and turned her nipples into hardened peaks, even as the warm water seduced her from below.

She shivered and closed her eyes, trying to control the intensity of her own desire as his warm, damp fingers traced a path from her shoulders and down her arms, before traveling back up her waist to the fullness of her breasts.

Her eyes snapped open, and she gasped as desire flared. She leaned into his touch, wanting more, wanting everything.

"I can't resist you." His lips were on her breasts, his tongue flicking at her sensitive nipples.

"Don't," she breathed. Flames shot through her, and she arched against him.

He groaned at her response. His hand moved down her stomach to the curls at her womanhood, tangling, caressing as he continued his exploration of her nipples with his tongue. Her heart pounded painfully, she couldn't breathe, her flesh was on fire. Hunger. Insatiable hunger, and she wanted more of the same. Her hands went around his shoulders and slowly slid to his neck to curl in the thickness of the hair at his nape. He raised his head to kiss her, and she met him halfway, buried herself in his scent. The desire to merge with his body, to be one, burned inside.

She pulled back to stare into Alan's face, catching every nuance of his expression. She was beautiful to him. She could see it in his face. She could feel the sensuous tug between them. He wanted her. His gaze clung to her and moved down her body in an almost tactile caress.

She lifted one leg to wrap it around his buttocks, then leaped upward until she straddled him. He gasped and reached for her, cradling her body against his powerful erection. Then slowly, she sheathed him, allowing only the shallowest penetration. He grasped her hips, trying to pull her fully upon him, but she wouldn't permit it.

"Jessamine, you're killing me!" he said in a choked tone.

She clenched around him. "Yes, but this time, I know you don't mean it literally. This kind of death is preferable. I want to love you slowly, thoroughly." Her gaze narrowed on his face. His lips were parted, his nostrils flaring, and he was beautiful in his need.

"Jessamine, let me come into you."

"Like this?" She moved farther down and he flexed within her.

He groaned as though he were in pain. "Nay, more."

At the sound, she allowed him access to her deepest self.

This time it was she who gasped as he drove into her with mindless, frantic hunger. He began a heated rhythm with more urgency than even last night's joining had brought. The rhythm increased, the tension built, and she grasped his shoulders as the world spun with feverish pleasure.

She heard Alan's heavy breathing, felt the slickness of his wet hands on her buttocks, lost herself in the wisps of steam that surrounded them. His wet chest pressed against her own, further igniting her senses. She gave a low cry of wild satisfaction.

The sound encouraged him all the more. He plunged deeper, harder, faster, and she hung on, moving with him until the tension inside her exploded with a force that sent a fiery release through every fiber of her being. An instant later she could feel Alan spasm again and again within her, shuddering helplessly as he poured his seed into her body.

He carried her, with their bodies still joined, to the side of the pool and laid her against the rocky ledge. He cradled her in his arms, still inside her, breathing heavily, his flesh hot against her own. Alan's breathing gradually steadied and slowed. "I lost control," he said, his voice uneven.

"We both lost control." She looked up at him.

"Maybe it's this place." His lips twisted. "An untamed paradise. Eden."

Paradise. Yes, but then why did she feel a strange sense of unease hovering just beyond her awareness? Something wasn't as it appeared here in this underground chamber. And years of court intrigues had taught her to trust her instincts.

She considered telling him her thoughts but hesitated. He seemed so at peace right now, more at peace than she had ever seen him.

He withdrew from her, then gathered her up in his arms as he stepped from the pool. He set her on her feet and dressed her, then himself, before scooping her into his arms once more. She lay against his shoulder as he strode away from the pool and back down the path that had led them there, back to the base of the stairs that led to the ark. He set her down, then moved to the saddlebag he'd abandoned at the base of the stairs. He withdrew his torn Templar cloak and spread it over the gold-lined rock. He shifted her onto the makeshift bed. "We'll sleep here awhile."

"Alan, what comes next? We found the ark. Now we must get it out of here, take it back to the port at Jaffa." She found she was holding her breath. What did come next for them, for her?

She'd never actually thought about what would happen after the prophecy was fulfilled. Her whole life, her every thought had always been on fulfillment of that duty.

He settled beside her and pulled her against his chest. She tried to relax, but the tension inside her refused to go away. She glanced up the stairs, to the ark that seemed to emit the light filling the cavern.

She forced her gaze away from the artifact and onto the man beside her. His eyes were closed. His breathing was slow and steady.

"Alan," she called softly, checking to see if he truly was asleep.

She waited. He didn't stir.

Slowly, careful not to disturb him, she slid out of his arms and stood. She glanced around the cavern, at the quiet stillness greeting her. Why was it so silent? If there were plants down here, then where were the other creatures of the land? She'd seen no evidence of rats or snakes or birds. Not even the smallest spider or fly. It appeared as though Alan and she were very much alone in this underground chamber.

She strode across the walkway through the trees and down the path leading back to the hot springs. She was eager to discover just what lay beyond the trees. But even more than that, she wondered if she might find a way out.

Because as far as she could tell from what she'd observed, they were trapped in this hidden paradise, along with the ark.

Chapter Sixteen

Alan opened his eyes and instantly felt Jessamine's absence. He shot to his feet. She was nowhere in sight. "Jessamine," he called.

His heart raced. Had she wandered off? Had someone taken her? As irrational as it seemed, he couldn't force the thought away.

He ran through the angel-lined path and through the trees beyond, all the while calling her name, over and over. He should have been more alert. Never had he slept so soundly as he had just then.

And he knew the reason why. He'd never been so content. A chill followed in the wake of the thought. Nor had he ever had as much to lose. Jessamine and the ark were treasures beyond price. What would become of him if he lost one, or both?

He picked up his speed, racing through the cavern that just hours ago had seemed a paradise. Now, the golden hues that danced on the walls seemed almost sinister, taunting him as he passed. "Jessamine," he called, louder this time.

"Alan?"

His heart stumbled at the sound of her voice. He followed it until he burst through the trees into an open space. A garden, he realized, as he raced to her side and pulled her into his arms. She trembled.

"Jessamine, what's wrong?"

Her eyes were wild, her face pale. "I've searched everywhere. There's no way out. We're trapped, Alan. The prophecy led us into a trap. We'll be stuck here beneath the ground forever."

"That cannot be," he said pressing a kiss to the top of her head. "Why would all the clues lead us here, only to trap us inside?"

Her trembling lessened.

"Have you ever felt that the prophecy would lead you to harm?" he asked, his voice gentle.

The fear in her eyes shifted to hope. "Never."

"Then there is no reason to believe that now."

She frowned. "What if the reason there are no more etchings in the chamber's entrance is because there is no more to the story?"

He reached up to smooth her dark hair. He inhaled her scent. "Jessamine, I'll never let anything happen to you. On my honor, I'll protect you with the same fierceness as I want to possess you, all the days of my life."

Warm color flooded her cheeks and her gaze dropped to the ground. "You don't understand. . . . The choice isn't . . ." Her gaze touched his face once more. "I haven't said I'd marry you."

"Married or not, Jessamine, I belong to you."

The dark centers of her eyes dilated. "What?"

"You know it's true. Say it."

She hesitated, then finally said, "You belong to me."

He nodded. "Just as you belong to me."

She buried her cheek against his chest.

"Why do you not speak?" he asked.

"I don't know what to say."

"Say you'll marry me . . . when you are ready. For I want you to crave my touch, my heat, with the same intensity that I crave you."

A flicker of pain crossed her face, then disappeared. "You are hard to resist."

He smiled as a sudden surge of tenderness swept through him. She felt the bond between them too. It was beyond either of them to resist the other. Alan turned toward the garden. He plucked the trumpet of a lily, then stepped back to her, sliding the ivory bloom behind her ear. The flower was a stark contrast to her dark, exotic hair. "I can wait until you say the words I long to hear."

Her fingers came up to touch the silken petals. She took a step back, putting some distance between them. "Let's find a way out of here first, shall we?"

He nodded, accepting her retreat. "Let's return to the ark and begin there. I have an idea."

They made their way back to the stairs. He folded his Templar tunic inside his saddlebag, then secured the bag over his shoulder. "Do you think you could help me move the ark?"

She nodded and headed for the first step. His hand on her arm stalled her. She turned to face him.

"Are you ready to leave now? Because I have a feeling once the ark moves, we'll have no time for anything else."

She drew a deep breath. "I'm ready."

He took her hand, and together they headed back into the presence of the ark. Alan moved to the far end of the holy artifact. "Place your hands on the poles and let me go first down the stairs so the bulk of the weight is on me."

Jessamine paused. "Why do you think moving the ark will cause something to happen?"

"The only thing that makes sense is that the ark is the light source down here."

Jessamine nodded solemnly and took the poles that

ran the length of the ark in her hands. With Alan on the opposite side, they lifted the ark, then paused expectantly, allowing it to hover above its platform.

Jessamine released a heavy sigh. "I almost expected another earthshake, or lightning to strike."

"So far, so good," Alan chuckled.

They headed for the stairs. The ark was heavy but not nearly as cumbersome as he'd expected. The builders of the holy vessel had balanced the weight well by placing the poles slightly below the lid.

Once down from the altar, they proceeded through the path with angels on each side. They walked side by side with the ark between them.

"Alan," Jessamine asked in a whisper. "Do the angels appear to be watching us as we pass?"

The lifelike statues did appear to follow them with their eyes as the couple moved slowly down the promenade. The golden feathers that made up their wings seemed to whisper despite the lack of a breeze. "Keep walking, Jessamine. It's an illusion. We're safe. You touched the angels yourself and found them to be solid and lifeless."

"What's this idea you had about getting us out of here?" Her voice sounded tense, but she pulled her shoulders back and kept pace with him.

"The third stanza of the prophecy."

She stumbled, then caught herself. "We've already lived through the predictions there."

"All except one passage." Alan tightened his grip on the ark, prepared to take the entire burden if need be. "'A whisper of I Am that I Am will pave the way,'" he recited. "The name of God given to the ancient Hebrews. It's the only part of the stanza that hasn't come to pass."

She frowned. "Perhaps."

"Say it with me."

"I Am that I Am," Jessamine whispered. "Nothing's happening."

"Keep saying it." They repeated the words over and over, their voices mingling, as they strode through the column of angels.

The golden path suddenly jerked beneath Alan's boots, tossing him to his knees. The ark crashed to the ground and Jessamine along with it. The path was splitting, great jagged cracks gaping like hungry mouths of stone.

"Alan!" Jessamine screamed. "What's happening?"

"Keep chanting." Alan was at her side, helping her once again to her feet. "I want you to run. Get out of here." He turned to look behind him.

The promenade of angels was shivering, undulating. He tried to remain steady, but the path shifted beneath his feet. It was like riding the back of a giant serpent. He turned back to Jessamine, hoping to see her far in the distance, only to find her next to the ark. "I won't leave without you."

"Do you want to die here?" He hastened to her side and gripped both sides of the ark, raising it against his chest. He took two steps forward, but felt as though the movement of the path sent him backward instead. "Dammit, Jessamine, get going!"

"Not without you." Jessamine's mouth was set in a grim line. "Give me one side of that ark to carry."

Alan cast her a glance of both desperation and exasperation. "If we get out of this alive, I swear . . ." He set the ark down and grasped the poles on one end.

She took her place on the opposite side. "We'd better hurry."

They ran with the ark between them along the path on which they'd arrived. They had to swerve many times to avoid gaping holes where the entire path had fallen away. The words *I Am that I Am* became their chant, the words matching their steps.

The earth beneath them quaked and shuddered, bringing down chunks of rock from the limestone walls. The rocks crashed around them, forcing them to stop and alter their path before moving forward again. Then the ceiling started to give way. Huge boulders rained down around them.

Jessamine screamed as a slab of rock dropped right in front of her. "Merciful God!"

"Not so merciful at the moment, I'm afraid." Alan ducked to avoid a rock coming at his head.

"Where are we headed?" Jessamine shouted when they came to a four-foot pile of rubble that blocked their way. "There's no way out!"

He set the ark down, forcing her to lower her side as well.

"We have to think about the clues," he growled in frustration. "I Am that I Am is the name of God. How can that help us here?"

Huge jagged cracks appeared in the rock floor on either side of them. Enormous rocks were dislodged from the walls, hurtling down behind them, in front of them, all around them. Crashing, roaring noises echoed in the confines of the cavern, vibrating until Alan felt the reverberations deep inside himself.

He focused his thoughts. He had to figure out what the clue meant if they were to survive. "God is the creator of Heaven and Earth. We are in the middle of the destruction of this bit of the world."

"Maybe the answer has nothing to do with biblical details and everything to do with the ark," Jessamine moaned in frustration.

Jessamine's eyes widened.

Alan felt the shock of an idea.

They both turned to the ark. "How can this get us out of here?" he shouted over the thunderous noise.

"Stones!" Jessamine said, her eyes suddenly bright. "Do you still have the stones of fire?"

He reached for his satchel and the precious treasure inside. "Here."

"You said whoever controls the stones, controls the ark and all its power."

He palmed the twelve stones and held them over the ark, between the angels' outstretched wings on the lid. "It's worth a try."

As he held the stones, a bluish light appeared above his hand. He extended his other hand out to Jessamine. When she placed her cool grip in his, he pulled her tight against his chest. He wanted to feel her heartbeat against his. "Close your eyes and chant with me."

"I Am that I Am!"

The stones warmed in his hand. A cool rush of air touched their faces. The ground beneath their feet shook. The air became a swirling rush, curling around them, carrying them upwards. Higher and higher.

It was as though the hand of God carried them from the paradise below to the world above. Jessamine clung to him. Her touch was the only sensation that seemed real as they floated for what seemed like an eternity. Then as suddenly as it had started, the wind died, leaving a deafening silence in its place. They descended until Alan felt something solid beneath his feet.

The first sight to meet his eyes was Jessamine. Her hair was windswept, her cheeks were rosy, and her eyes clenched shut.

"Jessamine?" He shoved the stones back into his satchel and reached for her shoulders.

Her dark eyes snapped open. She searched his face. "Are we safe?"

"I think so. Are you unharmed?"

She nodded.

Alan raised his gaze to the sky and crossed himself. "Thank you, most merciful Lord." He released his grip on her and turned to assess their situation. The glint of gold caught the corner of his eye. Alan reached for his sword as he turned.

"Alan." Jessamine's voice trailed off.

The ark rested not ten paces from them, glittering in the afternoon sun as though it belonged there, next to the spring at the summit of Jebel Madhbah.

The Spring of Moses? Whatever force had spat them from the depths below had sent them back down the mountain where their quest had begun.

His gaze met hers. A burst of unadulterated joy exploded inside him. He reached for her, twirling her around as he'd done in the cavern below. "We found the ark."

Jessamine laughed. The sound blended with the joy in his heart. "I don't care how it happened," she exclaimed. "I'm just grateful it did."

He sobered and set her back on her feet. "Now the real work begins."

She stared at the ark. "Transporting it to Jaffa?"

He nodded. "If only there were a way to disguise it."

She smiled. "There is. Look." She bent and gathered a handful of rock dust in her hand, then moved to the edge of the Spring of Moses. She created a thick paste before she returned to the ark and spread it over the gold finish, leaving a patina of reddish brown.

"Jessamine!" Alan stepped forward, then stopped. "You touched the ark."

"I didn't figure after all we've been through together that it would harm me."

"Your heart is pure." Alan smiled. "And your idea to disguise the gold is brilliant."

A smile started to form on her lips, then faded just as quickly. "Alan, where are the horses? Where's Will? This is where we left them."

"Will is familiar with the desert. He most likely took the horses where they would be protected from the storm last night." His gaze scanned the desert beyond them. "We might have to go find him when we are finished here. Until then, you keep covering the ark. I'm going to build a way to transport it, using the horses."

She nodded and returned to her work, alternating between preparing the paste and patting it over the gold.

Alan headed to a nearby tree, and using his sword, he struck the branches off until he had a pile of wood before him. He set about lashing the branches of acacia wood together with a length of rope he carried in his saddlebag, until he'd created a solid wooden platform to drag behind the horses.

When he was satisfied the transport would remain secure, he asked Jessamine to help him lift the ark onto it.

Jessamine continued covering the ark with the sandy paste as Alan searched the ground near the shrubs where they'd left the horses tethered. He didn't want to think about what would happen if Will had abandoned them here. They needed those horses to get out of the desert, with or without the ark.

He searched the sand. It didn't take long to discern the trail of hoofprints leading off to the right. Alan frowned when he realized all the prints belonged to the horses. There wasn't a single footprint mingled among them.

Had Will made it back down the mountainside after they'd separated?

Alan's gaze shot to the steep trail leading up the hillside. Could the old man have fallen? Was he hurt? Waiting for them to rescue him? At his advanced age, he wouldn't survive long out here without water.

Alan hurried back to Jessamine. She'd finished her task and was now cleaning her hands and face in the pool of water. As he approached, she turned toward him. "Any luck?"

"It's worse than we feared. Someone must have untethered the horses. It appears that they've wandered off into the wilderness." He hesitated. "And the evidence suggests Will never made it down from the mountain."

Her eyes went wide. "Poor Will. We have to go back for him."

"Aye, but when we find him, the horses will become more important than ever. Perhaps we should go after the horses first, then Will." He bent before his saddlebag and withdrew his Templar cloak. With a flick of his wrists, he unfurled the cloth and draped it, Templar cross down, over the ark. "It won't provide much protection from possible looters while we are gone, but the cloak will at least protect the ark from the elements."

He offered her his hand. "Come."

She hesitated. "Wouldn't it be better if we split up, and you went for the horses while I went to search for Will?"

He frowned. "I'll not leave you alone."

"Alan, we have no other choice. If Will is hurt . . ."

Frustration seared through him, stronger than ever before. "I don't like it."

A flush touched Jessamine's cheeks. "I know, but there is no other choice."

With a heavy sigh, he lifted the water bladder from

the saddlebag and handed it to her. "Take this. If you find Will, make him comfortable, give him water, but come back here, to me. Once I have the horses, we'll be able to move him. Agreed?"

She nodded.

"Come here." He opened his arms to her.

She moved into his embrace. He wrapped his arms around her, cradling her against him. She nestled her cheek deeper into the hollow of his shoulder. He felt heavy inside. He buried his face in her hair. "Be safe."

Why was parting with her so hard?

She stayed there against him for a long moment, letting her warm strength flow through him, until finally she pulled back. "I know what is in your heart, even if you don't say it," she whispered.

On those words, she started up the hillside without looking back.

Chapter Seventeen

It didn't take long for Alan to find all three of the horses. He rode one and allowed the other two to trail behind him as he headed back toward the spring. He hungrily searched the area where he and Jessamine had parted, hoping and praying to see her waiting alongside the ark.

At the sight of four dark-clothed men, his blood ran cold.

"Hello, Sir Alan. Is that not what they call you?"

"Who are you?" Alan asked, but he feared he already knew.

"Your enemy," the man replied in a thick accent.

These were the assassins who'd attacked Jessamine and him in the desert. As the men surrounded the ark, Alan returned his attention to the one closest to him, who bore a deep scar down the side of his face.

"Where's the girl?" the scarred man asked.

Alan forced himself to keep his emotions in check. Emotion always interfered with his ability to reason and plan. He kept his expression grim, assessing his options.

"Could it be possible we killed her with our poison darts?"

Alan's frown deepened.

The man smiled. "We had hoped to kill you both, but the woman was the easier target. I'm pleased to hear we were successful."

They thought she was dead. He had to keep them thinking that way. "You got the girl—what else can you want?"

"We want the ark." The men moved to surround him, as though they intended to kill him right here and now. "We've waited many years for the legendary Templars to come back for the ark they stole from us." His gaze narrowed on Alan. "Why did they only send one of you? We'd hoped to eliminate hundreds, as we did during the Crusades."

"Damn you to hell."

A sudden flare of anger darkened the dark-clothed assassin's expression. "You disappoint me, Templar." The man stepped closer and angled his hooked sword at Alan's horse. "You will dismount immediately, or I'll cut you down myself."

Alan slid to the ground and tensed, ready to fight. He let the reins dangle freely, then gave a shrill whistle. He drew his sword as he slapped his horse on the rear. Spooked by the sound and the motion, his horse reared violently. The other two horses shrieked, and they all bolted back toward the valley.

An angry cry rent the air. The man's eyes narrowed and his scar pulsed red. He leaped at Alan with his sword.

In a heartbeat, Alan blocked the strike. He gripped his sword tightly as the other three men charged. Four to one. He'd encountered worse odds on the battlefield.

Alan sank his sword into one attacker, then turned to the next. It was hard to predict the arc of his enemies' short, curved swords, and Alan felt the bite of their blades against the flesh of his upper arm and thigh. He spun away, gaining distance and a moment's respite. Suddenly, out of nowhere, a blinding blue light streaked around them, weaving in and out among the dark-clothed men. They screamed as the light touched them, leaving glowing red embers where it had struck.

Alan stumbled back from the familiar light which was moving like an overwhelming force against his enemies. The men ran for their horses and bolted from the scene, leaving Alan, the ark, and the blue light behind.

As the attackers rode away, Alan stumbled and drew a sharp breath. The wound in his thigh and his arm were not fatal, but they both stung as he studied the strange blue light. It hovered before him momentarily, then streaked away, following the dark-clothed men out into the desert.

Alan stumbled toward the ark. He leaned against it as he watched the light until it was no longer visible. That was the second time the strange blue orb had helped him and Jessamine in some way. He frowned at the thought, and he was even more perplexed when he noticed his wounds no longer stung.

He bolted upright when he realized he'd been leaning on the Ark of the Covenant. His gaze dropped to his thigh, to where the fabric of his robe had been split by one of the lethal hooked swords. Blood lingered on the fabric, but the flesh beneath looked as though it had never been injured. He brought his fingers up to his arm, touching his other wound. Once again he found the fabric sliced through and spattered with blood, but the flesh beneath was untouched.

A miracle.

Alan turned to stare at the ark. He'd touched it by accident and hadn't been incinerated on the spot as he'd very much expected to be. *A heart must be pure.* His own words drifted through his mind, and his chest grew tight. Even after everything that had happened in his life, the Lord still found him deserving.

Alan dropped to his knees. "Thank you for believing in me," he said, then rose. He flexed his leg and his arm and smiled, then turned toward the mountain and started up the steep incline.

Miracles did not change what he needed to do. He must find Jessamine. She should have returned from the mountain long before he'd come back with the horses. Something was wrong. His joy faded and fear took its place. He started to run.

He would find her. He had to.

It was almost time.

The conde sighted Jessamine in the distance. Every step brought her closer to him. Everything he wanted would soon be his. Everything.

He settled himself more comfortably against the rocks he sat upon to wait. He smiled as he watched her hasten up the path, oblivious to the trap he'd set for her.

Once he had her, he could do whatever he pleased. He would sample her delights right there on the mountainside, before joining his men below. The conde drew a thin dagger from his boot and pressed the flat side of the blade against his cheek, let the cool steel fire his blood.

Jessamine would soon experience the pain and pleasure he could bring to her. He closed his eyes. He drew in the scent of blood that still lingered on the blade from the last time he'd used it. It was almost time.

"Will. Where are you?" Jessamine called for the hundredth time. She'd searched everywhere on the Obelisk Terrace for their aged guide. But she'd found no footprints, no sign he'd ever been there.

Jessamine breathed a frustrated sigh. She paused near the altar, then slightly behind it at the sacrificial stone where she and Alan had first made love. Warmth pooled in her belly.

He'd asked her to marry him.

She bit down on her lip. If only the choice were her own . . . but it wasn't. Her uncle had the ultimate say in whom she married. She'd always been destined for some political marriage, no doubt to a foreign prince to help forge ties with Spain. And her uncle needed the gold a marriage could bring to Spain.

At the altar, she paused and brushed her fingers lightly over the rough stone. Alan would be considered unacceptable to her uncle because of his low rank. If she married him anyway, she'd be condemning him to death.

Her uncle would have no choice but to charge them both with treason if they went back to Spain. And if they didn't, there was no guarantee that her uncle wouldn't send men after them anyway. They'd be forced into a life of seclusion and poverty forever. And she wouldn't do that to Alan. She straightened. She cared about him too much.

Her chest heavy with grief, Jessamine wandered away from the temple terrace, over to the edge of the mountain, where the ground fell away into a steep cliff tumbling down to a red-gold valley below. On the other side, red mountains pierced the skyline, dominating the entire horizon.

The edge of the cliff where she stood seemed to end in a void of space and warm, dry air. The wind came up, plucking at the hem of her gown and tossing the length of her hair into wild disarray. She allowed that tempestuous wind to consume her, to fill her senses. She drew a sharp breath. Felt it cleanse the grief from her soul.

Grief had seemed to dominate her life in Spain, but today it had all but vanished because of Alan. With him, she felt a sense of freedom and joy that had been missing from her life for a long time now.

She didn't want to give up those feelings by returning home and resuming her place in the palace, by marrying someone else. Her uncle, the king, was growing impatient with her refusal to marry. Jessamine turned her face into the wind. Had the conde gone through the proper channels, she was certain the king would have entertained his suit. Even though he wasn't the foreign prince her uncle wanted, he had money to offer—money Spain desperately needed. A shudder ran through her.

She would rather stay here in the Holy Land and live among the Bedouins than submit to that Spanish pig's lecherous desires. And yet, if she returned to Spain, she might not be given a choice.

Were there any other alternatives for her? Tears dotted her lashes, but she wiped them away with the back of her hand. One more stanza of the prophecy remained. It was the stanza that frightened her more than any of the others. The first three seemed like the clues for a grand adventure. The last one threatened to send her to her doom.

The words filled her mind with the usual dread and pain.

The fate of the parents will not be yours as a sacrifice heralds the start of a new war.

Since she'd been young enough to comprehend the words of the prophecy, she'd hated the word *sacrifice*.

Jessamine stared ahead of her, focusing on the mountains in the distance. It was time for the fourth stanza to present itself, as the other three had. She closed her eyes against a surge of fear. What sort of sacrifice would be involved?

The soft sound of boot heels clicking on rock came

from behind her. Alan? An overwhelming sense of well-being washed over her. She turned to greet him.

The conde stood before her.

Her happiness died, and her blood ran cold.

His beady black eyes stared at her as he laughed. "Were you expecting someone else?"

His hand cracked against the side of her face with such force that she fell to the ground at the edge of the cliff. Her feet slipped into nothingness. She screamed.

The conde gripped her hand, dug into her flesh, as he pulled her back over the edge. "You're not getting away from me that easily, my dearest." He smiled. "My inconvenience has been great. And you'll pay for it all."

His cheeks mottled as his smile widened. "I can almost taste your fear. Perhaps you were worth the wait."

Jessamine shook her head, trying to clear it of the ringing pain from the conde's blow.

Once she was back upon the ground, he released her hand and gripped her hair, yanking her to her feet. "Tell me where the bastard you've been traveling with is hiding."

"I don't know."

Agony rocked her as his hand struck her cheek again. Her head reeled back and her vision blurred. Heaven help her. She couldn't lose consciousness in this man's presence. She had to stay alert. It was the only way she'd survive.

"Once again I'll ask you, where is the man?" he demanded in a too-quiet voice that sent icy rivulets of fear down her spine.

At her silence he continued, "I'll find him anyway. You know I will. That man must pay for taking you away from me."

"It was I who—"

Pain exploded against her other cheek this time. She crumpled to the ground, despite the conde's ruthless grip on her hair. A sharp rock sliced her lip and she felt the warm trickle of blood move down her chin, her neck.

"You are no match for me, Jessamine. Soon I'll have everything I ever wanted from you."

"What do you want? I have nothing to offer."

"Oh, but you do," he sneered. "As my bride, you'll help your husband to the crown of Spain."

"That's impossible. King Alfonso has too many heirs for my connection to the crown to matter."

"One good bout of plague, my dearest, and you never know who'll be left to pick up the pieces. I shall claim the throne by default. No one will argue, or they'll die trying."

"You wouldn't dare."

"Oh, I'll dare," he said, sliding a finger cruelly over her bruised cheek. "I'll dare that and so much more." He dipped his finger into the blood at her lip and brought it to his nose. He drew a slow, deep breath. His dark eyes filled with lust.

Her stomach lurched.

God help her.

Jessamine screamed. His blood thundering in his ears, Alan pushed himself up the hillside. He had to reach her.

He crested the Obelisk Terrace and skidded to a halt, searching the area for a sign that she had been there. Then he saw what he'd feared most—her small footsteps leading to the cliff. He hurried to the edge and looked over, praying he'd not see her body lying at the bottom. His breath rushed out with relief when he saw nothing but rocks below.

He crouched down, studying the rocky dirt farther

back from the cliff's edge. He spotted two sets of foot-prints, and signs of a struggle . . . along with several drops of blood. Terror more debilitating than he'd ever known suffocated him. His mind went blank. He stared at the blood upon the red-gold ground. Jessamine's blood.

He had to think. Come up with a plan. Alan clenched his hands. He needed a horse. But before he could try to recapture one of the horses he'd scared off, he had to discern the direction Jessamine and her captor were headed.

Alan followed the trail of footprints disappearing down the left side of the summit. He stumbled over the loose rock in his haste. By the look of the prints, there were only two of them—Jessamine's small prints and those of a larger man.

Alan followed the trail. At the bottom of the mountain, he paused where four more sets of footprints joined the others and mixed with at least five horses' hoofprints. Jessamine's captor had had reinforcements waiting for him.

Alan raced toward the spot where he'd found his own horses once before. To his relief they were there, munching on the grass as though nothing had happened. And standing there beside the horses was Will.

"Where in God's peace were you?" Relief and fury clashed, making the words sound harsher than he'd intended.

Will cringed as he hunched over his cane. "I must have fallen asleep." He frowned, his gaze searching behind Alan. "Where's Jessamine?"

"She's been abducted."

"By whom?"

"I don't know." Alan reached for his saddlebag and withdrew the mail he'd stored there when they'd first arrived in the desert. No matter how hot or heavy, the armor was necessary. His last encounter had warned him that he needed the protection. He slipped the mail on, then flung himself on the back of his horse.

Will's frown darkened. "Where's the ark?"

"By the Spring of Moses. Where I pray it will remain until I get back with Jessamine."

Will shuffled to the horse nearest him and mounted. "I'll take care of the ark."

Alan growled his frustration. "I can't leave you alone. There are assassins who attacked me. They want the ark."

Will's hazy gray eyes became shards of steel. "They would do well not to tangle with me."

Alan's frown deepened. He'd already made one mistake this day by allowing Jessamine to go off by herself. Was he compounding his failings by abandoning Will as well?

"I cannot leave you to such a fate."

Will straightened in the saddle. "I might not be as mighty a warrior as you, but I have ways of taking care of myself. Do not worry, and delay yourself no longer. I'll meet you in Jaffa with the ark."

"But how will you find us?"

"I'll find you. That's all you need to know." He kicked his horse and galloped back toward the base of Jabel Madhbah.

For a moment Alan hesitated. What if Will stole the ark for himself? Or was captured by the assassins the blue orb had scared off before? Alan frowned after the old man's retreating image. "I have to trust him," he said as he urged his own horse in the opposite direction. The gelding took off with a thunderous stride. Alan leaned over the horse's neck, encouraging even greater speed. He tightened his hold on the reins and searched for tracks.

He rode for nearly an hour before he finally caught sight of Jessamine on horseback along with five other riders, heading back toward Jaffa. Hiding behind acacia trees and rock ledges jutting out of the sand, Alan followed as soundlessly as possible.

A short time later, the abductors stopped near a rock face opening into a cave.

Alan dismounted about fifty feet from them, then strode forward, secreting himself and his horse in the shadow of the low brush. Heat seeped up from the desert floor, wringing beads of sweat from his brow. The only sound to score the silence was his own harsh breathing.

Four men had stationed themselves in the four corners of the camp, acting as guards.

Alan kept his gaze on Jessamine. She sat atop a horse with her hands bound before her. A dark man stood alongside her horse and roughly jerked her to the ground. His mouth twisted into a cruel smile. Instantly, Alan recognized the man they'd seen at the Temple Mount. The man Jessamine had called the conde.

Alan clenched his jaw, holding back an angry rush of breath as the man grasped her elbow and propelled her toward the cave.

"Come along, my dearest. I can wait not a moment more."

Jessamine walked beside him without speaking, but Alan recognized the fear in her eyes.

He clenched his fists, forcing himself to wait and watch for his moment to strike. He needed a plan to get her out of this place safely.

Suddenly Jessamine twisted out of the man's grip.

But she only took two steps before he grasped her hair and threw her to the ground.

The man growled, then straddled her on the ground. "I had the notion of preserving your modesty, but you've determined a different fate for yourself. Look at me while I ravage you, Princess!"

Alan's blood pounded in his veins. His body tensed, prepared to strike. He needed a distraction, just one small thing to balance the odds.

The conde lowered himself over Jessamine. He clawed at her bodice until it ripped open and clasped a meaty hand over her bare breast. "Are you weeping, Princess?"

She sank her teeth into his hand.

He shrieked.

The distraction was not as significant as Alan would have liked, but he couldn't hold himself back at the brutal violation. Alan surged forward, his sword drawn.

Darker shadows suddenly blanketed the sky. The wind picked up and sent stinging grains of sand to prick his cheeks, his neck, his hands. He bent his head just enough to block nature's attack while still keeping his gaze on Jessamine as he ran to her. As if sensing Alan's presence, the conde jerked back from Jessamine and shot to his feet. His eyes were dark and expressionless.

"We've been waiting for you," the conde drawled. "I knew you'd follow her." He signaled. Three men raced forward, swords drawn.

In the span of a heartbeat, Alan's gaze met Jessamine's. Even in the shadowed light, he could see the fear in her eyes, the bruises marring both cheeks. She scrambled to her feet, her eyes wide as she twisted her bound hands one way, then another, trying to break free.

With his gaze he signaled for her to run. She responded with an almost imperceptible nod.

His throat vibrated with the roar of a battle cry as old as the Highlands themselves. The sound echoed through the desert, and the charging men paused, their faces pale. Alan took advantage of their momentary fear. He slashed his sword across the chest of one man and brought the blade back up to sever the arm of another. Both men dropped to the sand and bellowed in pain.

The horses thrashed against their bonds and, breaking free, scattered, seeking escape. One man caught a horse's hoof in his groin and crumpled to the ground. Two others shot forward. Alan met them with a slash to one man's thigh and the other's shoulder. They collapsed in a heap amid a spattering of their own blood.

Several yards away, the conde caught one of the horses and mounted.

Alan braced himself for a renewed attack. He whirled and lunged out of the way only moments before a terrified horse bolted past him. He barely regained his balance before a second horse charged, carrying the conde, who slashed wildly at Alan's head. He ducked, avoiding the blow, but felt the whistle of air as it rushed past his shoulders. Alan twisted and brought his sword up to slash at the sides of the conde's horse, succeeding in also catching the saddle strap. The Spaniard hit the ground with a thud.

The wind gusted, pushing the conde's men back. Alan forced his mind to clear as he approached the conde. He raised his sword, prepared to strike, when a ferocious howl stole his focus. It wasn't the man before him who shouted out, but the desert itself.

In the rage of battle, Alan had not noticed the sky growing ever darker, or the wind that now blasted them. Alan hastened to Jessamine's side while he sheathed his sword. Without a break in his stride, he gripped her waist and carried her with him as he caught a terrified horse and mounted it. He set her in front and kicked the horse into a gallop.

One glance over his shoulder confirmed that yet another danger swept toward them—a sandstorm rolling closer at frightening speed.

Chapter Eighteen

An eerie stillness settled over the desert. Then came the howl of the wind as it moved like a dark, hovering blanket over the sand. Alan pressed the horse they rode to greater speed as they tried to stay ahead of the surge.

"We need cover," Alan shouted. "A cave, a rock outcropping, anything!"

Jessamine nodded. The wind tugged at her hair, whipping it wildly around her face. She caught the errant strands with one hand. With her other hand, she shielded her eyes from the merciless grains of sand stinging their skin and searched the hazy darkness.

"An outcropping," she shouted, pointing to the left.

Alan saw it, bolted for it as the very air around them seemed to suck them backward. He rounded the rock outcropping and pulled them to the ground in the shelter of a slight overhang. He pressed Jessamine back against the rock and hauled the horse in against her, stroking its neck, trying to calm the terrified beast. He urged the horse to its knees, then down. They huddled together.

Alan stripped his robe from his shoulders. Then he slipped into the space between the horse and the wall and tossed his robe over their collective heads. "Hold on to me!" he called over an unearthly howl.

The rock at their backs seemed to shudder as the sand hit. Alan cooed softly to the horse as the frightened animal quivered. A thunderous roar erupted around them. Sand slammed into their exposed legs and torsos. The weight of the robe over their heads became almost crushing, but Alan held the ends tight. His muscles strained with the effort.

"I can't breathe!" Jessamine gasped beside him.

"Draw slow, shallow breaths. God willing, it will be a short-lived storm."

The muscles of Alan's arms spasmed and shook with the effort of keeping the heavy weight of the sand off them. He steeled himself, finding deeper reserves of strength. He wouldn't let Jessamine suffocate.

They had waited for what seemed like an eternity when the absence of sound pierced Alan's defenses. The storm had passed. "We are safe," he whispered to Jessamine.

"Take a deep breath," he warned a moment before he thrust upward, throwing off some of the sand weighing down the robe over their heads.

He thrust up again. This time the robe shifted, allowing him to pull it back away from their faces. He blinked in the hazy darkness that greeted him. But even in the dim light, he could see the drifts of sand that had formed all around them. They were standing in one of those drifts. He simply had to break them free.

Alan dusted the sand from the horse's face and stroked its long neck. In the open air, the animal had stopped quaking. The beast struggled to its feet, straining against the heavy sand. The muscles of its flanks bunched and flexed as it struggled to free itself. Alan pressed Jessamine back against the rock, out of harm's way as the horse leaped up, fighting its way out of their sandy prison.

Alan turned to offer Jessamine a hand as she climbed to more even ground over the mounds left by the horse.

"The shelter worked," she said as she emerged, brushing sand from her face, her hair, her gown.

"Jessamine." He hesitated, trying to find the words to express what he felt. "What happened back there with the conde, and at the Obelisk Terrace . . . I never should have left you alone." He brought a finger up to her swollen, cracked lip. "We've upset many people by bringing the ark back to the world. Until we see it safely stowed with the other treasures the Templars protect, we can trust no one but each other. Do you understand?"

She nodded. "The conde . . . That wasn't your fault."

"I failed you," he said roughly. "It won't happen again." He reached out and dusted the sand from her cheek. "It would be best if we kept moving even though dusk is upon us. I won't feel safe until we set sail for home."

"Home." She turned away.

Alan looked at her retreating back. He knew her thoughts must have turned to the future they'd share, as did his own. "Let us be away from here. If the conde survived the storm, he won't be far behind us."

She'd made no pledge to him, but Alan was still hopeful that she would. He knew there was something she wasn't telling him, some reservation she had about accepting his proposal. She'd reveal what he needed to know when she was ready. They would have a long sea voyage back to Scotland. There would be time for talking . . . and more.

Alan mounted, then reached down to grasp her hand and pulled her up in front of him.

"What do we do next?" Jessamine asked, her voice more even now. "The ark is gone."

"Nay. The ark is safe." He set the horse in motion, guiding the animal over the newly formed drifts of sand. "I found Will after I rounded up the horses." He decided it was better not to mention the assassins. "He's meeting us in Jaffa with the ark."

"Then let's hurry," she said with feeling. "I can't wait to put this desert behind us."

He couldn't have agreed with her more.

After a full day's travel, the outskirts of Jaffa came into view. Despite the darkness, the market was crowded with people. Shimmering gold lanterns illuminated the narrow alley that led through the town and to the harbor beyond.

As the streets narrowed, Alan reined in the horse and dismounted. He offered Jessamine a hand down. A small plume of dust wafted around them at the motion, drawing several curious gazes. Several passersby frowned at their dusty, disheveled state, but Jessamine ignored them. She raised her chin and marched on by.

Winding her way through the market, Jessamine marveled at the sights. Colorful fabrics in the sheerest silk lay on tables next to coarse linen in dark, drab colors. The babble of voices assailed her—sellers hawking their goods, men with pushcarts shouting warnings, women cloaked in black veils, bartering over the price of fish.

Other stalls were filled to overflowing with apricots, dates, pomegranates, and bright red berries. The aroma of flowers and heavy incense mixed with the pungent scent of onions and garlic.

Beyond the market, the water of the Mediterranean shimmered beneath the light of a full moon. Several boats were moored offshore. Jessamine bit down on her lip as she recognized the conde's caravel. She quickened her pace. With luck they'd be on a boat, out to sea, and beyond his touch before he figured out where she'd gone.

At the shore, Alan approached a sailor leaning against a dory. "We need to hire a ship," Alan said.

When the man replied in rapid Arabic that he had no boats for hire, Jessamine stepped forward and asked in his language if he knew someone who might help them.

"Alan! Jessamine!" a familiar voice called from the crowd. Jessamine whirled to see Will hobbling toward them. "You're safe," he said as he reached them.

Alan nodded. "And are you well?" he asked.

Will smiled, creasing his weathered face. "Never better."

"Now all we need is a ship," Alan said.

The old man winked. "Taken care of and waiting for you. This way." He waved for them to follow as he turned and made his way toward an Arab dhow waiting at the dock. "I hired a ship for you. The Arab ships are the fastest, you'll find. The crew will take you where you wish to go."

Alan's expression was unreadable as he took her arm and led her through the crowd after the old man. Will stopped at the bottom of a gangplank. Alan raised his brows as he gazed at the ship. "How did you manage all this? The fastest ship, stowed cargo, a willing crew?"

"I have many friends to help me." Will shrugged and his smile faded, replaced with a note of tension. "Now those friends will help you and Jessamine. Please, Alan, accept what is. It'll be best for all of us, I promise."

After a slight hesitation, Alan clapped him on the shoulder. "We are indebted to you, my friend, many times over."

The tension in Will's face eased. "It is you who help me, Alan, not the other way around." Will started up the gangplank, then turned back when Alan and Jessamine did not follow. "Are you coming? We must sail this evening with our precious cargo."

Alan turned to Jessamine. "Go with Will. Make

certain the ark is on board as he says. I need to take care of the horse. I'll return in a moment."

Jessamine boarded the ship with Will, then turned to watch Alan disappear into the crowd. Her gaze moved over the lantern lights of the port town. The sounds from the marketplace faded away to leave only the soft caress of the water against the ship's hull and the shuffle of the sailors as they moved about the deck.

"May I see the ark, Will?" she asked.

Will nodded and guided her to the hatchway that led into the hold of the ship. Once she'd confirmed the treasure was there, Jessamine returned to the deck.

"May the evening soothe and welcome you," a voice said from behind her.

Jessamine turned to see a tall seaman in dark clothing bow before her.

"Allow me to show you to the captain's quarters."

She shook her head. "I'll wait here, thank you. I'd like to watch as we pull away from the shore."

He bowed once more, then was gone.

A welcome breeze drifted up from the water, cooling her flesh, and she turned to the railing again, waiting for Alan to return. They were heading to Scotland. His home. She thought of the days they'd spend together at sea, of the quiet mornings on deck watching the horizon. And she thought of the nights. The image had barely formed when Alan strode up the gangplank after being gone for over an hour, dressed now in a fresh muslin shirt and black breeches. He held several dark packages in his hands.

He signaled to the captain of the ship, who barked orders to his crew in Arabic, setting in motion a wave of activity as the men drew back the gangplank and hoisted the anchor. The ship was underway a few moments later, heading out into the harbor and the waters beyond.

Alan set his packages aside and joined her at the rail. "We did it." His lips gently brushed her temple.

"Yes, but I fear the worst lies ahead of us." The wind picked up as they left the harbor behind.

"For the next twenty days, we're safe from our enemies. After that, I must admit, you're right. Our task isn't done."

She nodded as her gaze wandered to the ship's deck and the efficient crew who raised the sails and secured the lines. "Are these men trustworthy with such a prize aboard their ship?"

"Will is with us. He selected these men. If he trusts them enough to sail with them, then we must also. And just to be certain, you will stay by my side every moment of every day. Until we are once again on land."

Her gaze lifted to his face. Warmth stirred within her despite the breeze. In the light of the deck lanterns, his expression was intent, his brow furrowed, as he stared into the black water beyond. She became acutely aware of the strength of his hands on the railing, of the taut muscles of his chest beneath his thin muslin shirt, of the thighs filling out his black breeches. He was dressed in the style of his countrymen. She liked the simplicity far more than the pompous clothing men wore at the Spanish court. Alan might be in plain clothing, but he was more appealing to her than any of those men had ever been.

Yet their situation had not changed. She still couldn't accept him, couldn't doom him to a life of running from her uncle's men, or send him to the hangman's noose if he was ever caught.

But what her head understood, her heart seemed to

dismiss. Her fingers tightened on the railing as she resisted the urge to press her hand to his chest or trail her fingers down the length of his thigh. She drew a sharp breath.

His gaze met hers. His muscles tensed.

She couldn't breathe. She couldn't look away from him.

"Jessamine?"

She knew he could feel her attraction. But she couldn't give in. She felt panic rise within her and she moved back from the railing. Where was that cabin the man had offered her?

Alan followed, wrapped her once again in his heat, his scent. Her heart pounded so hard, she was certain he could hear it.

"We can't," she murmured.

His gaze shifted out to sea. Conflicting emotions darkened his face. "Do you no longer desire me?"

"There are things you do not know. Obstacles that stand between us." She gazed up at him, feeling a familiar stirring between her thighs. No, she wouldn't give in. She had to stay strong.

"What?" His expression softened. "You can tell me anything, Jessamine. If there are issues, I can help."

She shook her head. "No one can help us."

The moonlight was strong and full on his face, and she'd never seen a grimmer expression on it.

"It might feel that way for you now. But know this, Jessamine. You belong to me. Nothing can change that fact."

"Alan." At the anguish in his voice, she reached for him, only to jerk her fingers back when she realized what she was doing. If she touched him, she would never be able to let go.

He must have read something in her gaze, because he

stepped back. "For once, you're thinking things through before reacting." He sighed. "Take the time you need. But know I am here waiting for you when you can no longer stand the pain of being apart." He turned away and strode toward the bridge.

She inhaled sharply and clenched her hands at her sides. She knew that pain already. Heaven help her, it took everything inside her to keep from reaching for him now.

Jessamine did not speak to him for nearly three days. Alan kept his word and was never far from her sight. He busied himself with charts and maps, but her presence drew him like nothing in his life ever had.

She stood at the rail several yards away as they approached the Strait of Gibraltar, the narrow strip of sea separating Spain from Morocco. They'd had favorable winds since they left the Holy Land. Coincidence? Or was the presence of the ark the reason? But even thoughts of finally having the ark safe in Scotland could not keep his gaze from moving back to Jessamine.

The strong afternoon sun stroked her dark hair with streaks of light as gusts tossed it about. Her face was raised as if she were drinking in both the sun and the vigor of the wind. Her features in the sunlight were exotically beautiful, but even the light could not brighten the strange, haunting sadness of her dark eyes.

He continued to watch her as they passed through the strait. His stomach knotted when her slender fingers came up to brush tears from her cheeks. Alan could take no more. He strode down the steps of the forecastle, then across the deck to where Jessamine stood by the rail.

"Jessamine?" He touched her hand.

She looked at him and smiled bitterly. "My mother was a Spaniard."

It was the first time she'd revealed anything to him about her family. He gazed at the tears shimmering on her dark lashes. "Tell me."

She hesitated. Her gaze darted back to the Spanish shoreline. "My father was a Moor," she said softly, with halting words. She told him about her parents' forbidden love.

As she talked, her words picked up speed. And he listened to her without displaying emotion, hearing what she said, accepting it all.

She explained how her parents had met, how they fell in love, how they defied their own parents in order to be together. She told him how they died—her father at the hands of his own people during an attack on the court by the occupying Moors. That had been many years ago. Her mother had died more recently by the hand of the conde, who had wanted to marry her, then ended up poisoning her instead.

Alan's gaze locked with hers. She truly had known how he felt when he'd confessed his childhood pain to her at Petra. Her life was no different. They'd both lived for years with others, but they'd both been seen as outcasts even among their own people.

Her voice shook when she revealed her position in the Spanish court and her inability to marry without the king's approval. The king would never agree to a marriage between them. She was slated for some nobleman or prince somewhere.

Alan released his breath in a slow, painful breath. He knew what a poor choice any king would consider him. And her status as a princess explained so much. Alan's mind whirled, but he put his questions aside, needing to hear the rest of her tale. "Was the conde the king's choice for you?" he asked, his voice strained.

"Never. Conde Salazar Mendoza is an opportunist.

He only wants me for the connections I can bring him." She dropped her gaze to her hands, then slowly brought her eyes back to his.

The reality of their situation tightened his chest. They couldn't marry without the king's consent, something they would never gain. He forced the pain away, deeper inside himself. He couldn't allow himself to feel just now, or he might shatter. "Do you seek the security of your uncle's court? Do you wish us to dock and see you safely to him?" He forced the words out.

She shook her head jerkily, then turned her face away. "I have realized during these three days past that I have no purpose in Spain. I don't want to carry the burdens of being a princess anymore. With you, I tasted freedom, and I don't think I can ever go back to the way things were before I left." She drew a sharp breath. "I cannot live as a princess, I cannot live as a commoner. Truly, there is no place where I belong."

Even though he knew he should not, he reached out and crushed her against his chest, his fingers buried in her hair. "You will always have a place with me."

His words sounded raw to his own ears. He focused on her pain instead of his own. He'd experienced similar agony himself when his parents had died and left him alone.

Jessamine shuddered at his touch. She made the mistake of looking up at him. His blue eyes captured her, held her in an entirely different kind of imprisonment. She stared at him with a mixture of fear and excitement. His smoldering gaze dropped to her lips, and Jessamine felt her body ignite at the same instant his mouth swooped down, capturing hers in a kiss of demanding hunger such as she'd never felt before. His hands pressed into her back, molding her pliant body to the rigid contours of his.

With a slight moan of desperation, she slipped her hands up his chest, her fingers sliding into the soft hair at his nape, her body arching against his. A shudder shook his body as she fitted herself to him, and his mouth crushed down on hers, parting her lips, his tongue driving into her mouth with urgency as their denied passion exploded.

Alan kissed her again and again until her breaths were coming in ragged gasps, mingling with his, and still he couldn't stop. The same uncontrollable compulsion to have her that had seized him at the temple complex overtook him again, and he kissed her until she was moaning and writhing in his arms and desire was pouring through him in hot, primal waves. Tearing his mouth from hers, he slid his lips across her cheek, her ear, her forehead.

He forced himself to grow still, to regain control, to gentle his caress, to gentle himself. He wanted her with the very essence of his being, but he'd meant it when he'd said she'd have to come to him. Especially now that he knew she was a princess. The divide between them was huge. A chasm. Was it too big to breach?

He wanted her in his life, no matter what. Could they find a way to make it work? His desire for her was real. As was hers for him. Desire crossed the divide of rank and responsibility, just as it had for her parents. They'd defied the world—and their love had ended tragically.

He didn't want that for Jessamine. She deserved so much more. The choice to proceed or break things off would have to be hers. He turned his face into the wind, allowing it to caress his heated skin.

She laid her head against his chest, listening to the sound of his heartbeat. "Is this what my parents felt? This explosion of passion every time they touched?"

"Probably."

"Why?" He heard the pain in her voice and understood what she was truly asking of him. *Why did such emotion spring to life between two people who were wrong for each other?*

"I don't know. It just happens sometimes. It's what we do with our passion that will matter from this moment on." He stepped back and let the wind swirl around them, cooling their heat further.

He glanced back at the coastline of Spain. "I know you're coming with me to Scotland because of the prophecy."

She opened her mouth to speak, but he held up his hand, cutting her off.

"If you want to return home after we settle the ark safely in Scotland, I'll escort you there myself. In the meanwhile, I set something out on your pallet to wear tonight. I have something special in mind. You'll meet me back up here on the deck at sunset for dinner."

With that, he turned and strode away, giving her no opportunity to refuse.

Chapter Nineteen

From the moment he'd met her, Alan had known there was something unique about Jessamine. But he'd never expected this. A princess. In hiding. An angry bridegroom who'd murdered her own mother pursued her. The wrath of an entire country, perhaps even two, could come down on Alan's head for what he'd done to her.

He'd ruined her. But he'd offered to marry her. Yet who was he to think himself worthy of her hand?

Alan headed belowdecks. He needed to think, to sort through his emotions. He reached the interior of the hull and allowed the dank darkness to seep around him.

Mother of God, a princess? With his hand fisted, he struck the thick planks that made up the hull. Pain reverberated in his hand. Better pain than confusion. He shook out his offended knuckles.

There had been clues to her identity from the moment they'd met—her fine clothes, her aristocratic manner, her hints about her education, her language skills, the conde's pursuit. The man had even called her Princess a time or two. And still Alan had failed to put it all together.

Because he hadn't wanted to.

He shoved his hand through his hair and leaned back against the cool, damp wood. Very well. So she was a princess. She'd stated on deck that she had nothing to go back to—only a future she didn't want as the wife of a nobleman. But to marry against the king's wishes would be an act of treason.

He would be willing to live a secret life if it meant living with Jessamine. But could he condemn her to that fate?

What did she want? Would she consider marrying him if they had to live the rest of their lives on the run? He drew a sharp breath of the stale, musty air. What did he have to offer a woman like Jessamine?

Only himself, and he wasn't even truly free to offer her that, not until he officially withdrew from the Templar order. He had given up his home and his inheritance to join the Templars. And once he was done with them, he'd have no employment either.

He could do what he'd done before. He was sure he could find a way for both of them to take on new names and find a new home. They could start all over again. Alan straightened, feeling somewhat lighter at the thought. He didn't have much to offer Jessamine except his protection and hope.

Would it be enough? There was only one way to find out.

With new determination firing his blood, Alan left the shadows of the hull and stepped forward into his future.

After Alan left her, Jessamine remained on deck for a short while before returning to the captain's cabin. She entered to find a hip bath had been set in the center of the chamber. Steam rose from the bath in gossamer threads, carrying a sweet, unfamiliar scent into the air. Was this the surprise Alan had said he'd left waiting there for her? If so, it was a welcome gift, indeed.

Suddenly, the grit of the desert seemed to weigh her down, and she peeled her torn and dirty clothes off, leaving them in a pile on the floor. With a sigh, she lowered herself into the scented water. She leaned back and closed her eyes in contented luxury as the hot water covered her. She felt the desert sand slough from her skin and velvet softness take its place.

She opened her eyes, entirely relaxed now, and noted a cake of soap had been laid out for her beside a length of linen for drying. She grasped the soap and brought it to her nose. The floral scent from the water came to her more strongly now. She'd never smelled the like before.

After dipping below the surface of the water to wet her hair, she lathered it. Feeling cleaner than she ever had before, she rinsed, then gazed about the small chamber she and Alan had shared every night since they'd left the Holy Land. Alan had not pressed her to make love. He'd said he would keep his distance, and he'd been a man of his word. He slept on the hammock in the corner, while she slept on the soft pallet at the opposite side of the chamber. Her gaze drifted there and caught on a soft green gown that had been laid out for her.

By Alan? Who else would have done such a thing?

Was that what he'd brought aboard the ship before they set sail? Should she wear the gown? Her gaze moved back to the butter yellow garment he'd purchased for her before they headed into the desert to find the ark. The garment was torn and dirty.

Jessamine stepped from the bath and grasped the linen, realizing this was the first time she'd ever bathed herself. Usually her maid, Sarafina, scrubbed her skin, lathered her hair, then dried her, helped her dress, and styled her hair.

Jessamine shook the loose ends of her wet hair, sending a spray of water onto the floor at her feet, and laughed. There was such freedom in doing these intimate tasks herself. She dried her skin and mopped up the wet floor with her sheet of linen, then brushed her hair until it fell in a cascade around her shoulders. When she was done, she slipped a clean chemise over her head, followed by the green gown, which laced in the front with silken gold ribbons. Finally, she slid her feet into a pair of gold-threaded slippers and felt like an entirely different person.

The clothing was different from the styles she had worn in Spain, with cleaner lines, less fabric, and no binding corset. Was this the style of dress the women of Alan's country wore? She was suddenly curious to find out. A whole new adventure awaited her in Scotland.

With a smile of satisfaction, Jessamine left the chamber. The silken fabric caressed her skin and drifted about her ankles as she ascended the stairs leading to the deck. When she cleared the hatch, lanterns set up about the ship's deck revealed Alan near the railing.

He was dressed in black from head to foot except for a snowy white shirt, which was so white it seemed to gleam against his dark tunic. His dark head was slightly bent as he gazed at the water. The muscles of his back flexed as he shoved his right hand through his dark hair. The sheer maleness of his wide, muscular shoulders, his broad back and narrow waist stole her breath. Jessamine must have made a sound, because he looked up sharply. He watched her from across the deck.

Stilled by the intensity of Alan's gaze, locked in the magnetism of his blue eyes, she felt as though she could hardly breathe. Suddenly the air seemed too warm, and she pressed a hand against her chest as though forcing the air in and out of her lungs.

And all the while, Alan's gaze held her until it seemed that time stood still, that they were the only two people in the world. Then Alan moved toward her and took her arm. Jessamine started, for his touch was warm and alive. Without speaking, he led her to a low table set up on the deck with two pillows placed beside it. Alan took her hand and helped her down to one of the pillows, his touch lingering for a moment on her shoulder before he sat beside her on the other pillow.

A seaman came forward then and set down a wooden platter filled with perfectly cooked vegetables, white fish, and the dates and berries she'd seen in the marketplace. They ate in relative silence, although all through supper, Jessamine was breathlessly aware of Alan next to her, of the soft slap of the water against the hull, and of the rhythmic sway of the boat.

"Have you seen the—?" She stopped and cast a glance about the deck, uncertain if anyone was listening to their conversation.

"Aye," Alan continued, understanding her unspoken question. "It's safe. Will insisted on sitting belowdecks with it until we reach the end of our journey."

"You said we were headed for Scotland. Where in Scotland exactly?"

"Dundee, near the North Sea."

She frowned. "I'm not familiar with your country."

Alan excused himself from the table. He strode to the forecastle, then returned a few moments later with a lantern and a large sheet of linen. He set it before her. A map.

She'd been educated with her uncle's children. And after having lived through times of war and hardship, King Alfonso had deemed it important that both his daughters and sons learn the politics not just of Spain, but of the world. She'd benefited from his beliefs and recognized the outline of Spain's coastline, but she'd never seen much beyond the Mediterranean Sea. "Is this where we are now?" she asked, pointing to a huge body of water.

"Aye." He smiled at her gently. "We will sail into the Atlantic Ocean, then up through the English Channel to Scotland."

She looked over the stern, seeing nothing but darkness. "Do you think the conde will follow us?"

"Someone is. We spotted a ship two days ago," he said. "I must admit Will was quite wise in his choice of vessel. The Arab dhow can outsail most ships. Whoever follows is at least a day behind us at present."

The knowledge didn't ease the sudden tightening in her chest. "We won't stop until we reach Scotland?"

"Nay, we'll sail straight for the next fortnight at least."

Her tension eased. They were safe for that long then. Her gaze returned to the starlit night around them. The sea's surface rippled with the wind, and a line of brilliant phosphorescence kicked up by the tiller trailed behind them for as far as the eye could see. "It seems as if we are the only people in the world tonight," she said softly.

"That's the way I want you to feel." He stood. "Dance with me, Jessamine."

His words brought her gaze back to him. "We have no music."

In the next moment she found herself in his arms. "We have the music of our hearts." She offered no resistance as he danced her away from the table and the lanterns, toward the bow of the ship.

Moonlight cloaked them in silver. His arms slipped about her waist. The warmth and strength of him felt like a caress against the lightweight fabric of her gown.

"You are a constant puzzle to me," she murmured. "Are you a warrior or a romantic?"

"Can't a man be both?" His breath was warm as he laughed softly against her ear.

"Irresistible, that's what you are." Her words were only a thread above a whisper.

He lifted a lock of her hair from her shoulders, drawing her closer as he did. He drew a deep breath. "You are beautiful tonight." He lifted her hair to his lips and rubbed the silken strands against them, whispering her name.

The hair slipped from his fingers, and his mouth found hers in a kiss that shattered the calm of the night and made her tremble with fevered longing. Once again it seemed as though time stood still. She could lose herself in his arms, in their passion.

Her heart thundering in her chest, she stepped away. She wanted Alan with an urgency so powerful it nearly consumed her. But if she gave herself to him one more time, she doubted she'd be able to resist him ever again. She wanted to marry him. She wanted to spend the rest of her life in his arms. But how was such a miracle possible, given their circumstances?

With a smothered cry, she turned away and ran back to the safety of her chamber.

The next morning Jessamine came on deck early.

"I'm glad you decided to come up for some air." Alan signaled for a seaman to take the wheel of the ship as he moved to join her at the railing.

She avoided Alan's gaze, searching behind them for the speck of black in the distance that might be the conde's ship. "Morning air is good for one's health."

"Aye." He came to stand beside her, leaning back against the railing so that he could stare into her face.

She couldn't keep her gaze from drifting toward him. The wind lifted the edges of his dark hair and molded his white shirt to his muscular body. For one brief moment she saw utter contentment cross his features before his usual mask fell into place. Yet that one glimpse told her more than he'd intended. He liked it here on deck.

"I thought you were only a warrior, not a sailor."

His gaze snapped to hers. "There's no 'only' in being a warrior. It requires not only discipline and skill but intelligence, if you don't want to find yourself buried six feet under."

"I meant no insult. I was simply pointing out you seem just as comfortable here on the deck with the wheel in your hands as you do with a sword."

His face softened. "In truth, I love the sea."

Jessamine's breath stilled at the sudden look of vulnerability in his face, his eyes. "Why did you not pursue a life at sea?"

"My father had other plans for me. I do believe it was because he loved me. He knew the life of a seaman would be a rough and uncertain one."

"Any more rough and uncertain than being a warrior?"

He laughed. "My father understood the land. Not the sea."

She frowned. "So how did you learn to sail?"

The vulnerable expression was gone. "After my parents died in the sea, I ran away from the clan and signed on as a cabin boy. For years, I worked my way up through the ranks until I had something that was mine—status, money, and skill. But it was never enough."

She frowned. "Was that when you returned to Scotland?"

He didn't answer for a moment. "I spent so much time alone out at sea. It gave me time to think about all that I'd lost in comparison to all I had." He looked away. "Then, one day, I decided my father was right, and I needed to prove that I could be like everyone else. So I went back to Scotland and learned to fight."

She waited for him to continue, but he didn't. She looked down at the sea below the ship with stinging eyes. "You gave up on your dreams."

"Nay, I just found a new one. The Templars gave me the family and security I'd lost."

Her gaze found his once more. "And if you give up the Templars, then what?"

He hesitated, then reached for her, trailing his fingers against the underside of her jaw to her chin. "By leaving the order, I'll be taking my dreams back, Jessamine. My dreams are about more than the sea. I want a family. I was quite serious in my offers of marriage to you. I know I have no right to offer for a princess, but that knowledge changes nothing. I still want you, more with each passing day."

"Alan—"

"Say nothing. Not yet. I want you to come to me in passion, needing me as much as I need you. Do you understand?"

She was beginning to, just as she was forgetting why she'd vowed to stay away from him in the first place. She could see the pulse beating wildly in his temple, and his breathing accelerated as he trailed his fingers down the length of her neck. She trembled in response and wild heat filled her core as it always did when he touched her. "Alan, please . . ."

"That pleases you?"

She drew a sharp breath as his fingers trailed across the rise of her breasts. "Very much."

He placed a soft, regretful kiss on her cheek, then moved away. "Enjoy your sightseeing." He offered her a bow. "I'm sure the distraction will have as little calming effect on you as my sailing the ship does on me." He turned and strode once more to the forecastle, taking the wheel in his hands.

She forced herself to look at him, then wished she hadn't. It was difficult to pretend to be casual with him when he looked at her with blatant seduction in his gaze. She swallowed roughly and twisted back toward the water. He was right. Staring at the water would have no effect on her heated nerves whatsoever.

The conde commanded his crew to put into port in Mijas, Spain. Alan Cathcart had proven himself to be a worthy opponent. If the conde was to successfully retrieve his bride and make the Scotsman pay for taking her away, reinforcements were essential.

He'd instructed his men to prepare his caravel for another fortnight at sea. While they did, he moved up the steep slope to the mansion the king used as his temporary home with as much haste as was possible, considering the bruises the conde had suffered when he fell off that horse in the desert. He was certain King Alfonso XI's court would remain in the area while they awaited the safe return of his niece.

Reaching the mansion, he was immediately ushered into the royal chambers when he stated he had news of the princess. The king sat in a low chair, flanked by two attendants, both armed. His secretary hovered nearby as the conde approached.

The haggardness of the king's face surprised the conde. Was it the war with the Moors or his niece's disappearance that was causing the man such distress? The conde held back a smile, hoping for the latter.

"My niece. You said you had word. Where is she?" The king's voice was anguished.

The conde bowed when he reached the king, then waited for the signal to rise, which came immediately. "Your Grace, she's been abducted by a Templar and is this very moment being swept off to Scotland. What the heathen intends with her, I don't know."

"How is that possible?" The king's hands trembled on the arms of his rather ordinary chair. "She was well guarded. My sister would not be pleased with my carelessness."

"Such things happen, Your Grace. 'Tis no fault of yours, and Jessamine is known as a, shall we say, willful child." The conde frowned. Any chair *he* sat in as king would be far grander, as befit his station. That dream would come true if he could convince the king his plan was the only option for rescuing Jessamine.

The king's expression darkened. "What is the ransom? I'll pay anything they ask."

"There is no ransom."

"No ransom?" the king said fiercely. "Whyever not? She is a princess. I want her back."

"I can bring her back."

The king's eyes narrowed. "I am familiar with your ambition, Conde Mendoza. What could you possibly want in return for such an act?"

The conde once again bit back a smile. Everything was fitting in place exactly as he'd imagined. "The girl's reputation will be in tatters, despite her royal status. I would be honored to serve my country and marry the girl." The conde paused, then added, "With your permission, of course."

The king's lips twisted. "Do I have another choice?"

"I regret that in this case, there is no other choice, Your Grace. Only I know where the girl is headed."

The king straightened and some of the weariness left his features. "You're quite cunning, Conde Mendoza. What will it take to get her back?"

"A marriage document, of course. And for her bride

price, I will give you two ships with a full complement of men and arms. Of course, they will accompany me before they will join your forces. I wish to teach this Scotsman a lesson for toying with things that are not his."

The king nodded to his secretary. "Draw up the documents."

"Urgency is essential, Your Grace."

The king stood, his gaze on the conde's face. The monarch looked weary and discouraged and ripe for plucking. As soon as the conde had the girl, he would be back to put the rest of his plan into action. Maybe then his mother would finally be proud of the man he'd become. She'd always told him he was nothing but a failure. Perhaps when he brought her the princess, she would finally know he could be successful.

As mother to a future king, could she be anything but pleased? The conde frowned. He wondered if even that would be enough for the woman. But he wouldn't know until he brought Jessamine to her.

As his bride.

It didn't take long for the king's secretary to provide the official marriage documents. Once he had them in his possession, the conde returned to the docks. As he walked, he flicked his finger over the royal wax seal of the House of Castile. Soon, he'd have everything he'd ever wanted. The girl was the weak link in the Spanish crown's armor. And he'd known it all along. A satisfied smile came to the conde's lips as he savored the pleasant prospects in store for him—a new bride, poison for the royals, and a throne. The joys that awaited him were many.

Now, to execute his plan. He would send three galleons after the ship carrying Jessamine to Scotland while he took one of the faster Arab ships and a small army with him to Dundee. He had to sail faster than the Scotsman in order to reach Scotland ahead of him. Once there, he would set a trap so the Scot received the full force of his fury when the man docked with his bride.

Chapter Twenty

As the next week passed, the tension between Alan and Jessamine grew thicker than the morning fog. Jessamine sat upon the deck each day below the forecastle, just out of his sight. But he knew she was there, and his body ached with need.

And the nights in the cabin became so unbearable that Alan did what he said he wouldn't do and left her alone to come up on deck, allowing the swift breeze to cool his thoughts and desires.

At least the weather remained constant. During the nights the wind was steady, rounding the lateen sails as they raced north. And every day brought perfect sunshine and strong winds that kept the ship flying over the water.

Alan feared their good luck might be too good to last. Three days later he was proven right when the carrack behind them drifted slightly off course, revealing three more ships.

Four ships were in pursuit.

Fortunately, his dhow continued to maintain its lead. From the crow's-nest, Alan tried to discern who their pursuers might be. Any number of people might be on their tail. The conde. The assassins he'd escaped in the desert. Even the Spanish military.

Alan headed back to the deck and to the forecastle, where the captain waited. "We have two cannons aboard?" Alan asked, drawing on what he'd seen below in the ship's hold.

"Aye, the ship is armed with two," confirmed the captain. "But speed and steady winds are our best weapons now. This dhow is faster and lighter than those who pursue us. Besides, I've seen the likes of those last three ships before. They are Spanish."

"Then speed is of the essence. Does the ship have any more speed in her?"

The captain barked orders to his crew, who scurried about, making certain the sails were taut and drawing all the wind they could. Under expert hands, the dhow shaved smoothly through the sea for the next week.

They didn't break sail until the familiar coastline of England came into view. Alan stood at the rail sorting out the facts, plotting strategy, drawing conclusions, and discarding information until he came up with what he hoped was a plan that would get Jessamine and the ark away from the ship, onto Scottish shores, and among his fellow Templars, before the Spanish arrived behind them.

The only thing standing between him, Jessamine, and success was the English Channel. They would have to risk entering it and hope and pray the English navy would be unaware of the violation of its territory.

The only chance they had was to proceed at night and make the ship as invisible as possible. Alan felt a smile tug at his lips. Perhaps the English would give them unwilling aid by ridding them of their pursuers, who wouldn't know what threat awaited them in the channel.

Alan glanced at the sky. Dusk was falling. Darkness would be here soon. He had to prepare.

The moon was a crescent-shaped sliver rising over the dark masses of land in the distance. Stars hung suspended by the millions, but the light they shed did little to illuminate the sinister shapes and shadows within the channel. Alan searched for English ships as the dhow glided silently over the water. They'd switched their two white sails for a dark-colored one. The lack of the second sail had slowed them down, but that couldn't be helped if they were to make it through the channel unchallenged.

The ship had to appear as only a dark shadow with no flag to identify it and no lights on the deck at all. The only sounds Alan heard were the soft lapping of the water against the hull and the rapid beat of his own heart. All hands had been banished belowdecks to keep the risk of movement or sound to a minimum. They could not risk discovery.

Only he, the captain, and two seamen remained on deck. The captain stood at the wheel. Alan searched the waters from the bow. One seaman lay flat against the deck below the aft sail. He could raise it in an instant if necessary. The other seaman lay against the deck above the cannon slats, ready to signal the men below to fire at a moment's notice. They'd prepared well for this part of the journey. With luck they'd make it through unscathed.

Alan's body tensed as he searched the velvet night. A shadow on his left brought a catch to his breath. He strained to see in the darkness. A ship? He couldn't be sure. Everything was so dark.

The shape vanished as quickly as it had come.

Had he only imagined something there? He took a deep, shuddering breath and stared into the black night. As the inky shoreline of England faded from view, Alan knew the worst was behind them. He allowed himself a comforting thought: the Templar army was almost within reach. On the shores of Scotland, they'd have all the help they needed.

* * *

The night faded away, giving birth to a new day. Twenty days after they'd departed from the Holy Land, the Arab dhow left behind the English Channel and the threat of discovery by the English navy. Sweet winds carried them up the North Sea toward a home Alan had not seen in almost a year.

A year could change many things. A year had changed him. He glanced out at the banks of the River Tay, which was taking them closer to the Templar headquarters. Were the brothers still occupying Trophichen Preceptory? One never knew what changes time would bring to an order in hiding. But for the sake of the ark, Alan prayed the order was as it had been before he and the other Scottish Templars had left for the Holy Land.

Alan felt a moment's ease as the familiar sights of the harbor came into view. With luck, they would stay ahead of their foes. Their day's lead could easily disappear on land. Yet he held the advantage because he knew the terrain like the back of his hand.

But the ark would slow them down.

The tension returned to his neck and shoulders. His hand left the rail to grip the hilt of his sword. He tugged the edge of his chain mail into place. He was prepared for anything. This battle was not yet won.

Where were they?

The conde paced restlessly back and forth in front of the docks of Dundee. The morning light had spilled across the land, and Cathcart and Jessamine had yet to arrive. As the night had vanished, so had his patience.

He'd made his journey on the Arab ship through the English Channel in record time, leaving the other three Spanish ships well behind. He'd brought just a few heavily armed men with him. They could take the

Scotsman. All they needed was for the bastard's ship to arrive in port.

So why didn't Cathcart come?

Had his intelligence been wrong? The thought brought with it a spark of fury. Had the old man on the docks of Jaffa lied about the Scots destination? The conde released a howl of animalistic rage and frustration. His troops edged away from him.

The cowards. He bared his teeth at the men, sending them scurrying back farther.

Then, just when he thought all was lost, the bow of a ship emerged at the mouth of the harbor. They were here. Power surged through the conde. He brought a hand up to his chest, to the marriage document he'd placed in his doublet over his heart. He felt the spread of glowing, comforting warmth penetrate his body, whispering of revenge and riches to come.

Once the ship had dropped anchor, it took some time to get the ark onto the smaller boat that would carry them all to shore. While waiting, Jessamine stared at the new world around her.

Her gaze took in the lush hillside, and her breath stilled in her chest. The red-gold hills of Spain that she'd found so beautiful all her life were utterly different from the rich emerald greens of the Scottish landscape. Nature had painted the soft rolling hills with a palette of every green imaginable. They seemed to stretch forever. On those velvety hills were swaths of deep purple, and the breeze carried the same soft scent Alan had used in her bath aboard the ship. Heather, he had called it. She drew the scent deeper inside her lungs, let it wrap itself around her soul.

Scotland had a softness about the land, the sea, even the air, that Spain did not. With a smile, Jessamine turned her gaze to the boat waiting for her to board. Will already sat in the bow along with two seamen who would help them move the ark onto a wagon. The ark was covered with a large linen sheet, but that simple disguise could not hide the outlines of the angels' wings beneath the thin fabric. Her smile slipped as she realized for the first time how vulnerable they would be transporting the ark to a safe haven.

Alan stood in the boat below, steadying the ladder for her. Jessamine hesitated for a moment as she reached his level. He smiled at her and the warmth of that smile moved clear down to her toes. She missed him terribly, and wondered more than once during their journey if resisting him was more torturous than a life on the run as traitors.

Once she was in the boat, he sat beside her, and her heart accelerated at his nearness. The boat lurched forward as the seamen rowed toward shore. Trying to distract herself, Jessamine turned her attention toward the Scottish shoreline ahead. In the early morning light, the docks were empty. Perhaps everyone else was still abed. The solitude comforted her as they approached the docks. "It's beautiful here," she said to Alan.

"Beautiful, indeed," he agreed softly.

Something in his voice suggested his comment was not directed entirely to the view. "If you find these hills intriguing, you should see the blue-black Scottish mountains. Savage beauty at its finest."

"I'd like to see those mountains. I want to see many mountains in my lifetime."

"You will." The morning light played with the breeze-blown bits of his hair, scattering them like threads of dark silk against the blue Scottish sky. The visual effect of the wind, the sun, the sky was intoxicating. It acted on her senses like a draft of sweet wine. She swayed slightly toward him and caught the scent of sandalwood and musk. She closed her eyes and sighed. Was it Scotland or the man beside her working this magic over her?

"Jessamine?" His voice was soft and thick.

She opened her eyes at the soft request. For a moment she couldn't move, trapped in his gaze. Her body tingled, from the palms of her hands to the soles of her feet. A blush heated her cheeks. She tore her eyes away.

"Where do we go from here?" she asked, scooting farther from him on the seat. Distance, that's what she needed.

He smiled knowingly. "We ride for Trophichen Preceptory, where we'll gather other Templars to help us battle whoever is following us."

"Who is following us, Alan?"

"I'm betting it's the Spanish and hoping it's not the assassins."

"It's because of me that the Spanish might be after us."

Alan's expression turned fierce. "Without you, I never would have found the ark." His voice was thick. "I'll protect you from them, if that's your choice."

She nodded. "That's my choice."

"Then come." He offered her his hand to help her from the boat as they reached the docks of Dundee.

She took his fingers and stood. Warmth pulsed up her arm as he led her from the boat to solid ground; then he released her fingers, leaving her feeling suddenly cold and alone.

"I must arrange for horses and a wagon. With luck, we'll make it to the preceptory before the other ships land," Alan said.

"Your luck is at an end, Templar." The conde's low, triumphant laugh echoed in the morning air.

Jessamine's gaze followed the sound to the slight rise above the dock. Thirteen Spanish soldiers flanked the conde with swords drawn.

In a blur of motion, Alan spun Jessamine away, toward the seamen who were carrying the ark. Alan unsheathed his sword with one hand and grasped a dagger from his boot with the other, then dove into the sudden flurry of action. Four soldiers rushed at him, flourishing their swords. He struck one man in the throat with his dagger while fending off three others with his sword.

Jessamine's heart hammered as she watched Alan engage the men with skill that was deadly and precise. The sound of clashing steel echoed loudly in her ears while they fought each other for their lives. But there were too many of them to Alan's one. Jessamine searched the abandoned docks. The ships in the harbor gave evidence that this was a working port, but where were all the people? Had the conde cleared the area so that no one would be around to help?

The conde broke away from the others and moved toward her. Jessamine stepped back, her gaze fixed on his dagger. She'd been so close to freedom.

He grasped her arm with bone-crushing force and pressed the tip of his dagger to her throat. "Are you afraid, my princess?"

A ripple of fear coursed through her. "Of course, I'm afraid. I'd be stupid not to be frightened."

"And you've proved to me, Jessamine, that you're not stupid. I see the fire has returned to your eyes. Good, I'll enjoy you all the more for it."

"You'll get no pleasure from me."

"You're wrong." He drew her against his chest. He started to lower his head, then suddenly stopped. His gaze shot to the ark, which had been abandoned by the seamen. Without swords or knives to protect them, they'd run off.

The conde tugged her forward with him as he moved toward the ark and slashed the covering. "Is that what I think it is? I've heard the legends." He stared at the dirt-covered ark with the same lust in his eyes that had been directed at her only moments before. "The Ark of the Covenant," he breathed. "Is it true what is written in the Bible, that only the pure can touch the ark and live? His gaze shot to hers. "Have you touched it?" he asked.

"Yes," she replied with a gasp as he forced her hand forward, dragging it over the muddied surface. The dry dirt crumbled, revealing the gold beneath.

He jerked her hand back. "I'd wondered what you were doing in the desert with that bastard. This is better than I ever imagined."

He twisted her back toward the battle. She gasped to see that Alan sported several wounds on his arms and legs, yet he continued to fight against overwhelming odds. Her heart lodged in her throat. "Stop it, you're killing him!" Jessamine cried.

"He deserves to die, my dear, for violating my property."

Across the distance, Alan's gaze met hers. He tried to move toward her, only to be attacked from behind by more soldiers. He flinched as their blades tore at his clothing, revealing his chain mail beneath. She prayed the mail would protect him. She prayed that someone would help him defeat these men.

The next thing she knew, she was jerked forward again. The conde signaled to two of his men to collect the ark while he dragged her toward a waiting wagon. She fought against him until he stopped and bound her hands.

She twisted back toward Alan as the conde dragged her forward. Would anyone help him? Could she? Her throat tightened. Perhaps not with a sword, but if she gave the conde what he wanted, then maybe . . .

She dug her heels into the dirt. She had to try. "Please," she begged. "Spare him and I'll go with you. I'll marry you willingly if you'll call your men off." Two men held Alan by the arms now while he writhed and kicked against them. Another man approached with a sword aimed at his heart. She sucked in a breath. Even his mail might not protect him from such a strike. "Tell them to stop!"

"You won't fight me any longer?" the conde asked, his eyes narrowing with suspicion.

"Make them stop now!"

With a shrill whistle, the conde called his men to him. The soldier with the sword brought the flat of his blade down against the side of Alan's head instead of striking his chest. The two men holding him released him, and Alan's legs buckled and he slumped to the ground.

The conde's lips curled back in a snarl. "I'll hold you to your promise."

She nodded. "You have my word."

Jessamine dared not move, or breathe, or do anything that might change the conde's mind. She shivered as she was tossed into the wagon. The vehicle lurched forward. Tears blurred her vision and ran in white-hot streaks down her cheeks.

She would have to give up what she wanted most in order to protect him. She only hoped Alan would understand.

Chapter Twenty-one

Alan awoke with a start. A dull thudding pounded through his head. He wrenched himself upright and reached for his sword. It wasn't there. At the sudden movement, his head spun. His heart pounded. His lungs labored to pull in a breath.

He swiped his hand over his eyes to clear them and felt stickiness on his fingers. Blood. His blood. His side burned, and sweat broke out on his brow. The thudding in his head intensified as he scanned the docks and the hillside above him. He was alone. The conde must have paid the townsfolk to vanish until he was gone.

And the conde *was* gone, along with Jessamine.

Jessamine. He'd lost Jessamine and the ark. Cold terror, more debilitating than the pain pulsing through his head, clenched his chest. That shadow he'd seen on the English Channel—it must have been the conde.

He'd lost Jessamine.

He turned his face to the sky and released a growl, a groan, a howl of sheer frustration and pain. The conde had taken her, and Alan had no idea where.

He drew a rasping breath, then another, until his breathing slowed and his thoughts cleared. He searched the planking of the docks, then the ground beyond, for his weapon. He had to find his sword. On hands and knees he searched until he caught a glint of silver beneath the afternoon sun and felt the reassurance of cold steel once again in his hand.

He had to think. He had to plan. He tried to get to his feet, only to collapse back against the soft earth. He tried again. This time he remained standing. But his head swam, and the world spun before his eyes. He sheathed his sword and took a step forward, then another. In order to save Jessamine, he had to find help. Templar help. Only his brothers could help him rescue the one thing more precious than anything else life held.

He had to stay in control. Instead of heading for Trophichen Preceptory, which he might find deserted, he would ride for Crosswick Priory instead. The monastery had at one time been his home. The Templars would still be in residence there no matter what changes a year had brought. The Templars could help him.

The words became a prayer as he shuffled toward the village of Dundee. To a horse that just seemed to be waiting there. Could this be the ark's doing? Stranger things had happened since they'd been in the presence of the holy treasure. Alan searched up and down the abandoned street for the animal's owner. Horse thieves were hanged in Scotland. Alan continued toward the animal as need drove him to take the risk.

The horse remained still as Alan tried to mount, but nausea hit him hard. He clutched his midsection, battling the urge to vomit, and concentrated on breathing. When the pain passed, he tried mounting the beast again. The animal whickered, then remained still, as though understanding Alan's need. He grasped the saddle and climbed awkwardly upon the horse's back.

When he set the horse in motion, he released a jagged breath as pain shot through him. He grasped the saddle with white-knuckled force and gritted his teeth against the pain that pierced his body and stabbed behind his eyes. He would endure whatever pain he had to. Nothing would stop him from finding Jessamine. Nothing.

By the time he finally saw the walls of the old monastery, Alan's body had gone numb, as had his mind. The late afternoon sun glinted off the stark gray stone, and if he hadn't gone so numb, he would have smiled. He'd missed this place—a place he'd once called home. At the gate, he slid off the horse's back and onto the ground. He pulled himself up with the help of the horse's saddle band, then tried to stumble toward the iron gate and the door beyond.

He made it to the door and knocked. He couldn't say who answered his summons, because at the very moment the door swung wide, the world before him went dark once more.

"Mother of God!" the Templar cursed as he caught the man collapsing in the doorway and hauled him inside. Alan Cathcart. They'd thought him dead. Alan's friend Simon frowned. By the looks of it, the man would be exactly that if they didn't get him inside and into the healing baths as soon as possible.

Simon slammed the door shut with his foot. "A little help, I beg thee," he called to anyone nearby.

"What in Heaven's name?" Brother Kenneth hurried forward. He gripped Alan by one shoulder, helping to support his weight.

"He's been in some sort of recent battle, and now he's out cold," Simon said as the three of them progressed down the long hallway. "Please hurry, Abbot. He weighs as much as a horse!"

Brother Patrick and Brother Bernard rushed into the

hallway just as the burdened men reached the first doorway on the right. "Alan?" they asked in unison.

"Help us prepare a bed for him, if you would," Brother Kenneth asked the younger brothers.

"Aye, Abbot." They hurried into the chamber and pulled back the covers of the serviceable cot in the corner.

Simon laid Alan down carefully and quickly removed his sword and sheath before he pulled the bloodied linen shirt Alan wore back to reveal a coat of mail beneath.

"He's injured very badly." Simon frowned down at the blood seeping through the links, not to mention the several gashes in the metal where the enemy's sword had penetrated. "We'll have to sew him up before we can take him to the healing baths."

"Aye," Brother Kenneth agreed. He turned to Brother Patrick. "Go get ale and linens." To Brother Bernard he said, "Go fetch a needle and thread and steel yourself for sewing him up." The young man nodded and hurried after Patrick as he hastened from the chamber.

"He'll not need any ale. He's already out cold," Simon said, frowning down at Alan's battle-torn body.

"The ale's for me," Brother Kenneth admitted. "Alan's presence here is good news and bad. He's returned to us. We praise the saints for that. But his condition . . ."

While they waited for the brothers to return with the supplies they needed, Simon ripped what was left of Alan's linen shirt into strips for a tourniquet here and a compress there, preventing any more blood from seeping out of his wounds.

When Brother Patrick and Brother Bernard returned, the abbot stepped back to let the young men work. But Simon hesitated, almost afraid to leave him now that Alan had finally returned to them. "We looked everywhere for him after the battle." Simon's gut twisted.

"Simon." Brother Kenneth placed a hand on his shoulder and encouraged him to step back. "Alan is with us now. That's what matters. God will see him through this. He brought our Falcon back to us. Come, let the others work."

Simon stepped back, but the knot in his stomach did not ease. "I should tell William Keith that Alan survived. He'll be relieved to know."

Again the abbot patted his shoulder. "In time, Simon. First we wait to see that he lives. Then we must hear what Alan has to tell us."

"Agreed."

Jessamine twisted the rope at her wrists, trying to work herself free. Not that it would do her much good even if she could manage to free her hands. Escape seemed impossible with so many soldiers nearby.

The conde rode at the front of their caravan on horseback, his men following on foot. He must have made port in Spain to gather more men and supplies.

Jessamine shifted so that her feet were under her as she searched for an opening, some way to throw herself over the edge of the cart and make her escape. A lump came to her throat. She had to do something to help Alan. They'd left him bleeding and battered, and quite possibly . . .

She couldn't finish the thought.

Her body coiled, preparing to leap, when a small voice beside her said, "That wouldn't be wise, my dear. There will be a better opportunity if you wait for it to present itself."

"*Will?*" Jessamine glanced sharply at the two men who strode nearby the cart. Neither of them looked at her.

She turned back toward the sound and lifted the edge of the linen that still partially covered the ark. Will was lying on the floorboards of the wagon. At the sight of the old man, her heart soared. Perhaps there was hope for escape.

"What are you doing?" she whispered.

He smiled. "I couldn't let them take you off alone."

She flicked another gaze at the men. "What about Alan? He needs help."

His smile faded. "He's alive. He's headed for Crosswick Priory, his old home. The monks there will help him."

Jessamine drew her first easy breath since they'd been attacked by the conde. "I pray you are right."

"Prayer would be useful here, my dear."

One of the soldiers looked her way. "Whom are you talking to?" he asked in a gruff voice.

Jessamine pulled the linen back down over Will's body. "I'm praying." She straightened and met his gaze. "Or will the conde take prayer away from me too?"

A low, dangerous chuckle came from the conde in front of the wagon. "Pray all you want, Princess. It won't help."

His comment brought the sting of tears to her eyes. Yes, it would. She squeezed her eyes shut. Prayer always helped.

Please, God, she prayed, *take care of Alan*. And for herself, she prayed for deliverance from a fate she'd thrust herself into.

Marriage to the conde . . . "Oh, God, please deliver me," she whispered with all her heart. She searched the small patch of unclouded sky overhead, which was now streaked with pink. Odd for what had started out as a sunny afternoon. They hit a deep rut and she slammed against the side of the wagon, crushed on the other side by the ark. "Will?" Where had Will gone?

He lifted the linen on the opposite side of the ark. His head poked around the edge. "I thought it would be safer for me to remain over here. Less risk for you too."

She lifted her gaze to the sky once more. The pink streaks had now turned red. She frowned. Had time passed so quickly? Usually a red sky suggested a time closer to eventide.

The hills she had found so beautiful upon her arrival now seemed eerily dark. The soft breeze died, the birds ceased their twittering, and the leaves of the rowan trees stilled.

Her skin prickled. Jessamine held her breath. An instant later rocks on the hillside opposite her started to tumble. A small rock zinged past her. Another hit her shoulder. She crouched down behind the ark.

A thunderous roar suddenly filled the air, followed by the shriek of a horse and the shouts of men. The wagon lurched to an abrupt stop. She flew forward and hit the front of the wagon. Pain radiated through her left shoulder at the impact. She peered around the ark. What was happening?

Large rocks tumbled down the hillside. Jessamine ducked. "Oh, please don't let them hit us," she whispered to herself. The wagon pitched to the right, then collapsed on the ground as a wheel snapped.

Jessamine's heart pounded. Dust choked the air. She coughed and wished she could bring her hand up to cover her nose and mouth. She ducked her head instead as the crack and roar of the rocks ceased, leaving only a blanketing silence.

She peered up over the ark at the world around her. Just ahead, the conde struggled to regain control of his horse. The soldiers had abandoned the cart to assist him and to examine the road, which had been ripped apart as though a mighty hand had severed it. Rocks littered the parts of the roadway that hadn't been destroyed.

Jessamine's gaze flew to the ark. She'd prayed only moments ago for deliverance. Was that what she'd been given? She wouldn't waste this chance, no matter how it had come to her. Taking her fate in her hands, she leaped out of the wagon and ran around to the side Will had occupied. She flipped up the linen. He was gone. Her gaze shot to the hillside. She saw him there. How had he climbed the rocky hill so fast? She scrambled up the hillside where she'd glimpsed him at the edge of the trees.

She found him quickly.

"My hands," she said, holding the bindings out to him.

"There's no time. You must run for the trees while I head for Crosswick Priory. I will tell Alan and his men where to find you."

She stretched her hands out farther. "Will, please." But he turned and was gone.

Angry shouts came from below. She darted into the trees and ran with her hands held tightly against her chest. She could feel the pounding of her heart with each desperate step she took. The branches of the trees and brush snagged her skirt and tore at the flesh of her legs and arms, but she forced herself forward.

Footsteps sounded behind her, fast and many. Her breath came in harsh bursts. She stumbled, caught herself, and continued forward, managing only a few feet more before a hand grasped her arm, wrenching her backward against the solid chest of one of the Spanish soldiers.

"Let me go. I am your princess."

"I follow the conde's orders."

Jessamine kicked and squirmed, but the soldier simply dragged her through the trees and brush back to the wagon. A shiver of apprehension coursed through her body when they approached the conde. His grin was little more than a dark, evil slash.

"We might be stuck in this godforsaken land a while longer, thanks to this rockslide, but you'll not escape your fate with me."

"I'd rather die."

"That can be arranged when I am done with you." He gave a harsh laugh as he grabbed a fistful of her hair, then jerked her forward, twisting her head painfully to the side. Her cry of pain opened her lips to the revolting touch of his mouth on hers, sucking wetly. She gagged. She brought her bound fists up and tried to beat him away, but the conde reached down, caught them, and dragged her arms painfully over her head.

"God's blood, you're going to be a worthwhile little treat when I finally do bed you, Princess. Until then . . ." His words broke off as he slammed his lips onto hers once more.

This time, Jessamine twisted her head away. The soldiers nearby watched, laughed, and looked at her in a way that needed no verbal translation.

In that moment the fourth stanza of the prophecy flashed through her mind. *The fate of the parents will not be yours as a sacrifice heralds the start of a new war.* A cold chill moved through her. Again, the word *sacrifice* stood out in her mind, as did the word *war.* She tried to wiggle free as the conde lifted her up and tossed her into the wagon, which was being repaired.

She'd be no one's sacrifice.

After she righted herself in the wagon, she looked toward the woods. At least Will had managed to escape. Maybe, with a little help from whatever divine forces seemed to be aiding them, he would find Alan. *Maybe,* her heart whispered.

It wasn't much of a hope, but it was all she had, and she clung to the words like a lifeline. She could endure anything as long as there was hope of a *maybe*.

Jessamine followed the conde into an old, dilapidated inn as darkness began to fall. Grasping her by her bound hands, he sliced through the ropes. "Try to escape again, and it'll be more than your hands I bind."

With an iron grip on her arm, the conde forced Jessamine to remain at his side as the innkeeper approached them from the dining room.

"How may I be o' service, milord, milady?" The innkeeper smiled as he wiped his hands on the front of his dirty apron.

"We need a church." The conde's voice was cold, his eyes colder.

The man's face went pale and his gaze shifted from the conde to Jessamine, then back again. "There be no church in these parts, I fear. We have tae travel half a day tae go tae the church two villages away."

"Mother of God! Will nothing go right this day?" the conde growled.

The innkeeper blanched as he raced to a small black desk and withdrew two keys, which he handed to the conde. "Our finest rooms are yers, as long as ye have need, milord."

The conde snatched the keys and signaled for the men behind them to follow him up the stairs. He forced Jessamine up the steps so fast she tripped, then found herself dragged until she gained her feet once more.

He kicked the door open and waved the men inside, instructing them to set the ark near the window. He pulled her inside behind him, then thrust her toward the bed.

The shadows of the room scattered a little under the

light of a single candle that sat upon a table in the corner. But it was the moonlight streaming through the window and onto the ark that seemed to banish most of the darkness. Pale silver light reflected off the tips of the angels' wings where the mud had been scraped off.

The light seemed to catch the conde's eye as he drifted toward the partly concealed chest. He tugged the linen away, revealing brilliant gold in places.

"Get over here," the conde demanded. He thrust a tartan blanket from the base of the bed into her hands. "Clean the ark off. I want to see it in all its glory."

"Why don't you clean it?"

He laughed. "And touch the ark? I've read the tales, Princess. You won't get rid of me so easily. Now, clean it!"

She knelt beside the ark and rubbed at the chest's sides until pure gold gleamed beneath the moonlight.

"The Ark of the Covenant," he breathed. "I never would have imagined it could be mine."

"The ark belongs to the world," she offered boldly.

"No, Jessamine, it is mine, just as you are."

"You might possess my body, but you will never have my heart or my soul."

He grinned and shifted his gaze to her. "Every part of you belongs to me, thanks to your uncle."

She frowned. "What do you mean? What have you done?"

He reached inside his tunic to withdraw a folded sheet of paper sealed with red wax. He tossed the paper at her. "Our marriage documents, with your uncle's blessing."

Jessamine stared at the bold red insignia pressed into the wax. Her uncle's seal. "He would never—"

"We came to an agreement. The king wants you back home where you belong." The conde strode toward the spot where she hunkered near the ark. He reached out and stroked his fingers harshly over her cheek, leaving pain in their wake. "And as the only one who could bring you back, he gave me exactly what I wanted. You."

She turned her head away. "Marriage to me will not aid you in your quest for power."

"Oh, it already has, Princess. Look at me." His fingers gripped her arm and tightened on her flesh until her gaze shifted back to him. "Your cousins, your uncle, and everyone in your royal circle are slowly being poisoned by their very own royal taster."

Jessamine gazed at him in helpless terror. "Explain yourself."

"Poison at every meal. Slow, but ultimately effective." He smiled a terrible smile.

The man was a monster. Jessamine could just imagine the pain and suffering everyone in the inner court was enduring now because of the conde's need for power. "Why?"

"Because my mother's only desire is for me to be king." The conde's face hardened. "And I'll do anything to make sure that she sees me as a success just once in this life."

She moved backward, up against the ark.

His eyes narrowed. "Don't look at me that way, or I'll cut your eyes out."

Jessamine flinched and tried to make her face an empty slate.

A knock sounded on the door.

"Go away!"

"Your Lordship, there is a messenger here for you," a voice called through the door. "He says he has urgent news about the Templars and their movements."

With a grunt of disgust, the conde turned toward the door.

Jessamine held her breath.

"Enjoy your respite, Princess. It won't last long." He slammed the door, then locked it behind him.

The stillness of the room wrapped itself around Jessamine, and a chill seeped into to her bones. The man would destroy her, the Spanish court, and the world, given half a chance.

Her gaze moved to the ark. With a weapon such as this one, that very thing might be possible. Someone had to stop him.

But who? Or what?

Jessamine stood and hastened to the ark. Her hand hovered over one of the angels' wings a moment before she drew a fortifying breath. She touched it. An immediate sense of peace moved through her, banishing her fears. She closed her eyes and allowed the sensation to move through her.

"Please," she prayed. "I beg you to do something, anything, to slow the conde so Alan can find me and put an end to his horrible plans."

Chapter Twenty-two

Alan opened his eyes, then shut them again as pain overwhelmed him. He allowed the pain to settle, then tried again to look around himself, this time with success. Slowly, he turned his head toward the light. A single tallow candle burned on the bedside table, and in the chair beside it sat the man who had been more a father to him than his own. "You'd better not be here for my soul, Reaper, because I'm not done with it yet."

"Alan," Brother Kenneth's big voice boomed in the small chamber. "You're awake."

Alan squeezed his eyes shut again, trying to still the chaos in his head. "Not so loud."

"I see surviving a close brush with death hasn't changed you at all," came a second voice.

"Simon?" A wave of relief washed over Alan. He drew a stuttering breath. So he hadn't left all his men behind to die. His chest tightened with gratitude. Simon had lived through the battle at Teba? Alan opened his eyes again and pushed himself up on his elbows regardless of the pain. He had to see Simon for himself and make certain his ears weren't playing tricks on him. He tried to sit up.

"Easy." Brother Simon came forward to sit on the edge of his cot. "We just patched your wounds. You need to go slowly."

"Simon." Alan reached out and touched his brother's

shoulder in the way they'd always greeted each other. "You're alive."

Simon's face turned serious. "William, you, me and Brianna." Simon shook his head, deep in thought. "She fooled us all with her disguise. Looking back now, she wasn't very convincing as a Templar, but *by the saints*, that woman could fight."

"Four blessings out of the horror we endured," Alan said, his voice as taut as his emotions.

"'Tis another blessing you survived today. Now lie back and let yourself heal," Brother Kenneth said.

"I can't," Alan said as he tried to swing his leg over the side of the bed. "Jessamine needs me."

"Ah, yes, Jessamine." Brother Kenneth leaned back in his chair and smiled. "You talked about her several times when we took you to the healing baths."

"Whatever it is I said, do not believe me." He looked at both men in turn, hoping he'd said nothing that would cast Jessamine in a negative light.

Brother Kenneth nodded, but Simon smiled. "I couldn't believe you didn't wake up when we soaked you in the cool bath. It was in the warm bath that you started talking."

Brother Kenneth batted at Simon. "You said nothing much. You merely spoke her name a few times. Who is she to you?"

"The woman I've asked to marry me. Twice."

Brother Kenneth raised an eyebrow. "We need to talk about what happened, Alan. How did you come to us in such a—" He paused.

"Who nearly killed you?" Simon interrupted.

"Spanish soldiers. Jessamine is a Spanish and Moorish princess." The words rolled off Alan's tongue easily, but the knowledge still brought a stab of pain to his chest.

"A princess?" Brother Simon frowned.

Alan continued. "Her bridegroom followed her here. He sprang a trap on us when we docked at Dundee and took not only Jessamine but the Ark of the Covenant."

Both men turned pale.

"The ark?" Kenneth breathed. "The real Ark of the Covenant?"

"Aye. Robert the Bruce bade me take on an additional task on the way to the Holy Land. He asked that I use the Templar letters left to us by William of Tyre to find the ark. He wanted it stored away with the Templar treasure so that no one country would be able to use it against any other."

"And the Spanish have it?" Brother Kenneth's voice was grave.

"The Conde Salazar Mendoza, to be more specific," Alan acknowledged, reaching for his satchel near the bed. He dipped his hand inside, then stretched out his fist to the other men and opened his fingers. "But the conde doesn't have these." He revealed eleven raw stones and one that he'd had set in Jaffa into a band of gold. The twelve stones of fire. "These stones are the power behind the ark. Only when the ark and the stones are wielded together does the ark manifest all its divine power."

"You're certain of this?" the abbot asked in a harsh whisper.

"Aye."

Brother Kenneth released a ragged sigh, but Simon's face grew dark. "This is not good news. One enemy on our shores was bad enough."

Alan placed the stones back in his satchel. "What is it? What's happened?"

"The French, led by Pierre de la Roche, attacked while you were away. The man was determined to rid this earth of every Templar. He burned many at the stake and slew many others."

Alan's jaw clenched. "He burned our brothers?"

Simon nodded. "And stole our treasure for his own evil purposes. The temptation of the ark might be the very thing that will bring him out of hiding."

"Nay, the man is dead," Kenneth said emphatically.

"We never found a body." Brother Simon visibly shuddered. "Does evil like that ever die?"

"Yes, Simon, it does." Kenneth crossed his arms over his chest.

"We must continue the battle. I need men, as many as you can spare," Alan said.

Kenneth and Simon shared a glance that Alan didn't understand. "Are there any men left?" Alan asked.

Simon dropped his gaze to the floor before he glanced back at Alan. "Our numbers are few. Here at the monastery there are only myself and three others who are ready to fight."

"Nay." Alan went still. "It would be like Teba all over again." He fisted his hands. "I cannot, will not do that to any of the men." He struggled to his feet. "I'll go alone."

Simon stood beside him and placed a hand on his shoulder. "You're not alone, Alan. You've returned to the fold. We took our oaths together. We stand together. Until the task is accomplished."

Alan forced a smile. "Our end could be in death."

Simon hesitated, then slowly nodded. "We've always known that risk. We'll leave on the morrow for Duna-guel Abbey. Kaden Buchanan resides there. He is young, but he and his men are ready to battle for such a cause."

"We leave tonight." Alan reached for his belt and sword.

Brother Kenneth stalled his movements with his hand. "Tonight you rest. You'll do Jessamine no good in your current condition. Let the healing waters work their holy magic. You'll be fit for battle again by first light."

Alan knew Brother Kenneth was right. He could feel weariness creep into the core of his being, but he stiffened, and reached for his belt anyway. "Jessamine needs me."

With a sigh, Brother Kenneth headed for the door. "Give me an hour at least to prepare food and horses."

Alan nodded. "Thank you, Reaper. I could always count on you."

"You always can," Brother Kenneth said before vanishing down the hallway.

Simon stood in the doorway. "I'll go prepare, and send word to William Keith that you're alive and well and in need of his help."

"Thank you, Simon. I'll be waiting in the courtyard."

Outside, Alan stared at the sky. Moonlight filtered through the trees and cast a thousand shards of white light upon the ground. A splash of blue invaded the white for a brief moment, followed by a rustling sound in the bushes beyond.

Alan drew his sword. "Who's there? Show yourself."

Will hobbled through the shrubs and hurried forward. "Sir Alan, I am so pleased to have found you."

The old man swayed on his feet. Alan reached out to grasp him, but Will steadied himself against a rock large enough to serve as a chair.

"How did you find me?"

"When you did not head to Trophichen Preceptory, I knew I'd find you here."

"What of Jessamine? You've seen her?" Alan knew he sounded frantic, but he didn't care.

The old man nodded. "I followed the conde and secreted myself in the wagon they used to transport the ark and Jessamine."

"Where are they? You must tell me."

"When I left them, they were headed for Marykirk."

"How long ago?"

"Half a day."

Alan nodded. "Or half a night. I must go to her at once."

The old man frowned. "Shouldn't you gather reinforcements first?"

"Jessamine needs me."

"You'll be no good to her without others to occupy the Spanish troops. Besides, the ark is taking care of Jessamine. Trust that it will continue to do so."

Alan stared at him. "Explain yourself."

Will coughed, then coughed again, the sound grating and harsh. "This old man needs some water, or better yet a mug of nice ale." He hobbled toward the monastery. "Been a while since I've wet my whistle." He fairly skipped inside the monastery doors and was gone.

As though Alan didn't already have enough to occupy his mind. How was the ark supposed to help Jessamine?

Chapter Twenty-three

The next morning, the conde escorted Jessamine from her chamber back to the wagon. When she hesitated, he lifted her in and set her down, none too gently, next to the ark.

"You'll not escape your fate today, Princess. We'll make that church by nightfall, so prepare yourself for a night of wedded bliss . . . with me."

Fear and revulsion tightened her chest as Jessamine shifted her gaze from the conde to the ark. He wanted her fear, and she refused to let him see how it filled her.

He left her with a biting laugh and mounted his waiting horse. His men gathered around him, ready to follow wherever he led them. Jessamine frowned. What spoils had the conde promised these men in order to gain their unfailing support? Her uncle's document of marriage would not obligate them to obey his orders. There had to be something else.

If she figured out what it was, perhaps she could offer them something more to change their allegiance.

Jessamine's hand moved to her chest, to the locket she kept hidden within the bodice of her gown. It was all she had left, and too precious to part with, even for her freedom. She had to think of some other inducement.

The ark was the only other thing of value that she had access to. But it was far too dangerous to barter with. Yet she couldn't help wondering if that was what the conde had done.

She studied the ark as the wagon lurched forward. The gold seemed brighter today despite the gray skies overhead. She reached out and with one finger hesitantly traced the ornate scrollwork surrounding the base. The gold warmed to her touch. A sensation of peace moved through her, and she turned her gaze to the landscape.

The wind swayed the tops of the rowan trees. And a purple gloom suddenly replaced the leaden skies of just a few moments ago. Jessamine knew an imminent storm when she saw one.

She raised her face to the sky and experienced a tiny thrill. Had the ark heard her prayers a second time? The cool breeze lifted her hair from her face, and she could smell the heady scent of rain, grass, and rich earth.

"You look pleased." The conde interrupted her thoughts. She turned her head to find him riding alongside the wagon. He glared at her.

"Another storm is coming. It's wonderful," she replied. Any moment the sky would split wide open and the rain would flood the roads, the hills, the rivers.

"I'd blame you for the weather if I didn't know better."

She let his comments roll off her with a shiver of anticipation as he stared at the sky. It made her feel . . . powerful, and important. As though her own thoughts and wishes mattered enough for the divine forces of the world to help Alan and her.

That was the power of love.

She drew a soft breath. She did love him. He might present a hard exterior to the world, but he had also revealed to her a gentle, passionate side.

And the conde would destroy all hope of fulfilling her love if they reached that church. Her emotions turned somber as she searched the sky once more. The rain began to fall, at first sporadically, then in huge drops.

The conde growled. "Turn back, men. We'll have to wait it out."

At that moment the heavens opened up. Rain poured down with stunning force. He kicked his horse into a gallop and sped back to the inn.

Jessamine simply tipped her head back and let the water bathe her face. A smile came to her lips. She was safe from marriage for one more day.

Inside the inn once more, Jessamine stood by the hearth in the dining room and squeezed the water from her hair. The warmth of the flames dried her skin, but her clothes were soaked through. She didn't care. The inconvenience seemed inconsequential, considering what she'd managed to avoid today. She settled into a chair before the fire and listened to the pounding raindrops hit the roof above her.

"Wipe that smile off your face." The conde gripped her arm and pulled her from the chair. It fell back against the wooden floorboards with a thud. "Come with me." He gave her no choice, dragging her from the room and up the stairs.

He jerked her into the open doorway of her room and thrust her inside. He strode after her and closed the door behind him.

She stood absolutely still at the realization that the rain had not saved her at all.

"Take off your clothes."

"What?" The word she feared most from the prophecy flitted through her mind. *Sacrifice.* Jessamine stiffened. No. She would not accept that fate. If her experience in the desert had taught her anything, it was that she controlled her destiny.

The conde unbuttoned his black tunic. "You heard me. Take your clothes off or I'll rip them from you."

"But the church, the marriage." She forced the words past a suddenly dry throat.

"I've decided not to wait. You will accommodate me. Now."

Her mind reeled as she searched for a way out. The ark had been returned to the corner of the chamber. Was there any way out this time?

"Your clothes!" he bit out as he draped his wet tunic near the fire he had demanded the innkeeper set on their arrival.

She started to unlace her gown, slowly and with trembling fingers. "Might I dry the gown by the fire?" she asked when she slipped the garment down around her feet.

At his sharp nod, she pulled a chair near the flames and hung her dress over the arms. As she bent to arrange the hem around the base of the chair, her locket escaped from the safety of her chemise. She gripped it in her palm and continued fluffing her skirt, hoping the conde hadn't noticed.

The locket. Her breath quickened as she remembered its hidden contents. The Bedouin herbs would help her if she could find some way for the conde to consume them.

She straightened and turned to face him. "Would you please call for some wine?"

He frowned. "You're stalling."

She nodded. "I'm nervous. I had hoped wine would help to ease my fears."

His face darkened and he clenched his fists. "I will indulge you this one time." Without replacing his tunic, he left the room to return a few moments later with a flask of red wine and two wooden cups. He set them on the small table near the door and moved to pour the liquid out, but she went to his side and placed a hand over his. "Allow me."

His eyes narrowed with suspicion.

"Will it not be my role once we are married?" she said sweetly, offering him her most innocent smile.

He straightened. "Very well. Serve me." He retreated to the bed and sat on the edge.

She turned her back to him and furtively opened the locket, then poured the powdered herbs into his cup before she filled it with wine. The powder frothed, and for a moment she feared discovery, until the froth settled and vanished, leaving only a rich clear liquid behind. She took the cup to him. "For you," she said in her most humble voice.

He accepted the cup and took a long drink, then nodded. "Pour for yourself and come join me." He took another long drink. "I've decided this little ploy of yours will work to my advantage."

Her heart stopped. "Why?"

He gave her a cruel, twisted smile. "Anticipation is hardening me even now. Look at me there." His gaze dropped to his groin.

She shivered. How long did the herbs take to work? The Bedouin woman had not told her that. She steeled herself and dropped her gaze to the bulge in his breeches. "Yes, I see."

He laughed. "Yes, my princess, you'll see all its wonder very soon."

She took a deep sip of her own cup.

He patted the coverlet beneath him. "Remove your chemise and sit by me. I wish to see you naked."

She swallowed. Her fingers drifted to the neckline of her chemise. She had reluctantly tugged the bodice down when the conde's cup fell from his hand. It hit the floor with a thump that drew her eager gaze.

She watched as the conde's eyelids fluttered closed and he slumped backward onto the bed.

Sweet relief surged through her. The herbs had worked!

She pulled her gown from the chair by the hearth and tossed it over her head. She fastened the damp garment quickly, then headed for the door.

While he slept, she would find freedom. She grasped the door latch and tried to push it down. It wouldn't move. Her heart thundered in her chest. He'd locked them in.

Hesitantly, she approached his body and with a light touch, searched his clothing for the key. Had he arranged for someone to lock the door from the outside? When she found nothing, she moved to the window. She had to escape. She threw the latch and opened it wide. The rain pummeled her hand, her head. The weather was no deterrent, but the four soldiers stationed below the window were. She released a cry of despair and shut the window.

Her legs went weak and she sank to the floor beside the ark. She was trapped in this room with that horrible man until the herbs wore off. Staring at his reclining figure, she hoped he wouldn't wake at least until the next morning.

Surrounded by the sound of the falling rain, she settled herself against the ark. She had no choice but to wait and search for another opportunity to leave the man far behind. She stared at the ever-changing brilliance of the leaping flames in the fire and breathed a sigh of relief. She'd eluded the conde for one more day, and it was probably the last opportunity she'd get. For when he awoke, he would make her pay for what she'd done.

Jessamine pulled her knees to her chest. Until then, she had made her own reprieve, and she intended to enjoy it. She closed her eyes and imagined the scent of the rain mixed with the familiar aroma of musk and sandalwood.

She pulled her knees tighter against her chest. No matter what the conde forced upon her tomorrow, it would be Alan whom she thought of, Alan whose touch she'd feel.

Alan turned his face to the sky and let the Scottish downpour cleanse him. He hadn't realized how much he'd missed the rain until now. After experiencing the heat and dryness of the desert, he would never again take the rain for granted. Especially this day, when he knew the weather would turn the roads into a treacherous mess no wagon would be able to navigate. The respite gave him time to gather more men.

Simon, Bernard, Will, two younger knights, and he had left the monastery while the world had been steeped in darkness. Morning was now fully upon them as the gray stone walls of Dunaguel Abbey came into view.

Help was within sight. As the frigid morning air wrapped itself around them, Alan spurred his horse into a gallop. The men followed right behind him. When they reached the gates, a monk in a brown robe with the hood drawn over his head came out to greet them. His hand moved beneath the fold in his robe. "How may we be of service to you?"

Alan's gaze narrowed. His hand drifted to his sword as he dismounted. "We need to speak to Kaden Buchanan. It's a matter of urgency."

The monk's hand relaxed. He brought his other hand

to his hood and pulled it back to reveal his face. A young man stood before them. "I'm Kaden Buchanan. State your purpose."

"Brother Kenneth sent us to you. He said you could help us gather an army."

"For what purpose?" His dark eyes remained wary.

Alan knew the time for truth was upon him. "To retrieve the Ark of the Covenant from a group of Spaniards. And rescue a princess they are holding against her will."

Kaden's eyes brightened, and a hearty laugh escaped him. When Alan didn't join his laughter, he sobered. "You speak truth?"

"By God, only truth."

Kaden frowned. "How did the Ark of the Covenant come to be in Scotland?"

"That's a long tale." Alan could feel his frustration rising. "Will you help us or not?"

"I'll give you all the forces you need." Kaden's gaze narrowed. "But you must promise me something in return."

"What?"

"That after we find the ark, we will use it to annihilate the French who remain in this country, threatening our lives and those of our Templar brothers."

Alan frowned. "To use the ark is dangerous."

"Not using it could be more so. Have you not seen what they've done to our brothers?" Kaden's voice was raw. "They've burned them alive."

"Do we do the same thing to them in return?"

"It would be justice."

"That's not justice. That's revenge." Alan frowned. "As Templars we must rise above the desire for vengeance. As Scots, we must show the French, the Spanish, or whoever comes to invade our shores, that we need no 'divine assistance.' That we, as men, will protect what's ours without undue cruelty, leaving punishment in God's hands."

Kaden's mouth tightened, but he nodded. "The code."

"We all live the code from the moment we take our vows." Alan paused. "So the question becomes, will you help us? Or shall we continue on our way?"

"The Templar in me cannot refuse you. I'll help." He stepped back and waved them through the gates. "Come in. We can gather the men and be on our way in short order."

Alan held back to wait for the others to proceed, then stopped before Kaden. He reached out and clasped the man's forearm. Kaden returned the familiar Templar greeting. "Thank you, my brother."

"You can thank me when we have your ark and your princess back." Kaden straightened and his eyes filled with determination.

"Until then," Alan said gratefully. *Hold tight, Jessamine*, he whispered in his thoughts.

Hold tight.

Chapter Twenty-four

The conde slowly opened his eyes and turned his head to focus on Jessamine, who was sitting on the floor next to the ark. "I should kill you for that little trick," he groaned and pressed a hand to his forehead.

Jessamine hastened to her feet. "Then do it now and spare us both the agony of what is to come." She placed her fingertips on the edge of the ark, needing the reassurance the artifact brought her.

The conde raised himself on one elbow and glared at her. "Just what agony would I be spared?"

"That of Alan Cathcart's blade slicing through your chest when he finds you."

The conde swung his feet to the floor with a ragged laugh. "He'll never find me in time." His gaze met hers. "It would give me such pleasure to punish you here and now," he said, his words slightly slurred. He gripped his middle as though in pain. "But the better punishment would be to marry you, then wring from you all the pleasure I can before I slay that bastard. Your death will not come so easily, my sweet. It will be slow and painful, like your mother's."

Jessamine forced herself not to react to the mention of her mother. "Kill me slow or fast, it matters not to me."

His face turned red. "You mock me?" The conde stood and took a tottering step toward her. "You'll pay for your insolence, Princess." He made his way toward her slowly.

Jessamine searched the chamber for somewhere to dart. There was nowhere to go. She already knew that, and still her instinct was to find a way to escape. She flinched as his fingers clamped around her arm and he pulled her away from the ark. "Come with me."

He moved to the door, and at his command, it was opened. "Get the ark and follow us down," he said to one of his men as he yanked her down the stairs and out into the inn yard.

Outside, Jessamine was startled at the change in temperature as they left the inn. Then she realized the cause. Deep white snow covered the ground. Snow. She'd seen snow from far away before, but never this close. She tipped her head back, allowing the tiny ice crystals to drift onto her cheeks. She opened her mouth and caught a flake on her tongue. Magical.

Jessamine's spirits soared. The rain had shifted to snow, once again making the wagon impossible to use on the rutted roads. Could she be so lucky as to escape this marriage one more time due to the mysterious weather?

"Go help with the ark," the conde yelled to two of his men, who lingered near the door.

"We weren't certain . . . The snow . . . ," one of the men stammered as his face turned as pale as the ground around him.

"Get the ark." The words were more a threat than an order.

As the men scrambled to do his bidding, Jessamine felt nausea rise in her throat. "We aren't going to wait the weather out."

"No!" The conde's tone was violent. "We'll walk the entire way if we must, but you and I will be married before the day is out." His dark eyes blazed. "If you ever put anything in my wine again, I'll cut you down where you stand."

Without waiting for a reply or an acknowledgment, he reached into the wagon and withdrew a length of rope. He pulled her hands together and bound them before he tied her to the railing of the wagon. "Don't forget, Princess, I'm the only one who can win our little game."

Jessamine suddenly shivered as the snowflakes fell all around her. Cold seeped through the thin fabric of her gown. She could feel lethargy attacking her body due to her lack of sleep. She straightened. She mustn't give in to her body's weakness or her fears.

She had to stay strong and in control of herself so she could take advantage of any opportunity to escape. With a groan, Jessamine tipped her head back and let the large snowflakes fall on her face and eyelashes.

The evening light began to fade from the sky as the conde and his men left the mountains behind. They had proceeded to the church on foot, carrying the ark along with them.

In the valley below, the peaked roofline of the church came into view. The conde pulled Jessamine along behind him as he trekked through knee-deep snow toward the church. As he pulled her forward, Jessamine dug her feet into the snow and tugged against him, resisting her fate.

With a roar of rage, he jerked her toward his body, then tossed her over his shoulder. She kicked and writhed until she knocked him off balance, sending them both into the snow with a thud. His hand snaked out and cracked against her cheek so hard, her head recoiled and hit the snowy ground. Abruptly, she grew still.

"That's better," the conde growled as he gained his

feet and tossed her limp body over his shoulder. He
continued toward the church.

The moment he'd long awaited was almost upon him.
With his marriage to Jessamine, and with the power of
the ark on his side, he'd be unstoppable. The sweet taste
of victory sat on his tongue now. Sweet as honey. And
now that he'd had a sample of what was to come, he
wanted more. He was no longer content with just rul-
ing Spain. He wanted an empire.

He had the Ark of the Covenant. With it he could
annihilate all who opposed him. Nothing would stop
him now.

As Alan surveyed the scene, he thought he detected a
smile on the conde's cruel and twisted lips before he
turned to enter the church with Jessamine. Alan dug
his heels into his horse's sides, encouraging the beast to
a faster pace.

The air grew still. That feeling of stillness before a
battle had always indicated danger before. Despite the
warning, Alan forged ahead, scanning the snow-covered
scenery before him. Tall, tumbled boulders lined the
path, as did a chest-high wild hedgerow, tall enough to
conceal a man, or many men, at the bottom of the incline.

He could be riding into a massacre, just like Teba.

He slowed his horse, forcing the men behind him to
do the same. 'Twas time to plan their attack.

Simon rode up beside him. "I see flashes of steel re-
flecting in the light of the setting sun from the bushes
near the church."

"Aye, 'tis what I sensed. They are waiting for us,"
Alan remarked with dire seriousness.

"Who?"

"The Spanish, no doubt."

Simon's hand moved to his sword. His gaze encompassed the men riding in tight formation behind Alan. "We are ready for them. You and I both learned from Teba," he said, as though he'd read Alan's thoughts.

Alan scanned the thirty men behind him, his own brothers and Kaden's men, all dressed once more in their Templar tunics. A moment of pride filled Alan's chest. They might be disbanded, but their warrior spirits would never fade. "This time we will remain together, all of us, as a unit," Alan said forcefully.

Simon nodded, as did the others behind him. "We stay together," they repeated.

Alan shifted his gaze to the church in the distance. "Then we are ready."

Simon nodded. "Until the end."

Alan drew his weapon. He sent a shrill whistle into the air and signaled for the men to follow. Every instinct was tuned to the battle ahead. Forcing his mind to remain calm, he ducked low over his horse and charged toward the church.

"Wake up," the conde's voice was soothing, but his hands on her shoulders were not. He shook her over and over, rattling her teeth until she forced her eyelids open just to make him stop.

The conde gazed down at her. "Good, you're awake. I was afraid I might have done some serious damage." He offered her a malevolent smile. "Can't have that . . . yet. The Spanish crown is just the start of what you and I will do together." He bent down and effortlessly lifted her to her tingling feet. "The priest is waiting."

The chill that had invaded her body made it hard to think or move. She swayed on her feet, then caught herself as she took in her surroundings. The church. They'd made it to the church.

When she hesitated, the conde gripped her arm and pulled her with him toward the priest waiting at the altar.

The ceremony passed in a blur. Jessamine stared straight ahead at the ornate gold designs on the sides of the Ark of the Covenant, which had been placed before them. As the dizziness and cold started to fade, she suddenly recalled the conde's words. *The Spanish crown is just the start of what you and I will do together.* She tensed. He had something even bigger planned than marrying her and taking over the Spanish crown.

She tugged at the binding that rendered her hands useless. She cast a quick glance behind her, only to see men with swords waiting by the church doors. There was no escape this time.

Jessamine did the only thing she could. She closed her eyes and prayed for deliverance for her uncle and his family, if not for herself. When she opened her eyes a moment later, it was to see the priest mounting the three steps to the high altar.

The conde grasped her hand in what might look like an affectionate squeeze to some, but was actually a brutal clench. He was dressed in black, as always. Today he looked more like Lucifer than he ever had before.

The Spaniard would soon be her husband. She shuddered. In the deepest part of herself she'd hoped the church doors would open wide and Alan would appear to save her from this fate.

But the service was almost over, and he hadn't come.

She swallowed against the raw ache in her throat and looked down at the green gown she wore. The hem was wet and dirty from the rain and the snow. Her only bridal touch was a lacy cloth covering her head that the conde had stolen from the bedside table in the inn.

She didn't look much like a bride. She didn't feel like

one either. This moment should be filled with joy and hope and love, not fear and revulsion.

As soon as the priest said the blessing over them, she would be expected to obey her husband and offer her body when he so desired.

She drew a shaky breath as the priest made his way back to them, his face solemn as he continued to say the words of the ritual.

"Kneel."

It was almost over. Any moment now, she would be bound to the conde for life. When she didn't kneel, the conde jerked her down. Her knees hit the stone floor and she bit her lip to keep from crying out.

The priest's voice droned on.

Alan hadn't come for her.

A single tear spilled over her lashes and onto her cheek.

She was another man's wife.

Chapter Twenty-five

As the first wave of Templars approached the snow-covered hedgerow, the Spanish troops erupted bearing swords, halberds, and pikes. The sound of steel on steel filled the evening air.

More Spaniards emerged, scores of them wearing breastplates and helms. Alan might have spent the past year away from Scotland, but he hadn't forgotten Scottish ways. His throat vibrated with the roar of a battle cry, which was picked up by the others. All over the hillside the call of war echoed from his men as they, too, surged forward.

The odds were more in their favor this time than they had been at Teba. Following Alan's plan, the first ten Templars charged together in a tight formation. Their strike of mounted warriors was as effective as always. Several of the Spaniards soon lay either dead or dying beneath the frenzy of panicked horses' hooves.

A second wave of Templars charged forward, with Kaden leading his men. The young Templar had added a new strategy to the usual Templar battle fare: five archers with longbows, who released a volley of wickedly barbed arrows. The arrows streamed over the heads of the Templars and into the bodies of the Spanish, adding to the carnage of writhing bodies and screaming horses.

Seeing an opening through the Spanish, Alan charged forward anew, intent on reaching the door of the church.

His men rode beside him, providing cover for him as he made his way to Jessamine.

While he kicked his horse toward the breach, the sound of bagpipes filled the air. He let the sound bolster him as his mind drifted to the smell of heather after a soft Scottish rain, the prickle of thistle as he ran through the open fields, the tang of pine and fir, the soft lilting sound of Gaelic—all memories, all things he wished to share with Jessamine.

He used those memories to fuel his spirit, calm his heartbeat, and focus his thoughts. He would reach his woman before the conde married her. He had to.

A Spanish horse and rider leaped toward Alan and his mount, bringing Alan's thoughts back to the battle. Acting on instinct rather than thought, Alan swung his sword and dispatched the man with a whistling sound. Another man on horseback fell into the place of the first.

Once more, Alan's blade came down, slashing the man's throat. He tumbled to the ground. Alan guided his horse out of harm's way as another man struck at him from the left. Alan's blade cleanly severed the man's arm at the elbow. The man's sword, with his hand still attached to it, tumbled to the ground.

With the way clear, Alan dismounted and surged toward the closed church doors. He nearly made it to the doors before two more men charged from the side, swords slashing violently at his arms and chest. Alan whirled and lunged, avoiding their blows. He readied himself for another attack, but Simon and Bernard were there, clearing the way.

Alan forced the huge wooden doors open. A thunderous boom reverberated through the church as the doors hit the stone walls.

"Halt!" Alan rushed with his sword drawn toward the spot where Jessamine stood at the altar.

The conde twisted around and Alan could see Jessamine's bound hands gripped cruelly in the Spaniard's grasp. "You're too late. We are married."

Alan drew a sharp breath. Then Jessamine's gaze met his. Her dark eyes were filled with emotion both rich and deep. He could see the truth of the conde's words written there, but he saw something else as well. Something precious, something beautiful, something even marriage could not take away from them.

He saw love.

Alan's chest tightened with pain and exhilaration. For a moment the sensations knocked him off kilter.

"Kill him!" The conde's angry voice brought Alan back to the moment. The Spaniards surged forward from the front and sides of the nave, their swords drawn.

Alan had nowhere to go but back. Yet he held his ground. This battle would not end the way it had on the docks of Dundee. Alan's hand tightened around the hilt of his sword, feeling the grooves of the intricate detailing fit themselves to the calluses of his palm. There were things worth fighting for, and dying for. All a man could do was choose his causes carefully, then follow the path of his heart.

And his heart and life were dedicated to protecting Jessamine. She deserved the freedom to choose her own destiny, not have it thrust upon her because of the station to which she was born.

Alan drew in a breath and held it, centering himself and his emotions. He exhaled, breathing out the turmoil that coiled within him.

He charged forward. Alan struck two of the conde's men dead without so much as a break in his stride. In that moment, the conde's eyes filled with doubt and fear. Simon and Kaden appeared at the doorway of the church and fought their way inside. Alan's spirits soared. Their presence inside the church could only mean the Templars had control of the courtyard. Alan strode forward, but the Spaniards turned and fled past him, out the door of the church. Simon and Kaden followed. Alan set his jaw as he continued forward toward the conde and Jessamine. These men would not fight to avenge a leader who cared nothing for them.

The conde howled his disgust; then his dark eyes brightened as a new complication, dressed all in black, stepped from the shadows. Four assassins, the same assassins who'd attacked in the desert, sprang forward. Deadly hooked blades glinted in the glow of the candlelight. Silently they surged forward, like snakes toward their prey.

Alan kept his thoughts focused and his body loose, avoiding their blows again and again.

"We will leave you in peace if you give us back the ark and never come for it again," one of the assassins said as he brought his blade down toward Alan's chest.

Alan easily deflected the blow. He caught the hook of the man's sword and sent it flying. "The ark needs protection from men such as the conde, who will only use it for evil purposes. The Templars can provide that protection."

"We can care for the ark," the man said as they circled each other.

Alan's gaze narrowed. "The ark is not safe in the Holy Land. There is too much strife among the people who live there. The area has known little peace. In that environment, the dangers are many. The Templars offer a solution."

The Arab assassin sent out a warbling call as he held up his hand. The fighting ceased. "Why should we trust you and your kind to keep it safe?"

Alan brought his sword hand with his weapon back

to settle over his heart, over the Templar cross of fiery red that blazed there. "Because we are men of God, both you and I, and we want the same thing. To preserve and protect."

The Arab's eyebrows came together and he nodded his understanding. "And if in the future we find some way to keep the ark safe in the Holy Land?"

Alan paused for a long moment, then set his sword on the ground. He unfastened his scabbard and let it fall, then drew his tunic over his head to reveal the mail beneath. He extended the tunic to the Arab. "Take this. When and if the time ever comes, bring this back and return it to one of us. We'll know what it signifies and we will return the ark to you for safekeeping."

For a long moment, the two men's eyes locked, each understanding what the other did not say. Then the Arab accepted the tunic and signaled his men to follow him out of the church, leaving Alan behind.

Alan stood alone in the aisle of the church and once again fixed his gaze on the conde.

"You've lost her," the man growled when he realized there were no more distractions. "Leave us, now."

"Never."

With a growl, the conde shoved Jessamine backward into the ark, snatched his sword from its scabbard, and leaped forward.

Alan charged. Their blades came together with a thunderous crash that sent the priest scurrying behind the high altar, leaving Jessamine alone.

The conde lunged, Alan deflected his blade, and the momentum of their thrusts carried each man past the other, sending Alan to Jessamine's side. He quickly cut through the bindings that held her captive a moment before he thrust at the conde.

The conde spun away.

Alan turned back to Jessamine. "Are you hurt?"

She rubbed her abused wrists. "Just married."

"We'll deal with that soon enough. Stay back."

The conde lunged at them both, his sword held high. He slashed down. Alan blocked with his sword and pulled Jessamine away moments before the conde swung again. His blade sliced through empty space, then struck the lid of the ark instead.

Alan sprang forward, his sword at the ready. But out of the corner of his eye he saw Jessamine clamp a hand to her mouth. Her eyes went wide as she stared at the ark. A swirl of blue light formed between the two angels' wings. Alan blocked out the sight, focusing on the conde.

"You've lost her," the conde said with a snarl, leaping forward with a savage thrust. Alan was forced to leap sideways, away from Jessamine. He recovered in a heartbeat, but in that split second, the conde grasped Jessamine and drew her back against his chest, using her as a shield.

"You wanted me. Come get me. But you'll have to go through her." The conde raised his sword to Jessamine's throat.

Icy fingers gripped Alan's spine. "This is between you and me. Let her go."

"Jessamine is my wife. My property." He stepped back, pulling her with him down the three steps of the altar.

Alan froze. He couldn't attack the conde with his sword, not with Jessamine's life at stake. He could, however, use his words to cut the man down. "There is nowhere for you to go." He took a step forward, waiting for the conde's reaction.

The muscles of the Spaniard's arm flexed as he tightened the grip on his sword. Jessamine swallowed visibly as the sword brushed against her skin.

Alan took another step down. "Your men have deserted you. Those Spaniards fighting in the churchyard aren't faring well beneath Templar swords." He took the final step down so that the two of them stood on equal ground. "They might have abandoned you too."

The conde's cheeks flushed red. "No one abandons the Conde Salazar Mendoza and lives. My mother's dead body is proof of that." At the admission, his eyes widened, then narrowed. "Damn you, Templar!"

The conde spun Jessamine around to face him. He gripped her throat with his free hand. She coughed and sputtered and brought her hands up, trying to free herself from his grasp.

Alan took two steps forward, but the conde tightened his grip on her throat.

"Marrying you was the one thing Mother told me I'd never be able to achieve," he told Jessamine. "I wanted to bring you home to show her withered body that she was wrong. I'm your husband, your lord and master. I'll take the crown of Spain in your name, even when you're dead, and I'll conquer the world with the help of the ark."

Alan could see the blood drain from Jessamine's face. The hands that fought the conde's turned limp. Her lips turned blue.

Alan ran toward her. The conde's gaze met Alan's. An odd smile twisted his face as he raised his sword, pointing it at Jessamine's chest.

A cry began in the pit of Alan's stomach. The war cry of his clan erupted from him, the sound as untamed as the hills that gave it birth. The conde's fingers tightened.

The pitch of Alan's cry heightened as he lunged forward, taking the conde with him. Jessamine crumpled to the ground and gasped for air.

It was the most wonderful sound Alan had ever heard.

The Spaniard scrambled to his feet, and the two of them circled each other, each taking measure of the other. "Are you ready to die, Templar? For that is your destiny, just as mine is to conquer and rule over all. Do you see the ark? It's preparing to strike you down, destroy you as it did the city of Jericho and Aaron's sons. Its raw power will annihilate you!"

"What makes you so certain of that?" Alan asked.

The conde sneered. "I possess the ark. It is my tool."

Even with his back to the ark, Alan could see what was happening. The conde's dark eyes reflected the swirling blue light.

Suddenly the man lunged. Alan parried and spun to the right. The conde brought his sword around in a sideways sweep, but Alan was ready, his sword stopping the blade's slice. As their swords collided, Alan kicked, catching the would-be usurper in the stomach and sending him staggering backward.

The conde kept his feet and grinned. "You are no match for me."

Alan kept his focus on the Spaniard, watching for signs of attack. When the conde's shoulder dropped ever so slightly to deliver an upward cut, Alan parried and spun. Primed to strike, Alan's sword cut deeply into the Spaniard's arm.

He heard the conde's gasp of pain. The man's grin was gone. His face twisted into a mask of hate. The Spaniard's blade arched toward Alan in a disemboweling sweep. The blood grooves on the blade whistled their deadly melody, but Alan ducked and let the blade slide through the space his body had just left.

Alan faced the conde. The two of them circled each other once more. The light in the church shifted from gold to blue, and ripples of light and darkness seemed to surround them.

The Spaniard's sword swung wide, and with the motion came the opening Alan had waited for. He spun inside and drove his elbow into the man's face as his razor-sharp sword sliced the conde's thigh. The conde screamed in agony, his legs buckled, and he hit the floor with his knees.

Alan's blade whipped to the Spaniard's neck. "If I let you live, will you take your army and go—leave this land and Jessamine in peace?"

"No," the conde growled. "I'll live. The ark will see to that. Once you're dead, this land and Jessamine will be mine."

Before Alan could finish his strike, a mist as thick and white as a winter's night crept through and around his legs to encompass the conde's body. When the mist became fire, Alan surged backward. He swooped Jessamine's body in his arms and carried her to the altar next to the ark. The blue light swirled and ebbed as the flames rippled across the conde's flesh. He screamed a terrible scream.

In that moment, Simon and Kaden charged through the church doorway, but they halted almost as suddenly as they'd entered, no doubt startled by the glowing blue light.

A flash of light as bright as lightning from the sky pulsed through the room. Alan closed his eyes against the unearthly brightness and shielded Jessamine's face with his chest. A prickle of heat touched his flesh, burning with an unstoppable wave of pain. Alan ground his teeth against the sensation and curled himself around Jessamine's body. "Take me, if you must," he said to the unnatural force. "But leave her here to find the peace she has searched for."

Suddenly, the light softened. The pain vanished, replaced by a delicate caress that filled his body with an overwhelming sense of peace and tranquility as soft and gentle as an early spring rain. As quickly as it had come, the bright light vanished, along with the swirling blue light above the ark.

Dizzying relief poured through Alan. He bowed his head to the ark. He didn't understand what had just happened, and he didn't need to. He was just grateful to whatever divine force had protected the woman he loved. The thought made his breath catch. He did love her. Alan's hands trembled as he brushed the hair away from Jessamine's face.

She opened her eyes and looked up at him. Her eyes were so serene, so filled with love. She raised a hand to his face. "You came for me."

"Always." He helped her sit up but couldn't stop the frown that came to his lips when he saw the purple bruise against the velvet skin of her neck.

"I'll heal," she said softly. "I'm more resilient than you think."

"You are a constant surprise." He leaned forward and kissed her forehead.

Jessamine clutched his hand as her gaze shifted to what remained of the conde's body. A pile of ashes lay atop a scorched mark on the stone floor. "He's really dead?"

"He's gone from this world." Alan's gaze moved to the open church doors. He nodded to Simon and Kaden that all was well. With a nod, they turned and strode back into the churchyard.

Alan smiled down at Jessamine. "It appears the Spaniards are gone, as are the Arabs. That just leaves you and me and the Templars."

"Then I'm no longer married?" Jessamine's voice was

a whisper. A slow smile came to her lips as she turned toward the ark. "I have been given everything I asked for in the presence of the ark, except for one thing."

"What is that?" he asked cautiously.

"You."

His heart swelled.

"You asked me twice before to marry you and I refused. Now I am asking you. Sir Alan Cathcart, would you marry me here and now? Not because you feel it is your duty, but because you cannot live without the love we share."

"You are the very air I breathe." He brought her fingers to his lips and kissed each one slowly. "I'm willing to risk everything for you. You're certain that's what you want? We'll be living with the charge of treason for the rest of our lives."

"That's not what I want, but I'm no longer willing to live without you. Perhaps in time I can make my uncle understand."

His lips moved from her fingers to her wrist, then down the length of her arm.

Her eyes dilated and he could see passion flare in their depths. "You must stop that until the priest can marry us, because I fear that making love on yet another church altar might not endear us to the heavenly forces that have watched over us these past few weeks."

Alan's laugh mingled with Jessamine's. The sound filled the church, displacing fear and violence. "I accept, and I couldn't agree with you more."

Chapter Twenty-six

Once the fighting had ceased and the injured had been tended to, Alan and Jessamine prepared to take their vows. As Jessamine waited at the back of the church, a small orb of blue light appeared before her. It circled around her in a flitting, jubilant way completely unlike the angry, swirling blue that had appeared over the ark.

Jessamine extended her hand. The blue orb accepted her invitation and hovered over her palm, warming her skin but in no way burning her. She laughed as a slight tickling sensation moved up her arm and into her core. "Are you here to wish us well in our marriage?" she asked, not really expecting an answer from the playful light.

It spiraled up toward the ceiling, then over the heads of the Templars who crowded the small church. Their voices quieted as the light swirled through them, then shifted toward the spot where Alan and the priest stood waiting for her. With a burst of brightness, the orb passed right through the stained glass window high over the altar, bathing the church and those inside it in a rainbow of dancing colors. Blues and greens and reds and yellows sparkled on every surface. Jessamine gasped at the splendor of it all.

There was no music, but suddenly the tinkling of imagined bells filled Jessamine's head. She started down the aisle, passing through the Templars' arced swords toward Alan. He smiled at her, and she was suddenly filled with a sense of joy as radiant as the light streaming all around them. The radiance swept through her, lifting her up until she felt as though she were sparkling with the same brilliance.

This was the way it should feel when you married the man you loved.

The vows passed in a blur of joy, and when the blessing was complete, Alan took Jessamine into his arms. There was a raw, unveiled passion in his eyes that she'd never seen before—an almost animal intensity that stole her breath. His mouth slanted possessively over hers. He kissed her slowly, gently, and the combination set her soul and body afire.

A rousing cheer went up from the crowd, which hastened forward to congratulate them. Alan broke the kiss, but took her hand in his. When the congratulations died down, the men scooped Jessamine and Alan up, creating seats for them with their arms.

"We've a surprise for you." Simon grinned up at Alan and winked at Jessamine as the Templars escorted the two of them from the church to a tiny cottage just past the churchyard. "No marriage is complete without a wedding night." A shout of laughter broke out amongst the men as they ushered the two of them inside.

"It's beautiful!" Jessamine breathed as they set her on the polished wooden floor. They set Alan down beside her.

Golden light spilled through the one-room cottage, illuminating the only article of furniture—a lone bed with crisp white linens sprinkled with blooms of heather. A pitcher of ale along with a platter of cheese and bread sat on a small table near the bed.

"Our gift to you both," Simon said with a bow. "The men and I cleaned it quite thoroughly."

As they were gazing about the chamber, two Templars brought in the ark and set it beneath the shuttered window opposite the bed. Alan had requested that the ark remain with him and Jessamine until it could be taken to a safer location. After another round of hearty congratulations, the men left and shut the door behind them.

Jessamine went into Alan's arms as though she had done so a hundred times before. "Alone at last."

"I missed you." Alan smiled at her, a slightly wicked smile.

Jessamine could feel her heartbeat intensify just looking at him. It had been so long. Too long. "Then let's not wait. I must touch you."

"Soon." He reached out and slipped her gown, then her chemise, over her shoulders. The garments pooled at her feet, and something hot and intense flared in his gaze as it ran over her naked body.

She could feel her nipples tautening, her breasts swelling, as his gaze caressed her.

"Come with me." He took her hand and led her to the bed. He set her gently on the side, then stepped back and dipped his hand into his satchel for a brief moment before removing his belt and swords and setting them aside. "There is something I want to give you."

"Now?" she asked, her heart beating so hard she could feel it thunder in every part of her body.

He smiled. "All will be well. I promise."

"What is it?"

He began to unfasten his white linen shirt. He stripped it off and threw it aside. "Bear with me," he said. "This all has a purpose."

"With each article of clothing you remove I care less and less about your purpose and more about touching you."

He laughed, a throaty, pleasant sound, then tugged off his boots. They joined his shirt on the floor.

Her hands clenched the bedlinens beneath her. She drew a sharp breath. *Dios*, he was beautiful. The early-evening sunlight streaming into the chamber bathed him in a golden glow, gilding his face, the tough sinewy grace of his torso and shoulders. Her chest was so tight she was having difficulty breathing. She swallowed roughly as he removed his breeches to reveal his brawny thighs.

He stood before her, his stance wide, his buttocks tight, every muscle tense, his manhood boldly aroused.

"I need no other gift but you," she said hoarsely as the very air in the room seemed to vibrate with the same arousal she saw in him. She stood and moved toward him.

"Nay." He pushed her gently back on to the bed. "Once you touch me, I'll not be able to talk. I must do this now."

She nodded. She couldn't think. Her bones seemed to have no substance.

"You gave me the gift of hope and faith, and something I never expected to feel again—joy." His chest rose sharply. "After Teba, I was dead inside. And you changed all that. Our passion changed all that."

He lifted her hand and brought it to his chest, put it over his heart. She could feel a rapid beat beneath her palm. He placed his hand on hers.

"I give you my heart, always and forever."

"Alan—"

"There is more." She felt something warm slip from his hand to hers. He drew his hand away.

She lifted her fingers slowly from his chest to reveal the gold ring set with a bright red stone that he'd had made for her in Jaffa. She gasped as she recognized what it was. One of the stones of fire.

"Alan . . ."

"If I am to be the guardian of the ark, then you are the guardian of the stones. Together, we must keep these treasures safe for the rest of our days."

She nodded, not trusting her voice.

His gaze fastened intently on her face. "I also want you to remember each time you look at this ring that it is you who set me afire every time we touch." He lifted the ring from her palm and slid it onto her left hand.

"Alan, I accept the gift of your heart and this ring, and all that it signifies. I willingly give myself to you in return." She could see his pulse beating wildly in his jaw. His eyes flared and sheer lust tore through her. "Please, I want nothing more except to feel you filling the aching emptiness between my thighs."

"Are you asking me to love you?"

"Yes."

He gathered her in his arms and reclined on the bed, placing her on top of him. "I'm yours, my princess, seduce me any way you please."

Suddenly she felt as though she was in control of her life and her destiny. She was entering a wild and secret world where anything was possible and nothing forbidden.

Her fingers stroked his chest. "Does this please you?"

"Aye, it makes me feel glorious."

"More glorious than this?" Her hand slid across his taut stomach. His muscles went rigid beneath her fingertips. Her fingers moved lower to tangle in the soft curls surrounding his manhood. He drew a sharp breath.

"And this, love . . . does this feel good?" She gently stroked his pulsing member.

"I ache," he said, arching his head back. "I need more."

She released him and shifted herself over him. Slowly, she slid down his length, until he filled her fully. She closed her eyes and tried to steady her breathing at the rich excitement pulsing around her. It was as though her every response was linked to his in some mysterious fashion. Every tingle of pleasure she gave him was her pleasure.

He lifted his head to hers and kissed her with a sweetness that wove a web of enchantment around them both.

"Let me give you more, Jessamine." He thrust upward, filling her with his hot hardness over and over again.

She moaned, clutching helplessly at his shoulders. "Alan."

"I've missed you so." His words were almost guttural. "The tightness . . . I feel you grabbing me every time I thrust into you."

She knew in that moment the power she held over him.

As she undulated over him, he gasped and shuddered. "You're making me lose control." He plunged deep, filling her, raising his buttocks off the bed to fill her fully.

She cried out with pleasure, trembling, quaking. Her arousal was too intense, the fullness within her too hot, too hard.

"Let me give you even more," he said, his breath coming in labored gasps. In a smooth, fluid motion, he flipped her onto her back and plunged deep. Hot lightning seared her. His palms cupped her bottom, squeezing her flesh with each bold invasion, lifting her to each thrust, encouraging her to take more of him.

She cried out with satisfaction as the very essence of her being aligned with his and spasms of release shuddered through them both.

Alan collapsed alongside her, pulling her tight against his side while she struggled to catch her breath. When she thought she could speak without gasping, she lifted her head to look at her husband. He was as breathless as she, smiling at her with a tenderness she'd never expected to find in any man.

"What are you smiling about?"

"Can a man in love not smile at his wife?"

She sucked in a small tremulous breath and quickly lowered her lashes to hide her eyes.

"What is it, Jessamine?"

"Nothing."

He lifted her chin with his finger, bringing her tear-filled gaze back to his face. "Tell me, anything."

"It's just that . . ." A tear spilled over her lashes onto her cheek. He brushed it away gently with his thumb. "I've waited so long to hear those words from you."

His smile returned. "I'm not the most eloquent man, but my feelings for you must have been obvious from the start."

"But a woman needs to hear the words."

His smile broadened. "I'll not make that mistake again." He leaned down and kissed her cheek where the tear had fallen. "I love you." His lips placed a gentle caress on her other cheek as well. "I love you." He pulled back and looked deeply into her eyes. In them she could see all the glory and all the wonder of his love. Then his mouth reinforced his words with a long and passionate kiss. When he pulled back, he said it once more. "I love you, Jessamine." His voice broke with emotion. "Always and forever."

She could feel his gaze on her for a long moment before his lips brushed hers with a velvet tenderness. He gathered her against him and lay down. "I think it best we get some sleep tonight. Tomorrow promises to be another eventful day."

She tensed. "The ark still isn't safe, is it?"

He shook his head. "Not until it is within the fortress of Stonehyve Castle. Even without a leader, the Spaniards may try to come after it again."

She sighed, her mind suddenly as weary as her body. "We are safe for tonight?"

"In my arms you will always be safe," he replied and pulled her more snugly against his chest. "Sweet dreams, love."

At dawn the next morning Alan and Jessamine started their journey to Stonehyve Castle. The pace was slower than Alan would have liked. The sooner they reached the protective walls of the castle, the better off they would be.

At dusk, their small army stopped. The men settled down for the night, setting watch fires to help guard against any possible enemies. Patrols scouted the area, while men took turns guarding each other and the ark.

But sleep did not come easily to Alan or Jessamine. They lay together watching the fire, wide awake and thinking.

"Alan," Jessamine whispered. "What do you think happened to Will in all the fighting?"

He sighed. The men had searched everywhere for his body. But they'd found nothing. "I'm hoping he wasn't involved in the battle and that he found safety elsewhere."

She leaned her head against his shoulder. "I'll hope the same."

"Never you fear about me," a familiar voice called from behind them.

"Will?" Alan shot to his feet, then helped Jessamine up.

"You're alive!" Jessamine ran toward the older man and engulfed him in a hug . . . except her hands moved right through him. She stared at her hands and then at Will, her eyes wide.

Alan's hand moved to his sword. "Will?" Alan regarded him warily. "What are you? Who are you?"

"William of Tyre." He bowed as far as his cane would allow.

Alan felt his pulse stumble. "The Templar William of Tyre? The man who wrote the Templar letters?"

His smile widened. "The very same."

"But how?" Jessamine asked, running her hand through Will's body once again. "Are you a ghost?"

"No," he said. "Over the years, I have been responsible for keeping the ark safe until a new guardian, or guardians, could be found. When I saw you in the tunnels beneath the Temple Mount, I knew you were the ones. I made it my task to protect and guide you when you needed me."

Jessamine's eyes widened. "You *were* always there when we needed you."

With a smile and a nod, Will's image shimmered, then faded, and a small blue orb hovered where he'd stood only moments before.

"The blue light!" she gasped. "That was you?" She held out her hand and allowed the blue orb to nestle in her palm. She chuckled as the light swirled over and under her hand.

As Alan watched, images of Will tumbled through his mind. When they'd first met him at Petra, he'd taken them to the Bedouins. As the blue light, he had guided them to the ark and to each other. "How could we have missed the fact that no one ever saw you when we did?"

The blue light took the form of Will once more.

"You weren't looking beyond surface appearance at first. But that changed along the way, as did you."

Alan's breath caught as another truth slipped into place. He finally understood why the Bruce had sent him on this quest. It wasn't because Alan was a mighty warrior, or because of his ability to reason things through, or because the king trusted him above all others. It was because of all the Templars in the brotherhood, Alan had needed something to believe in more than anyone else.

Alan grasped Jessamine in his arms and twirled her around. Their gazes met, their laughter merged, floated upward, and vibrated through the night sky toward the stars above.

"Thank you, Will," Alan said, his heart full to bursting.

"My time grows short," Will said, his voice fading. He took the form of light once again and spiraled into the night sky, disappearing among the stars.

"Is he gone?" Jessamine asked, staring up at the millions of glistening lights overhead.

"I don't think so." Alan put his arm around her. He pulled her close. "He's been guiding us all along. I doubt he'll abandon us until the ark is truly safe."

Chapter Twenty-seven

The next day, as the sun reached its zenith, Alan, Jessamine, Simon, and the rest of the Templar troops stood in the bailey of Stonehyve Castle. Within moments of the gate's opening, Jessamine found herself engulfed in the arms of William Keith's wife, Siobhan.

"We are so very pleased to have you here with us." Siobhan stepped back to look at her, but didn't release Jessamine's hands.

"'Tis a miracle, indeed!" William Keith grasped Alan in a playful hug, but Jessamine didn't miss the sheen of tears in the warrior's eyes. "How in Hades did you survive the battle of Teba? If we'd known, we would have stayed and—"

"William, I understand," Alan said with a gentle smile. "The memories of that battle are behind us."

"That they are," William agreed and nodded toward the ark, which had been placed near the two men. "I see your stay in the Holy Land was an adventurous one."

"I've brought the ark to you for safekeeping until it can be placed with the other treasures."

"Stonehyve Castle's walls are secure," William promised, then stepped forward to address all the men in the bailey. "Come inside. My good wife and I have prepared a wedding feast for Alan and Jessamine." He turned to them. "Come along, you two. It's time to introduce you to our guests."

Jessamine looked to Siobhan with surprise. "You shouldn't have."

Siobhan's hand squeezed Jessamine's arm. "We're family now."

"I'll escort my bride. If that's allowed."

"Yes, of course," Siobhan stepped back as Alan took Jessamine's arm and led her toward the open doors of the keep.

In the great hall Jessamine came to a sudden stop. "It's magnificent," she breathed, as she took in the chandeliers blazing with hundreds of candles and the rich tapestries lining the walls. Seated at tables across the chamber were the men who were Alan's Templar brothers. Retainers rushed back and forth, carrying trays of food that they served to the guests and filling silver goblets. The lilting strains of a flute and a fiddle rose above the voices, lending a festive air.

Jessamine found herself laughing for no other reason than the joy flowing through her. As a princess she had been to many fine feasts in her life, but not like this. This room was filled with color and light and friendship and love. By sacrificing her status just as her father had done, she had lost nothing and gained much. Jessamine smiled. She finally understood her parents' choices.

Siobhan and William ushered the two of them forward to the head table, where they were seated and goblets were pressed into their hands.

"To the bride and groom." William raised his own goblet in a toast echoed by the entire room.

When the toast was drunk, a man who'd been introduced as Brother Kenneth from the monastery approached them. "Greetings to you both."

Brother Kenneth turned first to Alan. "It pleases me you were able to find both Jessamine and the ark. And now you're married too." He offered them both a sincere smile. "I had a feeling you'd be leaving the brotherhood, as William did. So I brought you this." He pulled a folded and sealed square of parchment from inside his robe and handed it to Alan. "Consider it a wedding gift, though in truth it has always been yours."

Alan accepted the paper. He broke the seal, unfolded the parchment, and read the contents. As he did, Jessamine studied his face. At first his eyes darkened, then a sudden warm smile lit his face. "My father's property. You're returning it to me?"

"You granted the estate to the order when you joined us. But now you've chosen the sacrament of marriage, it is clear you'll need a place to call your own. It's a renewal of the cycle, Alan, and a fitting reward for your service. You'll accept Red Castle as your own?"

"I'll accept it. Thank you." Alan's voice was husky.

Brother Kenneth smiled crookedly. "I recall you dreaming about being a ship maker in your early days with us at the monastery. Lunan Bay below the castle seems a proper location to start a shipyard, wouldn't you say?"

"It'll be the perfect place to build a new life with the woman I love."

Alan leaned toward her and brushed his lips against her temple. "It won't be a palace, but it will be our home."

"Remember once you asked me what the most beautiful thing I had ever seen was?"

He nodded.

"I'm looking at it now." Jessamine smiled up into his eyes. "A husband I love. A new home. A new life. It is everything I've ever dreamed of, and all by my own choice."

Jessamine stood on the beach of Lunan Bay waiting for whatever surprise Alan had in store for her now. The

past ten months had been filled with one endless surprise after another.

She had a surprise for him today as well. She smiled
to herself, already knowing what his reaction would be.
Jessamine turned her face into the crisp, salty breeze
blowing along the coastline where Alan had set up his
shipyard. She tugged her tartan wrap closer about her
shoulders. What was keeping her husband?

"Alan?"

He appeared at the railing of the ship just then, and
his expression lit with excitement. "Are you ready?" he
asked as he slipped the gangplank into place for her to
come aboard.

She saw nothing, was aware of nothing but her husband waiting for her. She could tell by the smile on his
lips that he thought he was the most fortunate man
alive. The notion sent a ripple to her core.

Jessamine smiled as well. She was no longer afraid of
the physical attraction between them—it must have
been the same intense passion her own parents had felt
for each other. They'd also had the kind of attraction
that pushed past barriers, and had allowed them to
overcome the objections from both their families. She
realized now that she hadn't been an outcast, or half of
anything. She'd been born of love. How much more
fortunate could a person be?

That was the real prophecy of her life—the prophecy
of love.

"What do you think?" Alan asked as she stepped on
deck.

The first ship he'd built. He'd modeled it after the
Arab dhow they'd sailed on from the Holy Land. "It's
magnificent," she breathed, taking in the tightly stitched
and lashed timbers making up the hull as well as the
gleaming wood deck. Over the months of living with a

shipwright, she'd learned what quality workmanship her husband had produced. "It's a masterpiece."

"One that will take us to Spain as swiftly as any ship on the sea."

"I've been so worried. . . ." Her voice trailed off.

"I know you have. That's why I sent my men on the dhow along with your letter to your uncle, detailing the conde's scheme to poison the royal family and explaining our marriage."

"He wrote us back, giving us his blessing."

"Aye, but at times when we talk of your uncle's family, concern still lingers in your eyes. I want you to see for yourself that your uncle and his family are hearty and hale."

A half smile came to her lips. "I know I shouldn't still be concerned. In spite of your attempts to warn the king, all turned out well. The conde's plans to poison my family failed when the taster he'd hired to poison their food suddenly died."

"Do you think the ark could have been responsible for that?" Alan asked.

She shrugged. "I did pray for their deliverance, as well as our own. And look what happened for us."

"I'd like to believe that's what happened."

"Me too." She leaned forward and placed a tender kiss on his lips. As she moved to pull back, he drew her closer instead. She lifted her hand to his face and stroked his cheek. "I like my surprise."

He smiled mischievously. "There's more."

He took her hand and led her to the forecastle. The wind sharpened and tossed her hair about her shoulders. She gathered it with her hand and stood beside her husband, staring out at the sea. "This is my surprise?" she asked, suddenly curious why he'd brought her here.

"Nay." He took her hand and placed it on the wheel. "The wheel guides the boat. A steady hand keeps the crew and passengers safe."

Puzzled by his words, she looked down at the brightly polished wood beneath her hand. Her eyes widened. "The remaining eleven stones." He'd set them into the wood of the wheel.

"Is it safe to put the stones there?"

"There is no better place to guarantee the safety of those I love." He grinned. "I've named the ship the *Divine Fire*. It's our ship, Jessamine, yours and mine to use as we please, to return to Spain whenever you feel the need. The stones will guarantee steady winds and safe passage."

She smiled. "Those you love are pleased."

His gaze searched her face. His eyes brightened as comprehension dawned. "Are you well?"

"The two of us are fine."

His gaze was a warm caress embracing her and the child she carried. His arm slipped around her and he drew her against his chest. He placed a tender hand over the mound that hadn't even started to rise.

She tipped her head to look up at him. "I want you to know that although I'm Spanish and Moorish, Scotland is my home now." She laced her fingers through his. She steadied herself against the desire that flared at his adoring gaze. She had to ask him one last question that had burned in her mind since the time they'd spent at Stonehyve Castle. "Do you regret giving up the brotherhood for me?"

He tightened his fingers around hers. "I didn't give up the brotherhood—those men will always be dear to me. I gave up the Templar ways and causes." He placed a slow and gentle kiss on her lips that told her without words that she was his life, his heart, his soul.

The wind sharpened again, and this time along with the breeze came a small blue orb. The light chased the wind about the deck of the ship until it came to rest before the two of them. Jessamine reached out and put a finger to the blue light. She laughed as it tickled her hand, but her laughter died a moment later when the orb flared then curled in and over itself . . . as though waving good-bye.

"He's leaving," Jessamine breathed as her chest tightened.

"We don't need him anymore," Alan said, although his voice was as raw as her own. "We have each other."

The orb pulsed up to Jessamine's cheek. It lingered there for an instant before it spiraled upward and vanished in the blue skies overhead.

"It was Will who truly found the Ark of the Covenant," Jessamine said when she could speak once again.

"Nay," Alan said, pulling her against his side. "We found the ark because of each other, your prophecy, and Will's help. It took all of us."

"And now the ark is safe."

He nodded. "Until it is called forward from its resting place by a new and greater cause."

She leaned her head against his shoulder with a sigh. "The ark was a blessing in our lives."

Alan's hand moved down to caress Jessamine's abdomen with all the love in his heart. "I have a feeling our blessings have truly just begun."

She smiled. "Along with the greatest adventure of our lives."

He kissed her cheek as he whispered close to her ear. "How right you are, my wife. May our adventures go on forever."

Afterword

The hero of *Seducing the Knight*, Sir Alan Cathcart, was a real historical figure who was one of ten knights selected as King Robert the Bruce's inner circle. Their mission was to take the Bruce's heart after his death to the Holy Land for placement in the Church of the Holy Sepulchre. Their crusade to the Holy Land was symbolic of the journey the Bruce had longed to take during his lifetime but was never able to manage. Their journey came to a devastating end at the Battle of Teba in Spain.

As is the case with much of fiction, I used a little fact and a lot of fantasy to send Sir Alan Cathcart from the devastation in Teba into the Holy Land, where he would search for the legendary Ark of the Covenant.

In biblical history, the ark was where God manifested his presence on earth. The ark went ahead of the Children of Israel wherever they traveled. Not only was it the center of worship when it resided in the tabernacle, but the ark also protected the Israelites in battle, supernaturally defeating any adversaries that came before them (Joshua 6:3–4). The Israelites also went to the ark to seek God's guidance and wisdom for the nation (Numbers 7:89; Exodus 25:22).

But the Ark of the Covenant is also one of the most frightening artifacts described in all of biblical history. A golden box with the power to strike men dead, the ark, to the ancient Hebrews, was both a divine manifestation and a talisman so powerful that they carried it with them into battle. To their enemies, it was a treasure to be coveted, but once captured, a terrible punishment. It came to occupy the most revered spot in Jerusalem, the Holy of Holies at the Temple of Solomon, and then it mysteriously disappeared.

Where the ark went has been the subject of much conjecture over the centuries. Many theories exist: In 586 BC, the Babylonian emperor Nebuchadnezzar II sacked and destroyed the Temple of Solomon in Jerusalem, as a prelude to enslaving the Hebrews. But in the detailed biblical list of all the spoils the Babylonians took back with them to their homeland, the ark is not mentioned, which suggests to some that by then it had already disappeared.

Another theory surrounding the ark's disappearance from the temple is that it had been smuggled out of Jerusalem prior to the Babylonian conquest and spirited away by Solomon's son Melenik, the founder of the Ethiopian royal dynasty. Melenik was supposed to have brought the ark with him upon returning to the Ethiopian homeland of his mother, the Queen of Sheba.

Today, Ethiopian Orthodox Christians believe the ark resides in the Church of Saint Mary of Zion in Axum, Ethiopia. The sanctum where the ark supposedly is kept is guarded by a priest, and no outsider is allowed to enter, so the claim is impossible to substantiate.

Based on ancient Jewish writings, some have suggested the ark is hidden on Mount Nebo on the Jordan River's east bank. This site is presently in the modern nation of Jordan and there is no hint of the ark's presence there. Others suggest the ark is hidden somewhere near the Dead Sea, on the Jordan River's west bank. This location is usually considered in association with the ancient site of Qumran and the people of the Dead Sea Scrolls. The ark and other artifacts are believed buried in one of the region's caves, like the Dead Sea Scrolls.

Another view suggests the ark is located beneath Jerusalem, in a carved stone tunnel. Some say it is beneath the suggested site of the Crucifixion, Calvary. The Temple Institute in Jerusalem's Old City, an Ultra-Orthodox organization dedicated to rebuilding the Jewish temple, says the ark is under the Temple Mount and will be revealed when the temple is rebuilt.

While some ponder the whereabouts of the ark, others search for a scientific explanation of its miraculous powers. It has been proven that the ark's components of wood and gold, in the dimensions specified in the Bible, could accumulate and release an electrical charge strong enough to strike someone dead, as it might have done to Aaron's sons when they touched the ark.

And what about the strange manifestations of light documented in the Bible? Such as when God appeared to Moses upon Mount Sinai in a cloud of devouring fire (Exodus 24:15–17). Modern-day researchers have had similar experiences in the Sinai wilderness.

In 1993 a team of British archeologists were working around a shrine on the summit of Jebel Madhbah when they were caught in a rare thunderstorm. They were hurrying to get off the mountain when they saw a red ball of fiery light, estimated to be around six feet in diameter, hovering over the temple ruins. It was visible for about five minutes and moved slowly back and forth before vanishing. Some scientists explain the phenomenon as ball lightning, spheres of highly charged particles created by the electrified atmosphere of a thunderstorm. However, ball lightning tends to be bluish in color, not red, is not larger than a football, and is usually only visible for a few seconds.

Another explanation, which fits better with what was observed in 1993, is a rare electromagnetic anomaly known as geoplasma.

Plasma is an electrically charged gas that has been altered by an external energy source. The plasma can then ignite into an ionized "cold flame." It is capable of hovering in the air as a sphere or column of luminous gas that can move or remain static, depending on conditions, and can continue its state for several minutes. Geoplasma is believed to be caused by geodynamics. It occurs when certain types of rocks are rubbed together by seismic activity, ionizing the air above them.

Strange lights such as those reported at Jebel Madhbah have been reported at various locations throughout the world, usually in areas prone to earthquakes and tremors and in areas that host large amounts of rocks that contain arenite sandstone and carnelian granite.

Most geoplasma phenomena are also reported during or after heavy rainfall. The event on Jebel Madhbah included heavy rainfall, which was also the case in the appearance of the "glory of the Lord" as witnessed by the ancient Israelites. Exodus 19:16 reports "thunders and lightnings, and a thick cloud upon the mount." Was it geoplasma or a divine visitation?

In the pages of *Seducing the Knight*, I had to make many educated guesses about the Ark of the Covenant's location after it disappeared from the Temple of Solomon, about whether the Templars really had possession of the artifact at some point in history, about the location of the Mount Sinai mentioned in the Bible, about strange lights, guardian angels, and what powers the ark truly possessed. However, I believe this book is true to the essence of what the Ark of the Covenant was and how important it still is to millions of people worldwide.

EMILY BRYAN

Can an artistic genius . . .

Crispin Hawke, a brilliant sculptor, is revered by the *ton*. His works are celebrated in every fashionable parlor.

Transform an awkward heiress . . .

Grace Makepeace is determined to wed a titled lord, but her Bostonian bluntness leaves much to be desired among the well-heeled London crowd.

Into the most sought-after original . . .

Crispin agrees to school Grace in flirting and the delights of the flesh. But when she catches the eye of a marquess, he realizes maybe he's done his job a little too well. And suddenly he knows Grace is the one masterpiece he cannot bear to be parted from.

Without falling for her himself?

Stroke of Genius

ISBN 13: 978-0-8439-6361-8

CINDY HOLBY

An Elusive Huntress

She appeared out of nowhere, clad in form-fitting leathers and looking as magical as the mysterious woods she roamed. With flashing emerald eyes, she taunted the intruder, daring him to come deeper into her enchanted realm.

An Arranged Marriage

Rhys DeRemy owed his life to her father, just as he owed unswerving obedience to his king. If he took the heiress of Aubregate to wife, he could clear the debts of the tormented boy he had been as well as the battle-hardened warrior he'd become. But it was Eliane herself who called out to the man in him, whose fierce pride cast a spell on him, whose silken bed promised a . . .

Breath of Heaven

ISBN 13: 978-0-8439-6404-2

☐ **YES!**

Sign me up for the Historical Romance Book Club and send my FREE BOOKS! If I choose to stay in the club, I will pay only $8.50* each month, a savings of $6.48!

NAME: _____

ADDRESS: _____

TELEPHONE: _____

EMAIL: _____

☐ I want to pay by credit card.

☐ **VISA** ☐ **MasterCard** ☐ **DISCOVER**

ACCOUNT #: _____

EXPIRATION DATE: _____

SIGNATURE: _____

Mail this page along with $2.00 shipping and handling to:
Historical Romance Book Club
PO Box 6640
Wayne, PA 19087
Or fax (must include credit card information) to:
610-995-9274
You can also sign up online at **www.dorchesterpub.com**.
*Plus $2.00 for shipping. Offer open to residents of the U.S. and Canada only.
Canadian residents please call 1-800-481-9191 for pricing information.
If under 18, a parent or guardian must sign. Terms, prices and conditions subject to
change. Subscription subject to acceptance. Dorchester Publishing reserves the right
to reject any order or cancel any subscription.